Speaker

Cai Cherry

spectrum books

Cover designed by Spectrum Books.

Print ISBN: 978-1-915905-46-8

First edition, Spectrum Books, 2024.

For everyone who saved this wayward kid.
And for Rainbow Migration, who save so many others.

A.

Interlife

"It is better to endure patiently a smart which nobody feels but yourself, than to commit a hasty action whose evil consequences will extend to all connected with you."

— Charlotte Brontë, *Jane Eyre*

I

Hell With Better Lighting

Fuck.

My eyes open and I'm not blinded by the light. It's actually quite dull—faded, like it's hiding behind a clump of vaseline. I blink two or three times to try to clear the haziness, but it doesn't work; it still feels like there's a disconnect between my eyes and my brain. *Weird.* My head hurts as well. A deep throbbing pain, like the migraines I get, but somehow it feels more distant. It hurts, to be sure, but again, there's a disconnect.

"So… welcome?" a voice says, and only then do I begin to take in my surroundings. Firstly, I see my hands and I stare down at them. I'm not sure what they're planning on doing, but I watch them nonetheless. I'm wearing my favourite crappy clothes: a dark grey hoodie with my favourite singer's name scrawled across the chest in white graffiti font, and my black joggers, loose enough to be comfortable and tight enough to reassure me I'm not fat. I'm barefoot, which is uncomfortable on gristly green carpet, and odd, because I always wear socks. My head throbs.

The voice says my name and I look up. He's attractive—that's my first thought—kind of rugged, with smile lines around his eyes, and a broad white grin. He's got some stubble, which I'm usually not a fan of, but he wears it well, neatly trimmed along a jawline just sharp enough to be defined. He's what my sister Penny would call, "approachably attractive." That's not the point though, I have no idea where I am, or why, and I shouldn't be noticing the way his suit fits so snugly, or how his shirt buttons are pulled apart just a little bit by his…

I shake my head, as if to loosen the synapses. The man opposite raises an eyebrow and the corners of his lips curl into a smirk. An attractive smirk.

"Hi," I say. A strong start, but given the circumstances, I'm not sure what else I could have said.

"I'm going to assume you don't know what you're doing here?" he says, and I shake my head again, more purposefully this time, as if to say 'No'. He clears his throat slightly and continues, "This is, well I guess you could call it something like purgatory, but it's not entirely that. This is a space between life and the afterlife. An interlife. You're not completely dead, but you're also not completely alive... Are you following?"

What the fuck?

"I guess not. Well, take a seat and I'll tell you what happened."

I sit down on the green leather bench behind me. I hadn't even noticed it until now, but I just need to not stand anymore. My legs are so tired. I'm also sort of out of breath. Maybe I'm just anxious, I don't know.

"You were in a car accident. You were crossing the road on the way home from school and a van hit you. Your body is currently in the hospital, in the ICU. The prognosis doesn't look good, but the doctors are doing the best they can. This is one of those cases, though, where the decision isn't entirely down to the doctors. This is a place where we have to make a choice. It's down to you and me to decide what happens to you.

"This is like a courtroom, where we each make our case, and at the end you live or you die."

What the fuck? I repeat internally.

"So I'm dead?" I ask. It's not the smartest question, but the best I can do in this situation. After all, *I'm practically fucking dead.*

"No," he smirks again, and it's kind of endearing and infuriating at the same time. "Your body is still breathing, but not on its own, and your heart is still beating. If you were dead, we wouldn't be here. You wouldn't have a brain to ask if you were dead. This is just a place... in between."

"Okay," I nod, though I don't understand. "So what do we do?"

"Well, everyone is different. I mean, first of all, not everyone comes here. Not everyone gets a choice. But everyone who does come here has an opportunity to make their case, to prove their point, and at the end, we decide together, you and me, whether you go back or not. Everyone chooses how they do that in a different way. I had a Premier League footballer attempt to do it through a penalty shootout. I had a waitress do a rap battle. I've done sword combat and I've done cook-offs. It's really up to you, but it's not so much a conscious choice you make. You already know the arena you want to fight in, and that's where we are." He gestures around.

For the first time, I properly look around. It looks eerily familiar, but so out of place. You've got to be shitting me. My heart practically stops again, *I guess.*

The man opposite barks out a laugh: gruff and sudden. "I guess you've finally realised where we are?"

This is—to my embarrassment—the House of Commons. This is so humiliating. I could have picked gladiatorial combat, or an arm-wrestling competition. But no. If my sister knew, she'd never let me live it down.

"Yes," I sigh, looking down at the floor, my feet tucked under the bench. I feel an urge to apologise. I shouldn't though. "Sorry," I say. *Shit.*

He barks his laugh again. "Nothing to apologise for. This is your choice. Can't say I've really done…" He gestures around. "...*This* that often, but, hey, whatever works for you."

I look around and begin to notice the subtle differences,

the ones that are making this place feel so alien. The benches are empty, for a start, although that's not so bizarre, *amirite*? There are no names on plaques circling the chamber. There are no microphones dangling from the ceiling, and no bulletproof glass separating the equally empty gallery. *Anyone could throw a condom at me*, I laugh internally for some reason. *Not the time.* It feels cold too. My feet are cold, and my toes are being scratched by the worn carpet underfoot. I fold my arms and tuck my hands into my elbows. The rows of benches stare ominously at me, and I turn my head to see them doing the same behind me. The speaker's chair and clerks' desks are also barren. No papers lie strewn, and no books separate my despatch box from his. The mace is also missing. I guess Parliament isn't sitting right now.

I sit on the government benches. I'm not sure the relevance of that. Seeing as we're the only two people in here, I don't think either of us can command a majority. A hung parliament. *Hung*, I snigger, thinking of Tom who could always find a sexual pun in any vocabulary. Again, *not the time*. I have a lot of questions, but none of which I can articulate, and none of them seem any more or less important than the others, so what am I meant to ask first? My contributions to our conversation so far have been less than stellar, so I'm eager not to let the dialogue down even more. *Okay, this is what we know*: I was hit by a van on the way home from school. I don't remember that. I can't think of when I was last at school. Every day seems to blur together into one. And now I'm here. I'm in the *House of fucking Commons* and I have to convince this man to let me go back and live. It's not a lot to go on. He seems to have left a lot of blanks in here. Am I meant to ask about them, or just see what happens? Do I go with the flow? Well, that would put me at a disadvantage, surely. If I'm meant to be fighting for my life, shouldn't I at least know the rules of the game? We're in Parliament but I don't think we're making laws. What am

I meant to be doing? Should I propose an amendment? Should I table a question? I'm on the government front bench—do I answer questions? *This is a fucking mess.*

My sister would have hated that. No, she would hate that. If she were here. She never liked me swearing. She'd gasp and say with a giggle I knew she was putting on "You shouldn't swear." She'd call me by my name and punch me on the shoulder a little too hard for it to be a joke. She just didn't like me swearing. Still, I think the circumstances call for it here.

I have to say something, surely. The silence has gone on a little too long for it to be normal. I look up and see him staring at me. Him. *I don't know who the fuck this guy is, coming up in here and trying to judge me?* I feel a rage burning inside of me all of a sudden. My jaw clenches. His eyebrow cocks again, his eyes narrowing ever so slightly. I try to calm my breathing, but it seems impossible. I start counting in my head like Jo taught me: *One. Two. Three. Four. Five. Six…*

Fuck it.

"Who are you?" I say, standing, albeit slightly less confidently than I want. My voice cracks slightly halfway through, and my butt sort of awkwardly hovers between standing and sitting for a brief second, but it's enough for my thighs to want to bolt. I shake my head once. *Cool it.*

"Luce," he replies, walking around the despatch box and raising his hand. He pronounces it like 'loose', which is ironic given how tight he seems to keep it. This isn't proper parliamentary behaviour. The red lines in front of the benches seem to glow like fire. For some reason, I remember that they're two sword-lengths apart to stop the MPs stabbing opposing members during their debates. I guess it worked well back then, but this 'Luce' guy doesn't give a shit. Still, I meet his handshake as he rounds my corner of the table, and try to give it a few firm shakes, though his grasp is surprisingly gentle. I think my hands might be sweaty. *Fuck, he's so good looking.*

This seriously isn't the time. I think I might be horny? Is that normal? When people used to be hanged, they'd get an erection, so I guess death and boners aren't too far apart. That was a fun history lesson. Still, I just wish it didn't have to happen to me. He drops my hand and turns sharply before marching back to his side of the chamber. I guess marching might not be the right word. It's too driven for a stroll, but not stiff enough to be a proper march. *Never mind.*

I watch him as he returns to face me, shifting my weight from one hip to another, and I put my hands on the sides of the despatch box to steady me. The metal corners are cold to the touch, but the pattern, unlike the real thing, is clear and fresh, like it was cut yesterday. My politics teacher, Mr Whyssler, always joked that the government's box was so much more worn than the opposition's because the ministers would sweat and squirm to defend their policies, whereas the opposition could just lie back and criticise. It's easy, he would say, to criticise. It's harder to defend. Infinitely harder. Mr Whyssler's face flashes into my mind. He was good looking, too, but not like Luce. He was younger, but with thinning hair and a thin, wiry frame. His thick-rimmed glasses—the ones he'd call 'nerd glasses'—dominated his squirrel-like face. He was sweet. You could imagine drinking tea with him in the Cotswolds. Luce, you couldn't.

"Who are you, Luce?" I ask, as the anger dissipated slightly.

"I'm just the guy here to help decide what we do. I'm like a reverse hostage negotiator, or a therapist, or a judge. I'm all three." He laughs, this time a gentle chuckle, as if he found what he said genuinely amusing when he first said it, but with repetition it has died over time.

II

The First Time

We part ways shortly after that. I don't really have any questions to ask—none of it makes sense anyway—and we walk in silence to the door. Outside isn't a lobby though. It looks like a shopping centre, but blindingly white. No dirt, no chewing gum stuck to the floor, no tired kiosks collecting dust or dead flies in fluorescent lights.

Interestingly, there are other people here. People wander around, sit on benches, and speak to each other, but there's no sound. Well, not no sound, but I can't hear what they are saying. It's hard to describe: not like watching a video on mute, but also not like real life. *Weird.* All their clothes seem kind of faded, like they have been through a few too many washes, but everyone wears something comfortable: joggers; yoga pants; shorts; sun dresses; flannel and linen. I'm the only one who is barefoot, though. I notice that pretty quickly, and my face turns an upsetting shade of scarlet. I'm not sure why—no one else here seems to notice, and I guess it's not something that anyone thinks about when they're in the 'interlife' but I am painfully aware. My toes scrunch up as if to shy away from view.

I'm not sure what to do. I've never been one to mingle, and I don't feel like this is the kind of place to strike up a conversation with a stranger, anyway. Like a first day at school.

In fact, my first day of sixth form was pretty much like this, except I had shoes on that day, and was dressed fairly formally.

I'd gone to my secondary school with a group from primary, so I had friends there already, but no one I knew was going to my sixth form. It was my first time feeling like an adult. Feeling *really fucking alone.*

I hung back at the start, sitting at the back of the hall when they gave introductions, and scrolling on my phone instead of making conversation. I refreshed apps until it was clear I'd really shaken every last crumb out of that particular biscuit tin, and then I'd reread the same posts just to make it seem like I was doing something, anything. But the first day of sixth form was also where I met Abbas.

I had been pawing at my phone screen, hoping for some new content I could engage with and act like I was far too busy to meet new people. Like I didn't *need* new people. We had an induction talk by a teacher who seemed nice enough, with long chestnut-brown hair and a smile that was almost menacingly friendly, but I didn't pay much attention to what she was saying. I leaned back in my chair, slouching down slightly, and folded my arms, praying my relaxed posture would calm the panicked beating of my heart. *Fucking anxiety.* It was fine, I told myself. I'd spent way too long on my hair that morning, so every curl was perfectly coiffed into place, and I knew exactly how to clench my teeth and press my tongue to the roof of my mouth so my jawline would sharpen. My high cheekbones and dark green eyes also added to the whole 'mysterious bad boy' facade I was hoping to convey. It's not as if I'm bad looking; after a quick scan of the backs of people's heads, I was pretty confident I was one of the best-looking people here. *Arrogance.* I lashed my brain. *It's okay though, it helps make up for the fact that you're insane.* I was insane. Not in a quirky way. I didn't have a blog, but I do have a brain that doesn't know when to shut up, as hard as I tried to drown it out.

My internal dialogue drove me straight away from paying attention, and I snapped back when I noticed everyone standing up. The sticker I scrawled my name on in my devilishly messy handwriting had a blue dot in the corner, and everyone with a blue dot seemed to be making their way through the middle-left set of doors, so I breathed in deeply and followed them, hoping for the best. Loitering once again at the back of the group, I silently filed through to the classroom where, luckily, the teacher checked my name off at the door. I was in the right place. It was a geography classroom, with maps of the world littering the walls and the ubiquitous globe tucked behind a pile of textbooks on a filing cabinet. I grabbed a chair—at the back, again—and forced my brain to focus on the introduction the teacher was doing.

This guy was tall, with a long bushy beard and a pale complexion. He didn't seem quite as nice as the lady from the hall, but it's not as if I needed to befriend a geography teacher. I was here to get my A Levels and get out. And not repeat the events of the last few years. That's all. A trio of girls sat in the row in front of me, whispering and giggling as the teacher introduced himself as Mr Nathwani, the head of geography, and our form tutor. He asked us to raise our hands if we were sitting next to someone we knew, and mine remained messily clasped in front of me, my fingers intertwined. Almost everyone else raised their hand. *Great. Alone again.* He then asked us to introduce ourselves to someone we didn't know, the bastard. Like Jigsaw, coming up with sick games to entertain himself. Mr Nathwani, you son of a bitch. Everyone else leapt to their feet, laughing with their friends about the awkwardness of the situation. A group of boys at the other side of the room slapped each others' backs as they mock-introduced themselves to each other, despite having probably grown up on the same road. Mr Nathwani laughed indulgently. The girls in front turned around and shook my hand in turn, introducing themselves as Dana, Rubab, and Hope. I curled the corners of my mouth into a brief smile, my dimples popping out—*heart-throb, I know*—and introduced myself. I'd gone to a school in the next town over, but this sixth form was closer to home, so I'd switched after my GCSEs. Dana, Rubab and Hope had gone to school together since nursery, they told me with a somewhat unwarranted giggle. I continued my smile, not sure if it had crossed the line into creepy now, and told them how nice that was for them, trying to sound genuine but probably coming across as sarcastic. I've been told I sound sarcastic most of the time. I have a pretty flat voice, I guess, but I try to shrug it off.

The girls turned back around and introduced themselves to a new pair of girls who had wandered over. I didn't catch the names, nor did I want to appear as if I was eavesdropping. I looked around the room, trying to maintain a casual disinterest while my heart pounded in my chest. My palms started to sweat, which I'm sure made meeting me that much more pleasant. I wiped them on my polyester trousers, which were thoroughly non-absorbent.

"Hey."

I turn around, sucking in my gut to prepare for the tribulation of another introduction.

It was him. I didn't know it then, but there was the man who would ruin my life. Abbas. He once told me it means 'lion', which fitted him. He was beautiful and broad, his muscles struggling to catch up with his growing frame, and his brown eyes glistening and sparking like a wildfire. His dark curls, almost black, fell into broad strokes, like the kind you could make with a paintbrush and canvas, and concealed a faint scar above his left eyebrow, and his skin was like honey, or caramel, or something that doesn't fetishise a person based on their race. There were a few acne scars, and one spot that looked like it was beginning to erupt on his cheek, but while I would have freaked out over it, his imperfections were endearing, his complexion enchanting. He wore dark grey trousers which hugged what I could only assume was the best arse in the entire country. His white shirt had its sleeves rolled up to reveal his strong forearms, dusted with hair, and hands that engulfed mine as he introduced himself.

Fuck. Me.

Here he was. The man that a million songs have been written about. His voice was dulcet. I had never used that word before, and I doubt I will again in my life, but it was dulcet, and his perfect teeth under plump lips flashed me a smile as he shook my hand.

"Abbas," he said. His gaggle of mates stood behind him, staring at me. I collected myself, and shook his hand back, replying with my own name, and watching as the four other boys introduced themselves. Tom, Alonso, Lukas, and Liam. Honestly, I don't remember what they said that well. How could I, when I was staring into the eyes of a God? I repeated my story of moving to a new sixth form, and they nodded along politely, with grins on their faces. They told me that the four of them had been good friends since year seven, but that Abbas was new, too. They'd only met him that morning. I was surprised; they seemed like old friends. Abbas folded his arms as he watched them speak, and I zoned out of their story to watch how his eyes fixed on them. They weren't piercing, they were enveloping. You could bathe in them. I think my mouth might have dropped open a bit. I'm not usually this bad—okay, you might think so because of how I immediately stared at his ass—but when faced with perfection, you can do nothing but stand back and admire.

Then his eyes flicked to me. I hoped my tan from that summer hid my blush as mine darted away, instead darting between the other four. I nodded along vigorously, as though I'd been listening all along. *Definitely not staring at Abbas.* In my periphery, I could see a smile break out on Abbas's devastatingly handsome face. Tom, Alonso, Lukas and Liam: a nice bunch, but I was glad when Mr Nathwani interrupted their discussion of football they had tried to engage me in. I'd chuckled politely as they debated the merits of a match that happened either last night or a long time ago, I wasn't sure which. I shrugged with a smile and excused myself back to my seat. When seated, I glanced back over at Abbas, who was seemingly engrossed by Mr Nathwani handing out our timetables. I swore internally and forced my eyes back to my desk.

So, yeah, this is a little bit like the first day of school. Except no one here is that good looking. *Abbas*, I sigh.

I wander over to a bench and instinctively reach for my phone in my pocket, but there's nothing there. I purse my lips and wonder what I'm supposed to do now. What do people do when they're semi-dead? I think crying is a good option, but I don't really feel like that right now. I haven't been given a schedule, or any real explanation of what happens next, so I'm not sure if I should wander around, or wait here for something important. The shops that line the mall are all bright white, with signs printed in the faded colours that characterise this place, stating their purpose. The shops don't have brand names, but literally say what's inside: "clothes" or "food" or "games". I'm already in my own clothes, and I'm not hungry. Games could be cool though, and I think about what they might have inside. Despite the brightness of the atrium, I can't really see through the display-less windows—it seems too dark to tell what they actually have. I don't have cash or a card on me, and no contactless thanks to the phone situation, but a browse can't hurt, I guess.

I stand up, and have walked about five steps before I feel a tap on my middle back. It's soft but determined. I turn around and look down to see a girl, probably eight or so years old, staring up at me, her green eyes piercing me from behind long lashes.

"Hello," I say, my voice automatically going up an octave to speak to a child.

"Hello," she replies, her voice sharp and short. Unlike everyone else here, I can hear her perfectly.

"Um..." I pause and look around. For what, I'm not sure. "Can I help you?" I feel a heated intensity behind her eyes. Her demeanour is angry, jaded, cynical. But it's too serious to be cute.

"My name is Rebecca," she responds, disregarding what was, in fairness, an inane question. Rebecca extends her hand and shakes mine firmly, her tiny fingers struggling to wrap around my hand. "I need to tell you something."

She turns suddenly and marches off, not pausing to check if I'm following her. I watch her take a few steps before jogging a little to catch up with her driven strides. My bare feet slap against the white marble floor. Rebecca is wearing a jean jacket and a canary yellow sundress with tiny purple flowers embroidered on, too imperfectly to be done by machine. She wears little white flat shoes and her dark brown hair is pulled back into pigtails, each tied with a yellow ribbon bow. Rebecca dresses hauntingly similar to what my parents would force my sister into when Penny was younger; although old enough to have grown out of her princess era, but back before she was too old to be wrestled into anything but the jeans and hoodies she wanted.

We pass people who stare solemnly at the floor, too caught in their own worlds to notice us disturbing the moment. No one here is moving at speeds other than glacial, except Rebecca and I. The whole place looks the same to me, but Rebecca weaves confidently and expertly between lonely souls, fake plants, and benches, while I follow a pace or so behind. The hum of questions in my mind rattles on with none surfacing to be spoken. She turns unexpectedly into a small alcove, ornate yet whitewashed, and turns to face me as I cram myself into the tight space.

"I know who you are," she informs me, matter-of-factly, her eyes fixed on mine.

"And who are you?" I ask, my heart skipping a beat.

"I told you: Rebecca." She doesn't wait for another question. "I know who you are, and I need you to know something."

"What?"

"This whole thing… it's more important than you know." Her eyes sparkle, but her face remains stony. Tiny frown lines are etched between her eyebrows.

"What 'whole thing'? What are you talking about?"

"You know what Luce said, right? That you're here to make a choice?"

"You know Luce too?" I catch myself and pivot quickly. "What do you mean, it's important?" Okay, so the pivot question wasn't much better than the one I pivoted from. I'm under pressure here, and I don't even know why.

"I'm not allowed to say this, but you need to make the right decision."

"What's the right decision?"

"I'm not allowed to say, I just told you," Rebecca snaps, the tiny frown lines sharpening.

"No, you said... *Never mind.*" I sigh. "How am I meant to make the right decision if I don't even know what that is?"

"There's a lot of rules here," Rebecca says, and I cut her off.

"Yeah, I'm beginning to get that."

She ploughs straight on with her sentence. "And there are some that we can't break and some that we can. I'm not meant to be talking to you, but it's too important not to."

"Can you at least tell me why it's so important?"

"No."

"Great." My mind spins, but I can't place anything.

"Just…" she grabs my hands in her own, her soft skin pressing hard into mine, clasping my fingers with her angry fists. "Just please promise me you'll make the right decision?"

“Rebecca,” I sigh, exasperated. Exhaling is now becoming a prominent part of my dialogue. “Rebecca, I don’t know what decision you want me to make…”

“Need you to make,” she interjects.

“Need me to make,” I correct, “and I don’t know what’s going on, but… I don’t know.”

Her face screws up, her lips pursing into a tiny wrinkle, her tiny frown lines darkening, then she relaxes. “You’re important,” she tells me, saying my name.

“To what? To who?” Out of the swirling mess of my brain, I correct myself to ‘whom’. *Thanks, brain.*

“You’re important,” Rebecca repeats, her eyes never flinching from my own. “To me.”

III

It Begins

I can't remember much. I try to. I try to remember the van hitting me. I try to remember my last day of school, but my mind falls repeatedly into a black hole. I can't come up with timelines either. I have memories of school, of my family, of things I did, but I can't put them into anything by a vague order based on logic alone: 'of course I went to sixth form after secondary,' or 'a family Christmas must have come before my parents split up.' It's an imperfect science, but it beats the silence of sitting and waiting.

Somehow I end up back in the Commons, sitting in front of the government's despatch box, and staring emptily at the floor. I found some socks somewhere, though I don't remember when or how, so my feet are no longer chilled, but instead toasty inside some thick white cotton. My hands are numb, but I don't think that's from the cold. My mind reels from Rebecca's warning, if you could call it that. Does that over-dramatise it? A warning sounds ominous, but I guess it shook me. How could I be important to this little girl? I've never met her before in my life. I dig through hazy memory after hazy memory, but they feel more like dreams than experiences, and nothing renders any results.

Honestly, I'm exhausted. The last however-long-I've-been-here seems to have lasted an eternity. I haven't slept. I don't even know if that's something we do here, but it's something

I'd like to do if it's an option. I should ask Luce, if the bastard ever turns up. No timetable was ever given for when we have to 'decide' what to do. I assume the choices are I die or I return to Earth, which doesn't seem like much of a choice, but I guess Luce is the expert here, so I should defer to him. It's frustrating, waiting for him to appear, but I don't have much else to do here. Every time I try to go into a shop to browse, let alone buy something, I stop myself. It doesn't feel right, or safe, or... *normal.*

The door swings open, and in marches—again, is this the right word? Swaggers? Well, Luce comes in. He shoots a beaming smile at me. His outfit is nice; very '60s American, with a leather jacket over a white tee, dark blue jeans and, as the Yanks say, 'sneakers'. He stands facing me from the opposition's box with his hands rested on the corners. He wears a golden signet ring on his left middle finger, but the inscription is too small to read.

"Where would you like to begin?" he asks, looking at me optimistically. It's misplaced.

"I want to know what is happening, I guess?" I reply, trying to be sarcastic, but coming off more scared. That's more honest, I suppose.

"I told you, kiddo," Luce shakes his head with a tut. "You're here, and we have to decide whether you go back there, or whether you... move on."

"What is 'moving on'?" I say, not really expecting an answer. I don't get one either.

He laughs and shakes his head again. "I can't tell you that, kid." He's drifted off from his forward-facing stance, and now casually leans against the box, smiling down while positioned towards the Speaker's chair. "But you should enjoy this, I promise. This is the opportunity you need to air all your grievances, to say all your pieces, to not bite your tongue, and to really give it to 'em."

My eyes have dropped back to the floor, and my eyebrows furrow. I do this a lot, and people ask what I'm thinking about. I'm not thinking about anything though, and they never believe me. I'm trying to think, but there's too much to think about, and so it all boils down to nothing.

"Hey," he says, my name slipping out of his mouth like a page falling from a book. It feels weird. I look up at him. "I get that this is overwhelming. You're not handling this any better or any worse than anyone else who has come to me." His voice is soft. "But, y'know, this doesn't have to be scary. This is one of those situations where you have all the power. You pick the venue, the outfits, the world. You picked me." My eyes, which have dropped down again, perk back up at that. He senses my confusion. "Yeah," he laughs, "you even picked me. I mean, not that I exist—you can't help that—but you chose what I look like and sound like... I like it." He winks. My face burns scarlet red.

"So what am I meant to do?" I ask, gesturing deflatedly. "You keep talking about a choice, so should I just make it, or is there, like, a process?"

"Well, *we* make the choice, firstly." He smiles at me, but it feels bitter. "But there's a process. You can't just leap straight into it. You have to convince me, and you have to convince yourself."

"Well, I want to go back, obviously," I snap, the first time my voice has sounded confident. It cracks around the empty chamber, fading with each iteration.

"Hold your horses there, cowboy." He steps back with his hands raised in mock surrender. His words are jarring—that's what my dad says, or used to say, when I'd get myself worked up. My skin crawls. "I mean, first of all, you don't know that. And second of all, I'm not convinced yet, so you got some work to do."

"So I have to convince you that I want to be alive?"

"Yeah, that's right."

"So you think I want to die?" I ask, my brain spinning.

He sighs and shakes his head. "What I think is that this is a choice that people tend to *under*think. Lots of people don't get this choice, so the people that do always jump straight to a decision without thinking about it first. What does it mean? What are the implications?" He puts his elbows on the box and leans forward, his hands clasp in front of him. "Think of it this way: the world isn't the Garden of Eden anymore. Someone down there—not naming names—opened up a whole Pandora's box of sin. It's messy, it's ugly, it's brutal, and it's harsh. You know that. Do you want to jump straight back into that?"

"Yes."

He chuckles lightly again. "Convince me," he says, and sits down, his legs manspreading and his arms stretched out along the back of the bench. His broad, muscly arms. Stop.

I stand up. *Fuck, I hate public speaking,* I snarl to myself. It's not exactly the truth; I enjoy public speaking when I've had time to prepare well in advance what I'm going to say. I like to pore over every individual word, rehearse it a dozen times in front of the mirror so I can be sure that my face doesn't contort into a hideous monster while I'm making a point. I practise sucking in my stomach just in case the angles or the lights make me look fat. *What do I say? What do I say? What do I...*

"Uhhh... Mr. Speaker," I start, and the barking laugh of Luce interrupts me. My face turns crimson.

"Dude, this isn't the real House of Commons," he sniggers. It doesn't feel malicious, but it sure as hell feels like a fucking embarrassment, and hatred for him bursts back into my veins. Hatred for him and his stupid muscly arms.

"Alright, what the fuck am I meant to start with?" I try to brush it off, but my pink cheeks tell a different story.

"Just start with the truth."

Not helpful.

I shake my head again, clearing the clutter. It doesn't work. I introduce myself with the classic 'My name is' and then, with my mind blank, say four simple words that, ironically, I've never said before in my life: "I want to live."

They feel slippery, foreign, coming from my lips, and I stutter in silence. It's like jelly has just poured from my mouth. *Disgusting*. I sit back down.

"A strong start," Luce replies, rising to his feet. I assume we're ignoring 'Mr Speaker'-gate. "Well then," he says, looking me up and down with a half-smile and his eyebrows half-raised. I feel naked. "Let's carry on."

IV

The Clearing of Little Eden

The first session (sitting?) goes well, I think. I make some strong points that any seasoned debater would: "I want to live," and "I don't want to die." Not exactly the content I wheeled out for my sixth form debating competitions, but we all have to start somewhere, I guess. In fairness to me, those debates weren't literally life and death.

As the debate rolls on, with the clock speeding up and slowing down erratically, I become more cantankerous. It's fucking ridiculous: I have to argue with a man who thinks I don't want to live and who, as he speaks more and more, might actually want me to die. What the fuck am I meant to do? All the arguments that come to mind seem so elementary I'm afraid he'll laugh me out. Do I bring up the evolutionary drive to live? Do I mention that we're all God's children? Do I... I don't even know what. I mean, how should I have to debate this? You don't walk down the street interrogating people. 'Do you want to live or *do you want to fucking die*?' The presumption is that people want to live. Why do I have to prove I do? It might be childish, but, honestly, *why the fuck is this happening to me*?

When I was a kid, my parents always used to say I was a born debater. We'd watch the news and whenever a snippet of PMQs was played my dad would laugh and point at the screen. "That's gonna be you," he would say, a broad grin on his face. I'd beam back, not quite understanding, but pleased to have been singled out for a compliment. At least, I think it was a compliment. I always seemed to have a flair for the dramatic. I'd spend hours watching courtroom dramas or political thrillers, waiting with bated breath for the epic put-down or punchline. The bit where all the characters would stop and take in what they'd just witnessed. It's no surprise, then, that I joined the debate club at my sixth form, Queen Mary's Academy. I had a good rapport with our teacher, Ms Badden, a short and grouchy lady with wild ginger hair and a soft spot for the political. She rarely used to engage in personal conversations, but every once in a while, I'd pour my heart out to her, and she'd sit stiffly and listen, staring directly at me. She'd give me an awkward hug and a custard cream from the stash she was famed for keeping in her desk drawer before ushering me out of the classroom as her next class filed in.

Ms Badden wasn't a very pretty person, and her smile wasn't beautiful. I think the world was mean to her. I knew nothing about her personal life, except that she was a 'Ms' not a 'Mrs'. Rumours had floated around about her being a lesbian, but they were mainly just the ill-thought jokes of school kids who were too progressive to know that being gay wasn't a bad thing, but too young to come up with anything better. If Ms Badden were hot and married to a woman, the jokes would remain, and if she were ugly and married to a man, a new joke would arise from the sad tale of heterosexuality and the inevitable march towards a husband hating their wife. An inevitability even my parents couldn't escape. I don't know if she was lonely, and some part of me was cruelly embarrassed by associating with her. If she was a lesbian, I must be gay, I reasoned. I too must be condemned to a life of growing old, unpretty and alone. But I needed her, and I think, in my naive and self-absorbed way, she needed me too.

Ms Badden was technically an art teacher, but she started the debate club when a group of us were sitting around one lunchtime, arguing in her classroom about something or other—I don't remember exactly what it was now—but she believed a debate team was needed. We didn't have any opportunity to air our grievances. We watched day after day of politics fucking up our lives; not just the tuition fees our millennial forefathers would gripe about, but the clampdowns on protests, the demonisation of migrants, the political football they'd make out of our trans siblings. We were young. Idealistic. And Ms Badden sat there, marking a stack of tomato-red sketchbooks and munching on her standard lunch of salad with a (terrible-smelling) blue cheese sauce, silently listening before she broke our argument with a suggestion of a debate club. The next day we walked past her in the hall putting up posters: "An opportunity to discuss all things political," the heading screamed in a deep purple, next to a photo of the Prime Minister smiling inanely beside the Union Jack.

Tom joined the club with me, which made a change. I had gone from spending my lunches at my last school alone—when I actually turned up, that is—to now having competing demands on my time. It was nice to have friends.

June 2019 was the year my parents had decided to separate, though I'm not sure how mutual that decision was. My mum had gone through my dad's phone and found all the messages to women he'd met on business trips. They were legitimate business trips, mind. He travelled a lot for work as a consulting engineer for wind farms—both on—and off-shore, he would proudly remind you, despite you never having said anything to the contrary. The way he explained it, as I listened from the other room, was that he was tired. He was fucking exhausted of having to go to work every day in a new location, all across the UK and Europe, and come home to absolutely nothing.

He knew, *of course he knew*, what my mum sacrificed so he could do that. He knew she made sure we were up for school, that Penny's hair was braided and my shirt ironed. He knew she fed the dogs and the chickens, and made sure they were safe at night. He knew that she cooked and cleaned. But who did she think paid for that? It wasn't her salary as a librarian. No. It was his salary, his money, his work. So, yeah, sue him if it got a little difficult sometimes when his wife didn't want to kiss him when he got home. How every time he walked through that door, and she didn't tell him she loved him and she missed him, his smile would drop a little, and a little more, until he dreaded coming home. How he never saw his kids, because he was busy working for their future, so they didn't have to keep living on this shitty farm that was falling apart. Did she ever think about that? No. So he found another who wanted to spend time with him.

"Several others," my mother reminded him, her jaw clenched as she stared at the dining room table, tracing the grain of the wood with her index finger.

"Several others," he conceded, sighing. He stopped pacing the floor and turned to face her. I could hear the creak of a chair as he leaned on it. He told her that he was sorry. He wishes he had never done it, any of it. He wishes that it was all different. But those women were the symptom, not the cause. And he wanted to leave. Well, he clarified, he wanted my mum to leave.

The worst sound you can hear as a kid, and probably as an adult, is your mum crying. Her sobs, starting off quiet but growing guttural and pained, pounded my brain. He was wrong, she said. She didn't have to leave. She was sorry she made him feel that way. It could all be different. She'd do anything, she pleaded. She cried and crawled over the kitchen tiles to kneel in front of him. She'd been an awful wife, a bitch, the worst, but she still loved him more than anything. She still needed him. They were in love, she reminded him. They loved each other. And what about the kids? They need us to stay together, she said.

"Babe," my dad said, his voice strained, "The last thing our kids need is to think that two people can live a life with no love in."

That's when I decided to turn my headphones on and flood my simmering brain with music, starving it of the oxygen my thoughts needed. The crying stopped pretty soon, I think, and my mum had moved out within two days, back to her parents in the countryside.

He fucked up, and she begged him to stay. I'm not sure which hurts more: that he ruined it, or that she blamed himself. It all hurts.

Between June 2019 and March 2020, I barely saw my mum. We would visit her at the weekend, but as my life drowned me, I came up with more and more reasons not to see her. Whenever we did, her eyes would be hollow and sunken, and her clothes held the lingering smoke from her last cigarette; a habit she picked up after she left. She looked broken, like she didn't know what she could do without my dad, and so she did nothing. I didn't want to add more to her plate, so when shit happened, I swore she would never know. I only told her the good stuff: that I had received the top marks in my mock exams, and that my teachers had predicted straight 8s and 9s for my GCSEs next year. I didn't tell her that my arms were so scarred they felt more like scales, or that my girlfriend Olivia had called me a faggot when she broke up with me via a phone call with her friends stifling giggles on the other end, or that I cried myself to sleep wishing that there was someone who could hold me and take away some of my pain. I didn't tell her any of it.

Of course, then COVID hit, and we were all shut inside. Then the shitty, falling apart farm was a goddamn blessing. I ignored the Microsoft Teams calls and went outside, stalking the forest that surrounded our house, clambering over the gravestones of our ancestors, the ones that had condemned our family to the farmhouse, and squelching through the fields that he had long since sold off. The forest was the last bit of wild for a long while. A couple of acres that Dad had kept and refused all the offers for from our neighbours. He told me it was an ancient oak forest, something we should be so proud of having, not that we could ever have it, he would interject, without me saying a word: it was the forest who owned itself. Over the years we've lived here, it's always been my refuge. I knew the badger set beneath the hump of dirt; I knew the pond that would sit silently all winter until it would burst in spring with croaks and birdsong; I knew the clearing where an old maple tree had been felled after it rotted from within, and no trees had since grown over.

In that clearing, a small space that felt infinite, I would lie in the grasses that never seemed to creep above a few inches, and stare up at the sky. It always knew what I needed, whether it was perfect silence in the middle of the night, or warm sunbeams on my face in the middle of summer. It knew never to get too waterlogged or too dry and hard, and it knew that I would come back when I needed it.

I'd discovered the clearing when I was five and we had first moved to the farm from our house in Manchester. That's where my parents had met, my dad as a young engineering student and my mum as an English Literature graduate, determined on writing a novel to rival Brontë. They had bought a tiny house with just two bedrooms after my dad graduated, after years of living in scummy student flats (my dad's flatmates never cleaned apparently, and he was too head over heels with my mum to notice). They called it their Little Eden, as they painted the walls in bright colours, dragged abandoned furniture off the street, and scoured through garage sales and charity shops to find what my mum called 'hidden gems' and what my dad called 'absolute crap' to populate their home. When I came along, they were bowled over, and when my sister followed when I was four, the world was perfect. We'd walk hand-in-hand, blocking the entire pavement, to the shops and come back with our hands laden with groceries, laughing the whole way. It's hard not to romanticise a romantic past.

Then my dad's mother became seriously ill, only aged 52. We packed up Little Eden and moved halfway across the country to the farm to spend what would end up being my grandmother's last few weeks by her side. When she died, my father didn't cry. He'd lost his dad the year I was born, but when his mother died, he didn't shed a single tear. I remember standing at the funeral, holding my weeping mother's hand, and staring at him as they lowered her casket into the grave he had dug himself on our land. I don't think he even blinked.

And so, the farm was ours. Our Little Eden became our wilderness, as the arable land was sold to other farms, and we said goodbye to our smallholding of sheep, cows, and pigs, with only the chickens and sheepdogs, border collies by the names of Lasso and Rusty, remaining. It was in the weeks after my grandmother died that I found my clearing, while exploring the forest my dad had refused to give up.

I did a lot of thinking in that clearing in the summer after my mother left. The summer of the pandemic. The only virtual classes I went to were for history and English, with my teachers kindly chiding me afterwards for my absences in every other subject. The doctor wrote me a note, though, I told them. I could prove why I needed to be off. They would shake their heads and smile awkwardly.

It was in that clearing that some of my (no pun intended) clearest thoughts were fashioned out of the mess that was usually my brain. Even with sunrise and sunset, time stood still in that small patch of grass, and I would come up with the heart to match the logic behind my arguments and opinions. Even when arguing for something I completely oppose, I could infect it with such passion that I could make myself believe it, even for a second. I could argue for greater surveillance, I could argue for commoditization. My dad would laugh at me when I rehearsed my opening and closing speeches in front of him. I was always picked to do one or the other, *not to brag*. He would chuckle and say that I could switch sides so quickly. One week I'd be opposing carbon taxes and the next I'd be fully in support of them, arguing with such earnestness. He worried that I was fickle.

"With a brain like that," he'd say, with a smile on his face, and proffer another of his trademark sayings, "you need to be careful you don't go forgetting what your heart believes. You could sell saltwater to a sailor, kid, but you should remember not to sell it to yourself."

I'd brush it off and remind him that it was a debate club. We had to argue different sides, Dad. But looking back, y'know, maybe his joke wasn't too badly off. It's easy when you're young and your veins are pumped full of adrenaline and idealism and angst to wrap yourself up in things that you sell yourself, and forget what the fuck you're actually there for. That's why Penny never wore makeup. She said if she started, she'd probably never stop, and she didn't want to waste an hour every morning covering up a face that she shouldn't have a problem with. Her friends would laugh, and implore her to wear the bare minimum: just mascara and concealer, Penny. *Please*. "The bare minimum," she'd reply, deadpan, "is my face." And that's what we got. I was never like that, though. I leapt from one new obsession to another, with the painful yearning that one of them would eventually make me whole.

That's where Olivia came in. And Marcus. And Lewis. And Abbas.

V

Beginning With Olivia

"So let's talk about them," Luce says, leaning over his despatch box and looking me in the eye with his irises so black they might just be pupils.

"Talk about who?" I ask, shifting uncomfortably in my seat. I have pins and needles in my legs, and I don't know how long I've been sitting here, but I need to stand up sometime soon.

"Let's talk about Olivia."

***

I was homeschooled for most of primary school. My mum wanted to stay at home and raise us after we moved from Manchester, so she never worked after we started at the farm until we started school ourselves and she went to work as a librarian part-time in the next town over. Whenever I tell people this, they cock their heads and frown sympathetically. "That must have been hard," they tell me. It wasn't. It was a fucking adventure.

I was five years old and living in my own little kingdom. I'd burst out of the front door every morning after my mum had wrestled me into my wellies, with the dogs barking in circles around me as I sprinted for the shed where I knew Megan would be. She was awesome—a stocky country girl who had been working full time on the farm since she was 16, and who knew the fields like the back of her hand. Probably even better. She'd hoist me up onto her knee in the tractor cabin and let me steer down the wide dirt and gravel road to whichever field she had to work in that day. She'd make up stories, the most incredible ones I'd ever heard, about spider kings and their underworld lairs, about dragons and the brave princesses who'd tame them, about the crazy things our toys get up to when we're not looking. In hindsight, she probably ripped a lot of this shit off from books and films, but when I was five, *fuck me*, she was cool. I couldn't get enough.

But when Megan had gone home for the day, after driving her tractor around since sunrise, my mum would sit me down at the kitchen table, and go through numbers and sums, reading and writing, the water cycle and a frog's life cycle. Her hands, skinny and older than her years, would sit over mine as she traced my finger over the words in the books, as she taught me to hold a pencil and draw a house.

My dad used to say that homeschooled kids were misfits who didn't know what everyone else did—they'd been taught a handpicked selection of knowledge, and were left unexposed to the rest of the world. My mother would be damned if she was going to let that happen. She printed off every school curriculum she could find, and painstakingly charted out mine and Penny's progress over the years, until we had got to the point where we had leapfrogged what the other kids my age had studied, and my dad had to restrain her from teaching me Chaucer and Punnett squares. "They need to go to proper school, babe," he'd plead, his toothy smile barely masking his worry. "At least for one year before they start secondary school. They need to make friends."

And so, as usual, my father won, and Penny and I were shipped off to primary school, where I joined in year six.

So Olivia... I met her on the first day of my new school.

My mother dropped Penny and I off at the gate, and I stood and watched her wave goodbye and leave. Penny cried, but I just watched. Someone ran up and took my hand, and I turned around to see a cute brunette girl with big brown eyes smiling sweetly at me. "Hello," she said with her dimples lighting up her face. "My name's Olivia."

A couple of years later, when I was months into being her boyfriend, I found out that Olivia had been requisitioned by our teacher to be my 'buddy' while I got settled in. We howled with laughter when she told me, but at the time I just thought she was a uniquely precocious child who walked up to young boys and made herself known. It seems so long ago now. It seems even longer ago now that I'm dead. Well, dead-*ish*.

Olivia and I were pretty inseparable at first. She'd run up to me first thing in the morning, grab my hand in hers, and we'd spend the rest of the day side by side. We both hated maths and loved creative writing. We wouldn't participate in P.E., but we'd spend all of lunch and break running around until we were breathless, red, and panting. Our school uniforms would come home every day muddy from our games, our favourite being one that would involve us fighting imaginary dragons and monsters with six furry legs and huge green eyes that could spit corrosive venom. We spent so much time together, people would joke that we were a couple. The younger kids at school we would play with occasionally pretended we were their parents, and we'd act along, cooking plastic meals on a plastic stove, and telling them off for forgetting to do their homework. In just one year, she became my fiercest friend—the only one I'd ever had, aside from Megan. The first friend my own age.

***

"Hold up," Luce interjects, raising his hand to silence me. It works. My mouth is dry, having been talking for an unexpectedly long time. There isn't a glass of water nearby. I look up as his brow furrows, and he swallows in preparation for what he is about to say. "What happened to Megan?"

"Excuse me?" I reply, blinking at him.

"Megan," he repeats, "What happened to her?"

"I thought you wanted to talk about Olivia?" I ask, shifting in my seat. My mouth remains uncomfortably dry. I lick my lips, but it does nothing to help.

"Keep up," he snaps with a crocodile's smile, "I want you to tell me what happened to Megan."

"Then why ask about Olivia?"

"Why don't you want to talk about Megan?"

"Stop," I bark, my voice low. "You wanted to talk about Olivia, so we're going to talk about Olivia."

***

It's so long ago now, I barely remember how it started. I remember the night in mum's library when she was working late, and Penny and I were lounging on the beanbag chairs, she reading a colourful picture book on dinosaurs, and me staring heatedly at my phone. Most of the lights had been switched off, and the fluorescent bulb overhead buzzed irritatingly. My eyes were beginning to hurt from the strain of watching as the three little dots in a grey bubble flashed up and disappeared again, my heart pounding and my brain numb. I'm not even sure why I was so invested. Olivia was like a sister to me—a real sister, not the shite one Penny is—and I just didn't want to fuck up our relationship. It seemed like the natural progression of things, but it felt so unnatural. The fibres of my body knew it was wrong. The three dots popped up again, and were swiftly replaced by a short message: "Yes".

So we were boyfriend-girlfriend then. For reasons I don't really remember, we hid it from my parents at first. They just assumed we were still the best friends we had been for the last three years, and whenever she came over, they treated her like one of the family still, playfully teasing her at the dinner table, and making jokes about us being in a relationship, which we'd awkwardly laugh at, our hands interlocked under the table. We eventually told them—well, she did. Casually mentioned it one night after the movie we'd been watching had finished. My face flushed a dark red and my dad slapped me on the shoulder in congratulations, smiling broadly as my mum gasped and then berated us for not telling her as soon as it happened.

"Nothing's changed," I told her. "We're still the same people."

"Everything's changed," she replied. "Oh, you're so young."

She'd always do that, my mother. Exaggerate, particularly when it came to me. I don't even know what we were 'so young' for, but she didn't expand any further. She just went back to playing the game on her phone, shaking her head at the two of us in exasperation. My dad reminded us that we still had to sleep in separate rooms when she stayed over, and my face reddened again.

"Why?" Olivia asked. I shot her a look.

"Because you're still kids!" my dad laughed.

"I'm 13," she replied, ignoring my look.

"And he's 12, exactly." My dad's face turned serious, and he raised his eyebrows at her. "You're still kids."

Olivia huffed. I'm not sure what her problem was. When she went home later that night, my dad pulled me into the kitchen after we parted with a quick kiss on the cheek.

"Are you okay, kiddo?" he said, his hand on the same shoulder he had clapped me on.

"Fine, Dad. Why?"

"I'm just asking," he replied softly. I stared at the floor. "Your mum and I love you very much."

"I know, Dad." My eyes remained fixed on the yellow wall tiles. He didn't say anything more, and turned to grab a glass off the shelf. I stayed standing there, leaning on the counter. My face would likely never turn back to its normal colour.

As he filled the glass up from the tap, I suddenly noticed my heart begin to pound. I felt sick.

"Dad..." I said, and he replied with a 'Hmm?' I stared at his back while he drank the water, my stomach churning. Maybe I would have said something if he had turned to face me. Maybe. "Nothing," I shrugged and walked from the kitchen, up the stairs with the worn red carpet, and to my room, where I closed the door, and, my hand dropping from the cool brass handle, leaned against it, my forehead pressed on the painted wood. I tried to calm my breathing, which was slowly becoming more erratic. I jumped over a pile of laundry that had been lying there for a few days and fell onto my bed. My hands clenched the sheets—old white cotton ones with a dark blue pattern that had faded to a dull navy—and I drove my face into the pillow. I cried myself to sleep that night, with pins and needles radiating across my body.

When the sun rose the next day, light poured in through the window, the curtains having fallen down weeks prior after I tripped and, while falling, grabbed hold of the dense fabric and ripped them off the wall. The sunbeams hit my stiff body, and I sat up, dazed, to stare out at the clear sky. Some snot had dried on my face and I scratched it off, mildly disgusted with myself. My leg pounded and I pulled some painkillers off the bedside table, knocking a magazine onto the floor in the process, and swallowed the tablets dry. I pried my skinny jeans off me and felt the blood rush back into my lower body as I cursed myself for not getting undressed the night before. I had a few new ingrown hairs on my thighs, and I cursed myself again. There was a three-day-old cup of water on the table, and I guzzled it down. This truly was not my finest moment.

Walking downstairs, I stopped halfway and listened to the low tones of my parents talking in the kitchen. It had become something of a habit, to wait a beat before entering a room to make sure I wasn't interrupting anything. Twice I had walked in on them talking hushedly about my sister, and I dreaded ever catching them discussing me. I couldn't make out what they were saying, and the pit in my stomach grew deeper. Lining the staircase were photos of us all, the four of us, as we grew up. The only one featuring me that didn't arouse visceral disgust was one of me sitting in the garden of our Little Eden, the patchy dry grass and cracked ground parched from a heatwave, and I was dressed in a soft yellow vest—what my mum would call my 'tank top' in a way that felt derogatory, even if it was always coupled with her gushing over it—and blue shorts that cut off halfway down my skinny thighs. I was probably four or five in the photo, and cradled in my arms was Mr. Gumbo, a fat grey cat named after the dish my maternal grandmother would cook from her childhood in Louisiana, and my first word. He lazed in my arms as I grinned toothily at the camera, and I remember the heat radiating from his soft fur onto my skin in the cool breeze. He purred loudly, like a lawnmower at dawn, and I would giggle along as he nuzzled into my chest. *Fuck, I missed those days.*

I took a deep breath and walked into the kitchen—the site of my failure from the night before. I don't know why I didn't just tell him then and there. It was an opportunity, if not the perfect one. Do you ever get a perfect opportunity? This shit isn't a movie—it's messy, and it's disgusting, and it's life. I bottled it, basically. My parents were still in their pyjamas, leaning over the breakfast bar and chatting aimlessly while nursing their coffees from matching mugs Penny and I'd got them for Christmas one year. I knew my dad wasn't homophobic—he was too sensible for that. Too introverted to give a shit about what other people were doing, and too logical to think that just because you're fucking a man it makes you any less of a human being. Still, I don't know why I couldn't tell him, and now I was deep undercover into dating Olivia. I guess the longer it went on, the more impossible it would have been to tell them.

There I was, standing in the kitchen in some old joggers I'd pulled on and a t-shirt from a band I'd listened to religiously for one summer before immediately neglecting for the rest of my life, musing the impossibility of saying anything that would contradict the fact of my relationship with Olivia. I was quite clearly heterosexual; I had a girlfriend, for fuck's sake. In my mind, I could see us going to university together, moving in together, getting married, and having kids. That was what life looked like. It's what my parents did, and it's what my grandparents did, and it's what I would do, even if the thought of it made me nauseous.

"Hi, sweetheart," my mum said, turning to face me. I could smell the coffee breath on both of them from here, so I kept my distance, slinking round the edge of the kitchen to the cereal cupboard on the other side of the room. I grunted a 'Morning' to them both, and they went back to their conversation about the bulbs they'd planted together the weekend before. It was early spring, so they were eagerly awaiting the fruits, or flowers, of their labour once the cold snap had ended.

Lasso and Rusty laid bored in their crates in the mud room, a tiny square adjacent to the kitchen where we would kick off our shoes to prevent the dirt from being trampled into the carpet—my dad's worst nightmare. Their ears pricked up as the cereal sprinkled into the bowl, and I topped it off with a spoonful of sugar and milk, and their eyes watched me as I carried it through to the sitting room and flicked on the TV, but they didn't move. Since the sheep had gone, they were just dogs, and made no secret of the fact they had no intention of ever working again.

***

"Sorry, is this a story about the life of your dogs now?" Luce interrupted, with a 'hah' at the end, although it wasn't funny.

"I'm just telling you. It's not as if I've planned this whole thing out." I sighed. *I can't even tell the story of my life without doing it wrong.*

***

I did fall in love with Olivia. I mean, I loved her anyway. She had long been my best friend, my partner in crime, my other half. But I fell in love with her while we dated. I fell in love with all the things you begin to see when you date someone that you never saw when you were just friends: the way she brushed her hair while singing Taylor Swift songs under her breath like no one else could hear; the way she would bite grapes in half because "you get more juice that way"; the way she sent all the videos that made her laugh, because she knew you would laugh too. I fell in love with how she held my hand and stroked it with her thumb absentmindedly, and how she kissed me on the forehead, so softly.

It's not as if I was lying to her for the two or three years we dated. Maybe I did tell her I loved her because I thought I should, and how should I have known what love meant, anyway? She was everything to me. At the very least, she was the everything that I couldn't be, and if I lost her, I lost the chance to be everything I wished I was.

She could be cruel sometimes, though, like she was testing me and waiting for me to stumble. She would quiz me on all the other people we knew, from the popular football lads to the weird kids who seemed to always have tarot cards out during lunchtime. She would ask my opinion on everything they did, and then agree with me earnestly at the end, only for me to find out days later from her friends that she was telling them something completely different. Whenever she would ask me a question, I would wrap my head in knots trying to play out the scenarios that would lead to her finding me out, and, ever the politician my dad thought I was, I would end up concluding with a non sequitur and a convoluted analogy coupled with a forced laugh.

But every once in a while, Olivia would let her walls down completely. She would ask a question that would leave me stumped, not because I didn't know the answer, but because I didn't know what answer she needed.

Olivia's dad still hit her. Sure, my parents might have smacked me once or twice as a child, but Olivia's would still slap her across the cheek when she spoke back. Hard. It would leave a red stain on her face for an hour afterwards that she would hold a cold damp flannel to as she waited for the inflammation to recede. I told her it was wrong, that she should tell someone at school, but she would snap back that I didn't know what I was talking about. He wasn't a big man—kind of short, with a balding head, big nose, and the kind of attitude you find on a person who hates the world for his own absence of achievement. The kind of guy who hates participation trophies, but honestly, he needed one. He would make you laugh with his stories about growing up in London's east end, and then make your heart ache and burn and break when he hit his only daughter for telling him that she never touched his beer, when we both knew we had swiped one to drink only a few hours before.

That was the first time I saw it, and the last. I refused to go back to Olivia's house if she didn't do the right thing and report him, and she refused to listen to me. *Fuck.* It hurts just thinking about it now. Her own boyfriend abandoned her because he wasn't man enough to stand up to him.

***

"You were twelve," Luce says, his eyes staring down at his hands as he sat hunched over on the bench. I ignore him.

***

One time, lying in my bed together, on top of the covers with the door ajar when I was 13, almost 14, she intertwined her fingers with mine and rolled to face me. She said my name, so softly that I almost thought I had imagined it. I looked down to see her eyes, big and brown and deep, staring back at mine.

"Do you ever worry that you're running so fast and you forget if you're running from something or towards something?" she asked, blinking slowly.

My mind was blank in what I assumed was either ignorance or panic. Potentially both. My heartbeat quickened slightly. "I'm not sure, babe," I said. I had taken to calling her 'babe' when I saw a guy I fancy on a TV show doing the same to his girlfriend. "I guess so?"

"Me too."

VI

Some Answers

Luce walks out suddenly, with a gust of wind flying behind him. He doesn't say a word, or look at me, but he walks out, leaving me standing at my despatch box, my throat dry and my voice getting scratchy. I look up for the first time and watch the light pouring in from the skylights. Some dust particles dance in the beams, and I sit back down, my eyes never leaving them in their whimsical waltz through the rays of light. If it is the sun, I mean. Or just some random celestial glow. No one has explained to me the physics of this place.

It's a little irritating that he asks these questions, interrupts so often, and then doesn't even let me finish the story. If he asked about Olivia, I should be allowed to talk about Olivia. In my own words, in my own time, and in my own way. I haven't actually thought about her this much in a long time, but I guess you never forget your first—well, not love. You never forget your first heartbreak.

I haven't actually seen her in over two years. About six months after we broke up, before the end of year 11, her dad and her moved to Poland for his work, and although I gave her an awkward goodbye, with a tear in her eye, I never messaged and neither did she. Even when you're young, you know when it's over. It's not a bad thing, my dad told me. It's good, it's healthy. We had just sort of... run out of things to say. That's okay.

I take a deep breath and my eyes drift down, blinking to

clear the flashes of light etched into my corneas from staring at the "sun" for so long.

What the FUCK? I jump, my heart leaping into my throat. I let out a scream. It isn't manly.

"Jesus FUCKING Christ," I exhale, my ribcage struggling to confine my pounding heart. "What the FUCK are you doing here?"

"Oh. I just walked in," replies Rebecca, who is standing about a metre away. "You shouldn't swear."

"You can get in here?" My eyebrows furrow, my mouth agape. I ignore the last comment. It's a little too close to Penny for my liking, and the thought of her hurts.

"Oh, sure," she says, looking around curiously. The light coming from above illuminates the stray strands of hair flicking out from her pigtails. I stare at her expectantly, though for what, I'm not sure.

"What do you want?" I ask. I don't want to come across as rude, but she just walked into the one place I kind of assumed it would just be me and Luce. You know what they say about assumptions, I guess.

"I want to see how it's going," she replies, still looking around. I wonder momentarily if she's also watching the dust dance, or if she even knows what this room is. "How is it going?"

"Um," I pause, thinking back a little, "I mean, I don't know. He's just asking questions. You know what it's like? I mean, do you?"

"Mine is a little different," she says, looking at me for the first time since I've seen her.

Curiosity gets the better of me. I enquire as to what hers is like.

"Mine's just like therapy," she looks down at her feet, which are barefoot like mine were before I found these socks. "I used to have therapy back home."

"Why?" I ask. *Nosy, I know.*

"Lots of reasons." Rebecca is about eight, but she talks like she's eighteen. It feels weird to me. Like the girl who plays Matilda. She's precocious, for sure.

"Are you ever going to tell me anything, or is it just gonna be one cryptic remark after another?" It's getting a little frustrating. I'm a broken record, but honestly, I'm swinging from frustrated to confused to angry every five minutes in this potentially literal hellhole. It'd be nice to get an answer every now and then.

"I don't owe you anything," Rebecca says simply. She lets the statement hang in the stagnant air. It infuriates me.

"You're the one that came up to me! You told me you needed me, so you kind of do owe me an explanation here. This place is crazy enough without a strange kid coming up to me and trying to get me to promise things with zero context. You do owe me, Rebecca." I don't know why I use her name; I guess it makes me feel like a teacher. Authoritative.

Her face steels and she looks down at me as I sit on the edge of the bench, my arms holding me up on either side. "I. Don't. Owe. You. Anything." She turns and walks out.

I sigh noisily, and throw my head back to rest on the back of the bench, the hard wood digging into my neck. *Fuck.* I drag myself up and jog to catch up with her. Again, always one step behind this girl.

"Hey," I call out to her as she continues her march through the sparse mall. Nobody turns to look at us. I feel like I'm a sore thumb that no one notices. Eventually it'll turn septic and kill us all. Rebecca reaches a bench a few hundred yards from the door we left out of that doesn't seem to be there anymore. Maybe we turned a corner at some point, I don't know. Sitting down, she pouts and stares at the floor, breathing heavily. She's pissed.

"Hey, Rebecca," I say, sitting down at her side, looking at the side of her head as the tendons twitch in her temple. "I'm sorry." I'm not sure why I am, but I feel bad knowing she's mad at me, although the notion of what exactly I've done wrong eludes me. "I'm just confused here, and I'm kinda scared. I just want to know what's happening, and I want to help you, but I don't know how." I pause, feeling the pit return to my stomach with a vengeance. "I don't even know how to help myself."

Rebecca says nothing, but continues to stare daggers at the white floor, which remains unblemished despite her efforts. For some reason, *See You Again* by Wiz Khalifa and Charlie Puth is stuck in my head. The first rap verse. I can't remember how it ends.

"Do you wanna tell me, maybe, why you need my help?" I prompt. I want to put an arm around her, but it feels awkward. My hands lay in my lap, unmoving.

"Where are you from?" she asks, still staring into space. It's not an answer to my question, but I tell her anyway: a small town in the middle of nowhere. An old market town surrounded by fields and forests. But that's not my hometown. I'm from Little Eden, a perfect wilderness between four garden walls, and I moved to a bigger garden. She listens intently, but her fixed gaze never falters. I continue, telling her about my clearing in the woods, and the things I'd think about while I was there. I'd think about the people in my life.

"Your mum and dad?" she asks, interrupting my uneasy stream of consciousness.

Not really. "Sometimes, yeah." It seems like a harmless lie, but lying feels wrong to me, regardless. I feel a maggot pop up beneath my skin and begin crawling.

"Do you miss them?" Her detachedness was beginning to alarm me. Suddenly I'm very aware of how my breath sounds.

I hadn't really thought about it, to be honest. I do miss them, I guess. I don't know how long I've been here, in the Interlife, but it kind of feels like I've always been here. It feels normal to be here. I'm not homesick at all, but I do wish there is some more green. I want to be outside and breathe fresh air, instead of the staleness of inside.

"Yeah, I miss them," I reply. I'm not sure if I do, but what else do you say to that question? I do miss them, of course I miss them, but I don't miss them right now. I miss who they used to be. I miss when my mum would swing me into her arms and tell wild stories and would tousle the ringlets in my hair and laugh with that softly gruff giggle she would reserve for her family. I miss my dad's jokes and how he could get us all dancing in the living room on New Year's Eve, and I miss when him and my mum would cook together, and I would watch his hands on her waist as she stirred the pot, and how she'd lean back into his embrace, closing her eyes as the fragrant spices filled the kitchen. I miss the people they haven't been since I was a kid. I find myself ripped from my thoughts when I feel Rebecca's hand on my own. Her focus has softened along with the muscles in her face, but she still doesn't meet my eyes. Her soft skin is warm on my own long and bony fingers, what my mum would call my Tim Burton hands. My dad was kinder—pianist's hands. Rebecca wraps her fist around the four fingers of my right hand and squeezes gently.

"I miss my parents, too," she says. My heart aches for her.

"Do you know if you'll be able to go back to them?" I turn my hand around and squeeze her tiny hand slightly harder.

"I don't think so," she says softly, and my heart breaks. Goosebumps ripple over my skin. I look at her, and in her young age, behind the plump cheeks and the long eyelashes, behind a stray ringlet of hair curling down from her forehead, are eyes that speak multitudes. They far outstrip her youth, like the water that has dripped from a glacier into a river. She turns to me, meeting my eyes for the first time. I look into their ancient depths. "I don't need to see them again," she says.

"I'd like to, but I don't need to." My mouth is uncomfortably dry and sticky. There's nothing I can say even if I could make noise. Rebecca leans into me, her head too low for my shoulder, so she rests it on my chest, her hand still clasping mine.

There's a hand on my shoulder. I turn my head to see Luce standing behind me. He jerks his head gently, and mouths, "Come on." He turns before I can refuse, and I look down to see that somehow Rebecca has slipped away.

VII

The Beginning of the End. Or the Middle

"You've made quite a friend in Rebecca," Luce says, walking a step ahead of me. I don't know where we're going.

"I guess." I shrug, not knowing what to say. I don't know how he knows. I feel bad that I'm embarrassed to have befriended an eight-year-old girl; my only friend in this place. I feel bad about feeling bad.

"She's a sweet kid," he nods slowly while he walks, not bothering to check if I'm still following. I nod silently in reply. "Just..." he pauses and swallows. "Just make sure you're focussed on the right things here."

"Focussed on getting home?" I reply, my tone sharpening instinctively.

"Focussed on making the right choice, kiddo." The way he calls me 'kiddo' raises my hackles. My dad used to call me that when I was still young. I can't remember the last time he did.

By the time Luce turns to face me, I realise he's led us back to the Commons. We're facing each other across the despatch boxes. Again. "I realise I interrupted you when we last spoke." He acts as if it was a century ago. It feels that way, somehow. "I'm sorry."

I don't know what to say to that. I blink at him.

"Something urgent came up, and I had to go and deal with it," he shrugs, with his goddamn ruggedness meaning the non-chalance is practically dripping off of him. *The prick.* "But I'm here now, and I'd like you to carry on."

"With Olivia?" I ask, my mouth dry again. There's a glass of water beside the box, and I take a few sips, resisting the urge to guzzle. You'd think in the after, I mean, Interlife, you'd be less self-conscious about how quickly you drink, but here we are. I haven't pissed or shit since I got here, but what bodily functions remain, I'm going to be embarrassed about them.

"Hey, this is your venue," he waves his arms around, gesturing at the vaulted ceilings, "Your venue, your story, your choices."

"I mean, I can carry on with Olivia." Decisiveness has never been my strong suit.

"Then carry on, kiddo."

Kiddo.

***

I guess things started going downhill with Olivia when I first met Marcus. That's when I knew it was destined to end, no matter how hard I scratched and clawed at her to stay. No matter how many wounds I inflicted on us all.

Marcus didn't go to our school. He went to the boys-only school across town, behind the park next to the industrial estate. He was skinny, with a boyish charm I can only imagine one acquires from being dunked in testosterone seven hours a day. In my mind, everyone who went to the boys school was just being moulded into every closeted kids' worst nightmare and most perfect dream. His teeth were slightly crooked, and one of them at the back was missing, I later found out, but his smile could still light up the room when he belted out one of his signature howling laughs, clapping his hands like a seal. I'm not painting the most beautiful picture, but Marcus wasn't beautiful. He was just... intoxicating. His voice had a southeastern English twang to it that made it sound a higher pitch than it actually was, in that perfect frequency that drilled into your bones and your... well, another bone, I guess.

Marcus, unfortunately, was not gay. Marcus was straight, and Marcus was dating my friend Saira, and they'd been together since they were 12, a bit like Olivia and me. I didn't really have my own friends, I just shared Olivia's, and every day after school for months our squad would traipse down to the park next to the industrial estate, where Marcus and his boys were hanging out by the swings. Saira would run into his arms with a giggle, and his gangly frame would embrace her, laughing and looking into her eyes as they kissed quickly while the others hooted and hollered, and Olivia and I, holding hands, would blush and look down, avoiding the commotion. We were the 'couples' of the group, and would smile along while our friends would crack jokes about girls they liked and boys they wanted to fuck, secure in our belief that we were better, more mature, and happier than they were.

And as the group washed in and out of situationships, crushes, and 'talking' stages like the tide on the beach, Marcus and Saira and Olivia and I would watch above the fray as hearts were broken and lipstick was smeared. While the two of them would murmur into each other's ears and wrap their limbs around each other like horny spider monkeys, Olivia and I were satisfied with holding hands, a quick peck at the end of our goodbyes, and conversations about our favourite music, all the while I'd be dragging my eyes away from staring longingly at the boy next to us. It's a hard life. Sometimes, a very *hard* life.

It felt incomparably dirty to be kissing, albeit pecking, my girlfriend at the end of every day only to go home and pull up Marcus's social media and salivate and... expel other fluids over the photos of him in his football kit. The cheeky photos that would pop up in his close friends' stories of his team mucking about in the locker rooms, and, sometimes, just a selfie that had lighting to slay a Kardashian, with his cheeky smile and impish charm. Marcus was quite quickly becoming my motivation for going to school and seeing him after. He was becoming my obsession. I'd drag him into conversations with whoever I was talking to at the time, asking Olivia, jokingly of course, whether she thought Marcus was secretly bi, given how much he talked about his favourite footballers. Given how he admitted himself how he worshipped Kendrick Lamar and Lil Nas X and Taylor Swift because, he said, "Good music is good music." I asked the mates he hung around with whether he was such a twat at school too, in the hopes they'd tell another story of Marcus getting his cock out during a science lesson. A horny, closeted teen boy really is the worst conversationalist.

My stomach rolled and butterflies flooded into it whenever he clapped me on the shoulder, or squeezed my cheek in jest while grinning like a devil. While kissing my girlfriend or stroking her thigh while we lazed, I dreamed of Marcus. The thought of it, of it all, makes me feel sick even now.

It was only a matter of time, I know, before I would, like one of the killers in the true crime documentaries Olivia would inhale, strike. You can only fantasise so much before you're compelled to act.

***

"Do you think it's weird that you're talking about yourself like you're a murderer?" Luce interrupts. The question sounds too genuine to be a joke. So much for his earlier apology.

"Shut up," I roll my eyes and let out an exaggerated huff. "You said you wanted to listen."

***

So, I did strike. I went in for my first kill. My first taste of blood. *I labour the metaphor.*

I was 14, they were 15 (perpetually the baby of any group with an August birthday), when we went to a party to celebrate the last day of year 10 at our friend Aleksandra's house. Walking up the driveway, we were already tipsy, having spent the last few hours after school ended getting ready at Saira's mum's flat a few streets down. We endured what felt like endless rounds of 'Never Have I Ever' in which Olivia and I drank shamefully little, followed by a dozen rounds of Ring of Fire, in which Olivia and I rapidly closed the ground, and 'Who'd You Rather', in which Marcus flirtily grazed my thigh with a wink after choosing me over Abida, who was widely acknowledged to be the school 'hottie'. By the time we reached the imposing front door of Aleks's sprawling house, we were sweating cheap vodka from every pore.

Olivia and I, hand in hand as usual, kissed messily in a living room I faintly remember as having a strong smell of budget beer and aerosol air freshener. She grabbed my crotch, which I laughed off with a fumbled comment on how much I'd drunk. She frowned at me with her bottom lip pouting in a way that, even if I was straight, would have turned me off, and she strutted off to fill her cup. The bass beat rolled through the carpet, rattled the ceiling lights, and pummelled into my brain. I strained my swirling mind to recall the words to the song, but they were lost among the alcohol haze. I stuffed my hands into the pockets of my jeans that were once skinny but had grown increasingly baggy thanks to my new routine of press-ups before bed every night. *The things you do for lust.*

A hand grabbed my shoulder, and I turned around, grinning toothily, expecting to see Olivia returned with drinks for us both, but instead coming face to face with Marcus. He flashed me his heart-achingly enticing smile and pulled me into his firm chest. *Someone else hadn't been skipping their exercise regime,*

I sniggered internally. His hand snaked from my shoulder to tousle my hair. I squirmed away from him with a laugh, patting down the styling that took ages to perfectly sculpt. He batted my hands away and, with his arm wrapped around my neck in a headlock, tucked me into his armpit. With my hands gripping his biceps, and feeling them flex beneath the white polyester shirt with a sheen we had mocked him for, I called for mercy. Marcus's laughter barked out of him.

"Always so evasive," he chuckled in mock rebuke. I curled myself out of his grip and, steadying my swaying with a hand on his shoulder, smiled in reply. "Where's your girl?" He asked, but he didn't look around for her. His eyes were fixed on mine.

"Not my girl," I pulled a face, and he barked out another laugh. I held my tongue from telling him *I don't even want a girl.*

Marcus grinned and raised an eyebrow at me, absentmindedly biting his lip. *No. It must have been on purpose.* He placed his hand on top of mine and squeezed it. "You okay, bro?" He asked, leaning in slightly. His eyes still hadn't left mine.

"Yeah, I'm grand," I slurred. Perhaps I wasn't okay, *bro.*

"Come on, let's get you some fresh air."

Ordinarily I would have resisted the unwelcome reminder I was the youngest of the group and needed to be treated accordingly. But tonight, I followed silently, the blood in my head pounding against my eyes. Brushing past people I barely knew, or barely noticed, I allowed myself to be led, hand in hand, by Marcus, through the house and out the back door. On the patio at a glass table with metal legs rusting at the bolts sat a few girls, one of whom I recognised from my science class. They cheered as I stumbled out the door, making cute baby noises and commenting at how drunk I had let myself become. I gave them a mock salute—the reason why, I'm still not sure—and followed Marcus's humoured chuckle round the side of the house to a secluded bench between two landscaped hedges. Aleks's house was offensively big, and I imagined her parents must have hired gardeners, or a team of gardeners, to keep their property this pristine.

Plonking myself next to Marcus, I leaned into his chest, and he wrapped his arm around my shoulders. I nuzzled and he sniggered but gripped me tighter.

"How you doin', man?" Marcus asked, and I mumbled incoherently in response. "I figured," he laughed. The sound was harsh against the stillness of the night. I don't remember when it had grown so dark, but the only light was pouring out of the house windows. The night was cold, but heat radiated from Marcus.

He said something to Gaurav who had drunkenly stumbled round the corner, and waved them away, but his hand returned to my shoulder. I swear he started stroking me with it, caressing me. I *swear.* I was so tired, my eyes heavy and my head beginning to pound and spin. He whispered something to me—I'm not sure what, but I lifted my head up and saw him looking at me, his eyes staring into my own. Despite all my staring, I'd never seen the flecks of green that speckled the brown irises. My stomach exploded into butterflies that filled my lungs and fluttered through my veins.

I don't know why I did it. I really don't. I wish I hadn't. But I did.

I leaned in, my eyes drifting closed, and pressed my lips against his. I could feel his bottom lip grazing my chin, and I could taste the tequila and Diet Coke on his mouth. His fringe tickled my forehead, and my heart somersaulted in my chest. After what must have been seconds that felt like infinity, he pulled away. I fell forward before catching myself.

"Hey," he said, his voice strong and harsh.

Fuck.

"Bro."

FUCK.

I turned and ran without looking at him again.

VIII

The First Aftermath

So maybe running wasn't the smartest idea. I had barely got round the house and to the end of the driveway before my leg started throbbing in an unwelcome reminder this wasn't the first time in my life I had fucked up, and my head started to spin from the pain and the alcohol. Not wanting to turn, I doubled over, squeezing my eyes closed as if that would help anything, but it didn't, so I slunk into the shadows of the street, dimly lit by sporadic streetlamps, and began the walk home. I didn't hear anyone follow me, but the possibility flooded my mind anyway, the thought of Marcus running up to me, pulling me into a hug, or a kiss, or just to punch the shit out of me. My phone was eerily silent, and I checked it every few moments in case I'd missed a vibration, but it remained dormant, my empty home screen staring back at me. My mind was still spinning, my stomach sick with anxiety, with disgust, with sheer fucking heartbreak.

My mind probably should have been on Olivia—at the situation's most basic, I had just kissed someone else. I'd cheated, probably. If I had thought about her, the notion would have disgusted me. I had hated my dad for cheating, and I would have hated myself. But the idea never boarded my train of thought. Instead, my mind was fixed on myself. Myself, and Marcus.

I was gay, I had deduced from the incident. There was no denying it anymore. Sure, I had considered it in the abstract before, the fact lurking in the background of everything I had ever done, from my crush—bordering on obsession—with Olivia's favourite singer, Jacen Taylor, to the nights spent thinking about running my tongue over every inch of Marcus's body. Whenever I had touched Olivia, I had thought of him. Whenever I had touched myself, I had thought of a guy. So, yeah, I was probably definitely actually now, in practice, gay. The thought made me nauseous. But I didn't really think about Olivia except tangentially. I thought about her like she was living on the sidelines in my life, like a column that never moved, that never had an impact on me until she might be gone.

I'm a shit person, I know. This was my girlfriend. The first person except my family and except for Megan that I had ever told I loved them. And I treated her—even thought of her—like a side character in the story of my life. If that. Marcus was my main priority at that moment. The boy I had just kissed. It didn't feel like I wanted it to feel. There was no firework, no spark, no tenderness, nothing that felt like love. The thought made me want to break down and cry in the middle of the road. I wanted to scream and sob until my throat was raw, and until a lorry came along and put me out of my misery. I wanted it to rain hard, so my devastation would be muffled by the expansiveness of the world. I wanted it to not matter. I wanted to not matter. I wanted to be the only thing that mattered.

But no storm came. No pathetic fallacy to console me. Nor did I cry like I wanted to. I hurt like hell, but no tears came. Marcus didn't come either. I walked the six miles home in silence, a solitary car passing me in the night with a thumping bass that disturbed my misery. *Can't the world just give me this?* I asked myself as I watched its red rear lights disappear behind trees like the devil's eyes. Even he had given up on me.

***

Luce sniggers.

"Can I help you?" I look up, my voice raw and my eyes heavy with exhaustion.

"My sincerest apologies," he replies, and gestures for me to continue in my wallowing.

I drop my eyes to fix on my hands once more, and play with my fingers absentmindedly as I pick up the story again.

***

By the time I got home, the house was silent, and I figured everyone had gone to sleep. That's fine with me. I just want to go to bed. I want to lie in the black and replay the moment again and again. The kiss I had dreamed about for years had come and gone in an instant. A brief moment of present in between past and future. And now it had passed. I slipped my key into the door and turned, the lock janking noisily, and the door creaked open obnoxiously. I noted my annoyance, but wearily closed the door and headed for the stairs.

A polite cough stopped my heart, and my mind raced to picture Marcus sitting in the chair by the living room window; the reading light I hadn't registered being on. He was here, and my head twirled with the possibilities that might bring. Love or war. I turned around and peered through the ajar door.

"Hello, love," Lois said. She had been my dad's girlfriend for the last six months. She was a tall, slender woman, with short blonde hair, and a soft received pronunciation that soothed conversation around our boisterous kitchen table. Curled on the chair that seemed to cradle her graceful limbs with ease, her finger held the place in a battered paperback that I knew to be Jane Eyre even though its cover was pressed against her thigh—she had been reading it for the last few days and had cornered me into conversation about it several times. Her long eyelashes batted at me with more polite enquiry than concern or anger at my late and abrupt arrival. I had told them both that I would likely spend the night at Olivia's, or just crash at Aleks's if that was more the vibe, so me turning up at home in the early hours of the morning was not to be expected, particularly knowing the six miles of treacherous country road that stood between our farm and Aleks's townhouse.

"Is everything okay?" she asked. Her smooth voice trickled over the furnishings and fabric of the room like melted chocolate.

She didn't need to ask. But as she did, the tears came. I crumpled into the arms she wrapped around me as I sobbed and wept. My eyes bled salty beads and she said nothing, but held me in her soft embrace. Every time I opened my mouth to cough out an apology between hacking sobs, she silenced me with a gentle squeeze, and I continued to cry into her shoulder. Over time, for what felt like hours for me, but can't have been that long, my grief subsided, and my blotchy face stared at the carpet as I sat next to her on the chair that always seemed uncomfortably small for two, but now embraced us both like a blanket. As my tears dwindled from a gush to a drip, I told her of how I had been lying to my dad, my mum, my sister, everyone, for the last two years. I told her how I had fallen in love with Marcus like a kid falls in love with a new toy, and how I had thrown away Olivia just because I was too fucking stupid to hold myself back.

Not only that, but I told Lois everything. I told her how I hated myself and everything I was. I told her how my skin crawled with disgust when I thought about who I was, and I told her how I had cut away at it every night for a year in the hopes that one day it would all disappear. I told her how I had layered scar on scar, and how my body ached with the trauma I had been inflicting on it for so long. I told her how I missed my mum and told her how I was so scared of seeing her in case she saw what I had become. I told her how I was a cripple. How my leg had been fucked up in the outhouse that day with Megan. I told her how what hurt me more than the nerve damage was the constant knowledge that I was reduced to a lesser human, and that I was the reason my first ever proper friend left me. I told her how I wanted to be loved more than anything. How I had forgotten Olivia because I wanted the butterflies that lit up my heart to burst out in a firework of everything that I had spent my life wanting. I told her how all I remembered now was Marcus's eyes as he slowly wiped away the trace of my lips. I told her I just didn't want to be there anymore.

Throughout it all, I could feel Lois's eyes on me, blinking quietly. Their pale blue was never cold, but instead refreshing, like a summer river. She didn't say anything as I confessed my sins, but she just watched, her head cocked slightly to one side like a labrador. *Like how Luce is watching me now.* I wanted her to hug me, to hold me again, but she didn't. Not until I had spluttered out the last of my admissions. I sat there, breathless from the exertion, and instead of feeling lighter, like the websites said I would, I felt hollow. Hollow and tired. The realisation I had just turned a corner from which I could never retreat flicked through my mind, but I was too exhausted to consider it.

Lois leaned forward, her long legs unravelling beneath her. She put a hand on my shoulder and squeezed it gently. There were no perfect words she could have said at that moment. Nothing that could've changed how I felt. No magic phrase or secret spell she could have uttered that would have sparked a new dawn on the life I had brought upon myself. I don't even remember what she said. I didn't look her in the eye, but mumbled an excuse and apology, and dragged myself to bed.

***

At this pause, Luce stands quietly, and steps to his box. I watch him. The pressure behind my eyes tries to force some tears out, but I steady myself and focus on breathing in and out.

"You skipped quite a portion there, kiddo."

Kiddo.

"What do you mean?" I say. My voice is shaky and quiet.

"You'd never told me what happened with Megan. You'd never told me you hurt yourself. You'd never told me half of this stuff." Luce's voice is steady, and it irritates me, but I'm exhausted. At the mention of my leg, it starts throbbing again.

"I don't know what you want me to say."

"We'll have to come back to this later, but I think you should finish your story first."

***

When I woke the next day, my sheets were stained brown with blood, and I cursed myself. My head pounded in my skull, and I gulped down a glass of water that I don't remember having left there. The skin on my forearms was taut and painful with the effort. I was careful not to strain it so much that the scabs split. I put my head in my hands and began to pray that last night was a dream. *Chance would be a fine fucking thing.*

"Kiddo," my dad said, and my head spun round to see him sitting at my desk on the adjacent wall. I hadn't seen him there when I woke, and I instinctively burrowed back into my duvet. Maybe he hadn't seen my arms. Maybe he doesn't know anything. But I knew I was lying to myself. *As per.* "I think you need to talk to me."

"What are you doing in my room?" I yelled, my voice an octave higher than usual, and strained with incredulity. He was silent. "Get out!" He didn't move. "Dad. Get out." He was still.

I wanted to run out from my bed and straight to the clearing, but my head was spinning with the terror that he would follow me there, and my one sanctuary would be breached. I couldn't risk that. But I couldn't get out of bed to go anywhere. Then he would see my arms. *If he hadn't already.* I'm trapped.

"I know you had a talk with Lois last night," he began, and I clamped my eyes closed. "She told me what you said to her. Now I want to give you a chance to say it to me."

"What?" I'm confused.

"I want you to tell me what you told Lois."

"But you said she already told you."

"I want to hear it from you." His tone was clipped. His eyes bored holes into my skull.

"Dad," I exhaled. Tears threatened to break the dam. My leg and head battered me. It was too much. "Dad. Please."

The tears began to stream from my eyes. My body was racked with harsh sobs, and my muscles ached from the strain. Dad sat there, at my desk, facing me, and watching with a stony expression. I pulled my knees to my chest and felt the sweat soak into the fabric of my pyjamas. *Too. Much.*

"Son," he said. He never called me that unless I was in trouble. I felt five again. "Come and find me when you're done." And he left the room.

IX

Last Night

Rebecca is already outside the door when Luce finally releases me from the Commons. I sit beside her on the bench silently, and she rests her head on my shoulder. Well, my upper arm. I don't have the energy to say anything. I never knew how exhausting it would be to recount one of the worst days of my life. From kissing Marcus, to breaking down in front of Lois, to the endless talk my dad subjected me to when I finally ventured downstairs. Not my finest hours.

"Can I show you something?" she says, and I glance down at her. She's not looking at me. I nod, and, taking my hand, she stands up and begins to tow me.

My head, overflowing with thoughts, doesn't even register where we are walking to until I feel sand underneath my shoeless feet. I look up and see the sea, stretching out until the horizon, with pastel grey clouds floating ahead. The cool breeze of an English seaside is cleansing, and I take a deep, salty breath in. Rebecca is still holding my hand, and I see her looking up at me. Her eyes are wide.

"How did we get here?" I ask, and she shrugs.

"I know the way." It's not an answer, but I allow her to pull me to the tide line, with the waves breaking and the foam climbing up the sand to inches from where we sit. The sand is cold, but not wet. I smile and close my eyes, hearing the expanse of the sea swirl against the wind.

"This is where I come sometimes," Rebecca says. "When I want to think or when I don't want to be with the other people."

"The other people?"

"Everyone else."

"You mean all the other people in the mall?"

"Yeah. Sometimes they get too much," she says, staring off into the distance.

"Do you ever talk to them?" I know I hadn't.

"Not really."

The conversation dies. Rebecca is scratching patterns and spirals into the sand, and I pick up handfuls and watch the grains slip out of my loose fist. There's something about the beach that just makes you feel so small. It's like staring at the stars.

"Do you know what your decision will be yet?" Rebecca asks.

"I don't think we're getting very close. He keeps making me talk about my life. Like he asks one question about my girlfriend, and then a question about my friend, and then a question about my family. I don't know where it's going," I reply.

"Yeah, it feels like that sometimes, but he tells me he knows when you're getting close. He told me it is like how you know when you're hungry or tired. You just know."

"Are you getting close?" I ask.

"Maybe. But I suppose that I will have to wait for you first."

Aaaand we're back to the mysteries.

"Why can't you make a decision without me?"

"Because my decision depends on your decision."

"Is that allowed?" I ask. It feels like it shouldn't be. It's a lot of peer pressure. This girl is telling me she's going to decide whether to live or die based on my choices. You'd think you wouldn't have to put up with this shit in heaven.

"Luce says it's not normal." I snort. "What?"

I shake my head, and glance at the shells she is arranging. "Do you ever feel Luce knows everything and tells you nothing?"

She giggles. "Yes." I laugh with her, and don't mention the fact that she's exactly the same.

We spend the next hour or so playing on the beach. I dig a hole using my cupped hands as spades, and Rebecca decorates the edge with rocks she thinks are pretty. We find a grassy dune and scramble after the grasshoppers that flee from our path, and Rebecca squeals when one lands on her bare leg. I examine the pebbles she hands me in turn, as she points out what makes each one special. For one, it's the band of silver flashing across a black orb. For another, it's the speckles. For another, it's a tiny stone wedged in a hole of another. I ask if she wants to take them home with us, and she shakes her head slowly, twisting her mouth to one side. Neither of us notice that I just called it 'home'.

The wind slowly picks up over time, and as we begin the walk back, I feel the pit returning to my stomach. I start to say something, but Rebecca has already begun a sentence.

"My mummy used to take us to a beach like that," she says. "She gave us money for ice creams and we could paddle."

"That sounds really nice," I reply, twiddling a strand of beach grass between my fingers.

"I think that was the only time she was happy. Because daddy wasn't there."

"How come?" I ask.

"Daddy was mean to her. I think she was scared of him."

"How was he mean?" My own mother would've scolded me for such a probing question into another family's personal affairs.

"He was in charge of everything. He wouldn't let her speak about anything," Rebecca says.

"Why?"

"Because he didn't want people to know what he was doing."

"What was he doing?" *Curiosity killed the cat.*

"I'm not meant to say."

"What do you mean, Rebecca?" I stop walking. She is silent. "Did he… touch you in places he shouldn't?" She nods slowly.

There's no satisfaction to bring the cat back.

***

Rebecca's confession weighs heavily on my mind. *No. Not a confession. She had nothing to confess.* I'm also not too stupid to realise that this likely had something to do with why she needed me to make the 'right' choice.

I don't even know how much time had passed when I barrelled back into the Commons, and saw Luce sat on his bench, awaiting my arrival.

"So, I thought we'd circle back to the things you mentioned last time," he says, before I'd even sat down.

I grasp the sides of the despatch box, and cut him off before he can finish the final syllable. "You know about Rebecca, don't you?"

"Yes, I know Rebecca," he replies, bemused.

"No; you know what her dad did, right?"

His tone changes. "I know about Rebecca, yes."

Fire flashes in me. "What the fuck is she doing here?"

"She's here for the same reason you all are."

"She doesn't need to be here. She needs your help."

"That's not my place."

"Not your place? What do you mean? She's a kid. Who doesn't help a kid?" I'm yelling now.

"There are rules."

"Rules?" I bark at him. "What possible rules could there be to stop you helping a little kid whose dad is fucking abusing her?"

His demeanour is defensive and quiet. "Kiddo, I don't make the rules here."

"The rules are bullshit."

"But they are the rules."

"Well, I've made my choice," I say, straightening my back. "I want to go back."

"You haven't made the choice," he replies, and the flames creep higher.

"It's my choice. I've made it. I want to go back."

"You rushing into a snap decision isn't helping anybody," he says slowly, as if to average out the speed at which we are talking. "The decision, which is *ours* to make, has to be made properly. This is life or death. You can't flip a coin."

"Flip a coin? This kid is being abused by her dad. She's being fucking molested, and yet me wanting to stop that is a rash fucking decision? Who the fuck do you think you are?"

"She's not being molested, kid. She's here. She's safe here."

"What if she goes back?" I cry, gesturing wildly. "If she goes back, if she makes that choice, then what? Then what the fuck happens? We all just go on our merry way while she's getting raped?"

He shouts my name, silencing me. My breath is hard and shaky, like I've run a marathon. I stare at him from behind hooded eyes. "It's very noble what you want to do. It's very noble. But unless you focus on yourself—unless you focus on your choice, and making that choice for you—you won't be of any help to anyone. Not to Rebecca. Not to you. Not to anybody. Not when you don't know the full story."

"Then what am I meant to do?" I pant.

"This," he gestures around the room. "This right here is what you're meant to do."

***

Luce asks me about my favourite book, so I tell him.

I feel like everyone who reads, reads countless books, and each one affects them in some way. My mum's favourite book was always *The Tenant of Wildfell Hall*, so much so that on the birth of my sister, my father bought her a gold signet ring inscribed with part of one of her favourite quotes: "*I would rather have your friendship.*" My dad's favourite book was *The Stand* by Stephen King. It's probably no wonder they didn't stay together, when you go from a Brontë to a novel that quotes Bruce Springsteen, but for the time they were married, literature never divided them. My mum could devour *Carrie* before my dad had finished the BBC adaptation of *Pride and Prejudice*, and when they were ready, they'd discuss.

In a twisted turn of events, when I was banished to my room which had had the door unscrewed from its hinges and hidden in the garage (robbing me of what little dignity, not to mention privacy, I had left), I found Lois had left her battered copy of *Jane Eyre* on my nightstand. In my teenage angst, feeling utterly betrayed by the fact the one person I had confided in had breached my confidence not even a day later, I tore open the front page and began reading. My phone had been taken off me, and my laptop had been locked in my dad's desk drawer, so there was really nothing for me to do than get to know a fictional governess.

I finished the book the next day.

"I think," I tell Luce, "that when you feel that alone. When you feel that shit. When you feel like you can't even watch the world fall down around you because someone is holding a blindfold over your eyes, you latch onto anything that helps you escape."

Therefore, *Jane Eyre* is my favourite book.

As I read, I began to scrawl my favourite quotes in the margins in blunt pencil. From "*I am no bird*" to "*Your mind is my treasure.*" In the cruellest way, I, a recently de-closeted teenage boy, had fallen in love with a woman from 200 years before. I did not love Jane, nor was I particularly fond of Mr Rochester. I fell in love with Charlotte Brontë's writing. Her poetry. Her turns of phrase, and her winding prose.

Much like my friend Saira, who became obsessed with *The Big Bang Theory* after her sister died when we were in our final year of GCSEs, I never try to defend *Jane Eyre*. I don't have to. Some people loathe it, and others love it. All I know is that Jane and her creator saved my life.

By the time my father had seen fit to give me my phone back, I turned it on to find dozens and dozens of missed calls, messages, and notifications.. The separation from the outside world had not eased the anxiety that burrowed into my soul when I saw Marcus's name flash up.

`Hey bro. Can we talk?`

I had a million things I wanted to say to him. A million different ways to say it. But no words came. I knew eventually I needed to talk to him, but was there any way I could hold off until we were both adults? I stared at the message, the only one from him. There were reams from Olivia, getting increasingly angry that I was ignoring her 'for no reason', and others from our friends, asking where I had gone for the past few days. I couldn't tell them that I had had my life taken away from me. That after my sins had been confessed to my father, he had deprived me of my independence and banished me from my solitude. I couldn't tell them that I wasn't permitted to shower with the door closed, or that he had set up camp on my bedroom floor so that even while sleeping, I wasn't alone. In what he promised was for my protection, he stole away the last semblance of humanity.

And still, here I was, facing a question I knew I had to answer, from the one person I wanted to talk to more than anything. *What would Jane do*? Probably something witty and ferocious that would lead the man to fall in love with her spirit, if not her plain face. But, alas. I was a 14-year-old kid who didn't have a bedroom door. I wasn't quite Jane Eyre.

My thumbs squirmed as I tried to come up with what to say to Marcus. The fact that I was messaging him before I had even contemplated replying to Olivia didn't cross my mind. I typed and deleted, then typed and deleted, one message after another, desperately trying to put all my scattered thoughts onto the page.

The phone buzzed, and I dropped it on my carpeted bedroom floor. I hadn't hoovered it since my dad had moved in, and I found myself disgusted with the veneer of hair, broken nails, and dust that covered the carpet like a film. I picked up the phone as it continued to vibrate, turning it over to see Marcus's name and photo flashing up at me. He was calling me. My heart pounded, and I began to sweat. *What the fuck do I do?*

I clicked answer.

"Hey, man," Marcus said, his voice low and raspy.

"Hey," I replied. My voice cracked halfway through, and my face beamed a bright red to my empty room.

"Listen, I just saw you were online and…"

"I know, I'm so sorry. I didn't mean to... y'know. I was just drunk and stupid and tired and I didn't know what I was doing," I blurted, my brain quickly running out of mindless thoughts to load the machine gun that was my mouth.

He said my name, cutting me off, as I continued my rampage of nonsense.

"Yes?" I replied, my voice quiet and desperate.

"I know that you're gay, and…"

"I'm not gay." I cursed myself again for denying it. At least the one upside of this situation should have been that the cat was out of the bag.

"You are, mate. It's not a problem. It doesn't change the way I see you." My heart continued to pound. "But being gay also doesn't change the situation. I have Saira, and I love her, man. You have Olivia, and that's your thing. I don't know what you want to do with that, and it's not my place. But I need to tell Saira."

"Why?" Tears threatened to claw from my eyes.

"That's just what we do. It's the right thing to do."

"You're going to tell Saira I'm gay?" The chain of consequences was inevitable. Saira was Olivia's best friend. And Saira loved to talk. Everyone would find out.

"No, of course not. It's not my place." He sighed. Nowhere seemed to be his place. "But I need to tell her that you kissed me." "No, you don't. You can…"

"Look, I know this sucks. I'm sorry, I really am, mate. But you kissed me. I didn't want this to happen. I don't want to out you, but it's not as if it's a big secret, anyway."

"What?" I whispered. My throat was tightening every second.

"Everyone knows you're gay, man. It's okay, honestly."

"But, how?" A tear streaked down my cheek. My eyes burned. It was a stupid question. Why was I doubting people knew the truth? "Does Olivia know?"

"I guess so. I don't know."

"But you're still going to out me, Marcus."

"Not to her."

"No. Saira will tell Olivia. You're going to out me. You can't do that." I was going to keep clawing until I saw a glimmer of hope.

"I'll ask her not to tell Olivia. You deserve a chance to at least do that yourself."

"Marcus, I'm gay. I'm fucking gay and the very least I could do is get my own fucking opportunity to tell people." I remembered when we saw *Love, Simon* together at the cinema, all of us. I remembered how I would glance over at him, watching Simon fall in love with Blue, a grin on his face. It made me fucking mad.

"I don't want to out you," he told me. He sounded tired.

Resigned. "You kissed me," he said. "You kissed me. I can't just forget that happened."

"So what am I meant to do now?" The prospect of a glimmer of a hope died.

"I think you should talk to Olivia. She's been asking about you. She said you haven't spoken to her since the party."

"Yeah," I whispered, barely audible.

"Listen, man." He paused. "I really am sorry."

"Yeah. Me too."

***

At least Marcus gave me a goodbye. I hated not being able to close chapters like that. The last time we saw each other was a few months later outside school, when I was leaving for the day and he was waiting for Saira so they could go to the park as we always did. After that phone call, it had been without me.

I never got to say goodbye to Megan. By the time they had discharged me from the hospital after setting my leg and prescribing me a cocktail of painkillers I was too young to fully appreciate, Megan would never show up again at the farm. I was still a kid, and my parents were still together, and I cried as my parents informed me after asking many times that Megan would not be returning. They were in the process of selling the farmland anyway, so Megan would have left eventually, but they didn't trust her after that. They said they wouldn't let her be around me again. It was for my own good, they told me, but I knew it was for their sake.

I had been playing in the barn, a game of hide-and-seek with Megan that could last for hours as she went about her tasks. Usually I was forbidden from being in the barn, by both my parents and Megan herself, but that time I thought the game could go on much longer if I hid somewhere she would never find me.

I could hear her calling for me as I wedged myself behind a piece of machinery that looked terribly dangerous, but that only excited me more. *She'll never find me here*. Her calls got more and more urgent, and I tried to suppress my giggles, but before long I couldn't hold them back anymore. On hearing my burst of laughter, Megan's heavy steps ran into the barn and I could see her from my one eye poking out behind the metal look left to right frantically. A few moments later, she traced my laughter to its source and tried to pull me free.

"What are you doing here?" she was saying, "You know you're not allowed to be in here." I just laughed, but it soon became apparent that I was wedged in. Her tugs got more aggressive, and I could see the worry printed across her face slowly turn more and more frightened. I stopped laughing and watched her silently and still as she tried to free me.

"Wait here. Don't move. I need to get your dad." She gave me a stern look before turning and hot-footing it out of the barn and through the dirt path to the house.

This had concerned me greatly. I knew Megan would have let me get off from this infraction with nothing more than a quick talking-to. My dad wouldn't be so lenient. I started to twist my body and jerk it back and forth, trying to find some contortion that would free me. I started to pant and struggle and cry. With one momentous push, I freed my torso from behind the machine, but my right leg was still trapped. I pulled. I pulled harder. I knew I didn't have long before my dad got here, so, in my panic, I tried to run.

The machine gave a loud creak, and before I could turn round, my leg had pulled an imposing metal arm from its position, and I saw out of the corner of my eye as it fell to the floor like the felling of a great tree. It landed on my leg, still trapped, and I could hear the bones crunch and pain radiate up my body like an earthquake. My dad said he could hear me screaming as he jogged down the path, but I don't remember making a noise.

As I grew up, I began to understand more and more of what the doctors had been telling me since I was six. The bones had been repaired, but the nerve damage was unlikely to ever fully recover. I was prescribed drugs for the neuropathic pain that would haunt me as I got older.

My classmates would jest in jealousy when I was sitting by the side of every P.E. lesson I ever attended, while they were forced to run around in freezing weather or the cold. I wished I could be there with them. I would sit and think of the times I would be running with the dogs, and begged every night to be able to do that again, and not be a cripple. That was another thing they used to say, even though they didn't even know what had happened to me. I couldn't run. I was a cripple.

I never got to say goodbye to Megan, but at night, I often dream that I never had to.

Last night, I dreamt of her again.

X

Words Hurt

I haven't seen Rebecca in a while. I ask Luce about her, but he says she's fine, and I shouldn't worry. I have so many questions for her, knowing her answers wouldn't satisfy my itching for a happy ending. I want to know why she's here. If her family is okay. In truth, I also want to know about the beach. I want to know how we went there.

The mall we're all confined in is expansive. I walk for hours and hours but find nothing to give me any answers. Every day I'm here, the questions build and build, and they never get any easier to grapple with. The questions Luce asks—well, the things he mentions that I then monologue on—are solidly depressing. But the decision I—*we*—have to make hangs over my head. I now know how Damocles felt, except I don't even have any power. It's hard not to think about it, but eventually my mind wanders to other things. My family. My dogs. *Abbas*.

Try as I might, I can't remember the day I got here. I don't remember the accident Luce told me about. I don't remember the events leading up to it. He asked me, early on in the 'process', if stepping in front of the van was an accident, or whether I did it on purpose. An accident, I swore, but the truth is I don't know. I know the thought of jumping in front of traffic crossed my mind more than once, but I'm not sure if I actually would have ever done it. Too messy.

I once googled how to write a suicide note. I don't think

I was genuinely suicidal—just depressed—but, ironically, the article I ended up scrolling through made me laugh. It recommended leaving some money behind for pizza to cheer up your family, or personalising it by apologising to your mum for the mess. It was dumb, but needed. Like me, the article said: *dumb but needed.*

I smirk to myself as I pace the third floor. This isn't the top floor; I think there's one more mezzanine level, but for the life of me, I can't seem to find the staircase. The third floor is the quietest, with the fewest people, and it's also the darkest. The way the light falls down from the blinding white ceiling shadows much of the third floor, particularly closest to the walls, where the benches are. Sitting next to the plastic plants in the still air, it's not idyllic, but it feels safe. I sit there and, quite literally, twiddle my thumbs. For some reason, no one but Rebecca has spoken to me. I guess I haven't spoken to anyone else myself, though. Conversations are, quite famously, a two-way street, and I have no intention of going down that particular avenue. Everyone here looks bloody miserable. It's understandable given the circumstances, of course we're all here to decide whether to live or die, but it wouldn't hurt someone to crack a smile every once in a while as they roam the endless halls of the Interlife.

It's not as if it's impossible to talk to other people here. I mean, Rebecca certainly did it. But just like every time I try to go into one of the shops, something inside me guides me away. Every time I think about talking to someone else, something stops me. It just doesn't feel right. I'm not sure if it's some super-natural force, or if it's just social anxiety, but either way, it's the situation we're in.

I wish I had a book. After *Jane Eyre*, I couldn't stop reading. First it was *Wuthering Heights*, then *The Tenant of Wildfell Hall.* Naturally, I had to devour the Brontës' collected works, and then I moved onto everything else I could get my hands on.

It was like a drug that released me from the monotonous hell that was my life. The best drug you could get in the English countryside, anyway.

It was a startling change. I had rarely read beforehand, preferring to absorb my somewhat limited knowledge from documentaries or podcasts, and as I grew obsessed with politics, I tore through news app after news app like a Very Hungry Caterpillar, watching all the videos and clips that the free (and by that, I mean not-hiding-behind-a-paywall) press could offer. But once Lois had left *Jane Eyre* by my bed, the thought of sitting and watching something, with the risk my mind would wander back to reality, became terrifying. And it soon became apparent that, after weeks of silence, the one way to get me to talk over the dinner table was to ask me about a book I was reading. At first, my dad strictly censored the content. I wasn't permitted to read anything gay, for fear it would antagonise my emotions and lead to a relapse into depression. Once I heard Lois argue with him over it. I had crept from my room when the sun had set, believing my dad had left for a work trip, and Lois was in her own home, when the hushed tones froze my hand before it could turn the doorknob.

"How is he supposed to feel okay about himself if you never let him find other people like him?"

"He's gay, Lois, he's not a mutant. He knows gay people exist."

"Look around, Dan. There's nobody gay in this godforsaken town," Lois hissed.

"Wayne's kid is gay. Y'know, Seán from the museum?" The museum my dad was referring to was the sorriest excuse for history our town had to offer. Century-old broken pottery does not a tourist trap make.

"He's not gay, Dan. He has a speech impediment."

"No—he's genuinely gay."

"Oh... I didn't know that." There was silence. "Even so, he

needs to be allowed to read. He's depressed, he's lonely. He's just got out of his first ever relationship, and he needs a friend."

"What do you want him to read?"

"Something... *gay*."

I rolled my eyes to mask the pit in my stomach and went back to bed. Water wasn't worth the trouble. But when I woke up in the morning, I found a door on its hinges, and a few days later, there was a stack of fresh books on my shelf. I ran my finger over the embossed type on the covers, muttering the author's names as I traced them: James Baldwin, Hanya Yanagihara, E.M. Forster, Madeleine Miller, Casey McQuiston. I couldn't bring myself to mention it, and neither, as it turned out, could my dad or Lois. It was our silent understanding now that I was gay, and I read about gay things, in my room with a door.

***

"Did you forgive her?" Luce asks.

"Lois?"

"Lois."

"I mean... she didn't do anything wrong. I'd just confessed a lot to her, and she wasn't even part of the family, not properly. She did what she thought was right. She was the first person I'd ever told, even implicitly, that I liked boys. She was the first person I'd told about the self-harm, about wanting to die. She was the first person in a long time I'd told about what happened with Megan."

"But did you forgive her for telling your dad?"

I sighed and looked down at the despatch box. Its original shine had started to wane over the hours I'd stood at it. "I guess not."

"Why not?" His tone wasn't unkind. The question was unwelcome, as were most of his, but Luce seemed to have no malice.

"She was the first person I'd told. I trusted her, and she didn't give me any warning that she'd told my dad, or that she would tell anyone. I just woke up the next morning, literally, and found my privacy had gone, and my life was turned upside down. I didn't want that."

"Did you forgive Marcus?"

The about-turn derailed my train of thought. "What do you mean?"

"Well, you said you didn't forgive Lois because she didn't warn you she would tell someone else. Marcus told you that he would tell Saira. He even waited to tell you before he did tell Saira. Did you forgive Marcus for telling someone you kissed him?" Luce sat down and leaned forward, resting his head on his interlocking fingers. His lips were pursed in thought. *Man, he still looks attractive.*

I knew how to answer. I didn't know how to justify the answer. I studied the box's detailing as my eyebrows furrowed in frustration at the illogicality. "No." If I couldn't justify it, I wouldn't. He hadn't asked me to.

"Why?"

Rats.

"It's not the same... Lois betrayed me because I'd trusted her and she didn't give me any indication that she would breach that trust. Marcus betrayed me because... Marcus meant a lot to me. I guess he gave me a chance to straighten things out with Olivia, but..."

"But what?"

"But that's not what I wanted from him. I didn't want that chance. I wanted him not to tell. I wanted him to keep it a secret, for me. I wanted him to protect me."

"And he didn't protect you?"

"No."

"So what did he do?"

***

I realised then that I probably should have taken Marcus up on the opportunity he had given me. I should have told Olivia. I should have got in first and tried to deal with it and be in control of the situation. But I pussied out. Of course, by the moment I realised that it was too late, because that opportunity had been taken from me.

"Saira told me what you did."

My gut twisted itself into an agonising knot. "Did she?"

"Yes. I know you kissed Marcus." It was a small—a very small—consolation that she couldn't see my face over the phone.

"Yeah."

"So you did?"

I didn't realise the point was still up for debate. "Yes."

"So you're gay?"

Her prosecutorial aptitude shone through in moments like this. It was no surprise when she announced on Facebook her intention to study law. And yes, she became one of those people who uses every social media platform as LinkedIn.

"Yes."

"Okay."

"Olivia, I'm sorry."

"Why are you sorry?"

"It was wrong of me to kiss Marcus, and it was wrong of me to lie to you."

"It's me who should be sorry," she said.

I was confused. "What for?"

"For dating a faggot all this time."

My heart sank like I'd been punched in the gut. I could hear distant muffled laughter from the other end of the phone. My brain swam with thoughts of our friends, *my* friends, laughing at me. Laughing at me for being a faggot. I hung up the phone. I got into bed, and I cried.

*****

"I'm sorry, kiddo." Luce looks into my eyes.

"Yeah." I sigh, looking back into his.

"Did you tell your parents what she said?"

"I told my dad, eventually, yeah. Not my mum, though."

"You haven't mentioned your mum in a while," he notes.

"She wasn't around much. I saw her once or twice in those few months, maybe, but she was always just so... hollow. She didn't smile like she used to. She was thin and gaunt and she smelled of smoke. I didn't like being around her, and I didn't want to make it worse by telling her about me."

"Did you tell her you were gay?"

"Eventually, but I never even properly told my dad. Lois did that for me. I waited a long time to tell Mum though. I was scared she would ask for the whole story; she always did. She loved a love story, but I didn't want to tell it to her. I didn't want her to know how bad I was hurting in case it made her hurt even more."

"And Lois, what happened to her?"

"She left a few weeks after those books appeared by my bed. She cleared her stuff out one weekend when my sister was at a friend's house, and when I was in the woods, in the clearing. I'd only been gone a few hours, but when I came back, her mugs had been taken off the shelf. I imagine she'd cleared the drawer she had in my dad's room. There weren't any shoes of hers by the front door. She only left *Jane Eyre* on my desk. Dad didn't mention anything. We just went along, pretending she had never existed in the first place."

"Do you know why she left?"

"No," I say. It's the truth. "But I worried she left because of me."

"She didn't."

I look up at Luce, surprise on my face. He's still looking at me, but his eyes are vacant, like he's remembering.

***

Rebecca appears after that session ends, plonking herself next to me as I sit on the third floor bench I have christened my own. "Hello," she smiles, handing me a daisy.

"Hi," I smile back, and take the flower, spinning it in my fingers and watching the petals blur in a circle.

"I'm sorry if I made you sad," she says.

"Of course you didn't. I'm just sorry that happened to you. I can't imagine what..." Words don't do it justice.

"I know. I know what Daddy did was wrong. It's okay." She nods. "It's okay."

"It's not okay," I reply softly, more for my benefit than for hers.

"I'm here now, and Luce says I'm safe here."

"You are," I nod my head slowly, emphatically, with the kind of certainty you only get when someone else needs it, no matter how little you actually know.

We're silent for a few moments. I stare down at the flower in my hands. There really is nothing I can say to make either of us feel better. Not that she seems to need cheering up. I look down at her, swinging her bare legs back and forth under the bench. She seems so small. She looks back at me.

"Do you want to go back to the beach?"

Her question reminds me of my own, and I welcome the change of topic so I can shed my discomfort. "Hey, Rebecca?"

She nods with a grin.

"How did we go to the beach?"

"We walked there, silly."

I chuckle lightly. "I know we did, but does that mean we can walk to other places?"

"Sometimes."

Her cryptic way of speaking never ceases to disappoint. "But does that mean I can go to other places I want to go to?"

"Like your home?"

"Yeah, like home."

"Luce has to let you. You can't just go there."

"How does he let you?" I ask.

"He knows when you need it."

XI

I Want to Ask You a Question

"I want to ask you a question," she repeated.

I rolled my eyes. "It's like Mamma Mia in here, because here we go again," I laughed gutturally. It was awkward.

"Why is it that you cut yourself?"

Okay. *Heavy shit.* I sometimes forgot therapists are meant to ask you this sort of stuff.

It was the day before I started sixth form, and my therapist was worried. Jo, her name was. She was middle-aged, and she smiled easily and laughed quickly. She looked more like a Vicky to me though.

"I don't know." I tugged at the cuffs of my long-sleeved tee. It was hot outside, and my sweat was still drying from the walk across town to the centre, but the air-con was a refreshing change of pace. The room we were in was fairly bland, with soft tones like lavender and baby blue splashed across the blank canvas of a numbingly clinical building. It was haphazard and off-putting.

Jo sat a few feet away from me in a classically corporate armchair a deep shade of grape purple. Like most therapists, she wore a neutral palate that complemented her light green-blue eyes, and spoke softly, as if that would soften the blow of the interrogation I am subjected to twice a week. She's the third therapist I'd seen there. The first made me quit after one session because I couldn't stand the way he tugged at his inch-long stubble while he listened. The second I lasted four sessions with before I begged my dad for a new one. She treated me like an exam question, with right and wrong answers up every alley. By the end of the second hour, she'd already diagnosed me with several personality disorders, anxiety disorders, and labelled me high risk of developing an eating disorder. A fascinating process to watch her work, for sure, but I had enough of a self-preservation drive left to get out of there.

Jo was nice, though. She was kind and seemed genuinely interested in me. In therapy, I tried to say as little as possible—torn between wanting the medication and avoiding hospitalisation, something I dreaded subjecting my parents to—but Jo had a knack for getting me monologuing. She asked questions I genuinely cared about the answers to, not just about myself, but the things and the people I loved. I don't know how she did it, but I honestly thought she knew more about me than I did, and I knew myself better than anyone.

I couldn't avoid the question in front of me, though.

"Let me tell you why people cut themselves," Jo said, butting in just as I had opened my mouth to spout out a load of crap to stall answering properly.

I nodded at her, pleased for the escape.

"When you're in pain—any kind of pain—your brain rushes endorphins out to make you feel better. It's like a natural painkiller. So sometimes people hurt themselves to get that same rush of endorphins, and they start to crave it. They become addicted to the one thing that makes them feel even a tiny bit better."

I nodded again. I didn't agree, though.

"You're a smart kid," she said, and I smiled at the ground politely. "Your brain is tangling itself up in knots, and you're just sat there with no way to make sense of it all. So when you cut yourself, you get a rush of endorphins, and it gives you a moment of clarity. It might even bring you back down to earth and remind you that you're not your brain. You're a body too, and you're real, and it reminds you of that fact."

Maybe I did agree.

"But what therapy does is help you untangle your brain, and give you that same clarity and that same sense of self and that same reminder that you actually do exist, but without you hurting yourself."

"I know," I replied. I was uncomfortable, and starting to sweat again, despite the cool artificial breeze emanating from the ceiling.

"Next time, I want you to take a deep breath—the deepest you can—and I want you to start to count. Count the in-breath, *'One'*, the out-breath, *'Two'*. Keep counting until you're more focussed on your breathing and on your numbers and less focussed on wanting to harm yourself." She said it with a sympathetic smile.

I paused and closed my eyes for a moment. This shit was why people didn't want to go to therapy. I wasn't going to kill myself, I was sure of that. I didn't want to die, I just needed a moment's fucking relief from the storm that perpetually raged inside my head. It was unbearable.

***

"This is meta, can we stop?" I say, chuckling.

"Meta?" Luce replies, smiling at me.

"You're interrogating me about an interrogation. I don't like it"

"You picked the topic," he throws his hands up in surrender. As a thing he did, it teetered between irritating and adorable.

"You asked me what happened after the whole Marcus thing!"

"I meant more like, you were out of the closet, you were a young, attractive, newly single guy out on the town. What did you do? Who did you meet? I didn't mean a soliloquy about the most depressive topic on the roster."

"Oh, I'm sorry," I say in mock defence, "Let me gloss over the morbid parts of my life and skip ahead to the bit where me and the other town queers linked arms and danced under a rainbow to Shania Twain."

"Kiddo, your story has been incredibly depressing thus far. The only time I've seen you smile is when you mentioned Abbas's name in passing." He pronounces the 's' before and after the apostrophe, and the sibilance is snake-like. "And you haven't mentioned him since."

I nod slowly. "My life wasn't depressing, I don't think. I was happy. I was happy as a kid, when we were in Little Eden, and then when we went to the farm. I was happy when I started school, and I was happy until the end with Olivia."

"It wouldn't kill you to tell everyone else that." Our patter and back-and-forth has grown in the hours we've spent together, and I find myself looking forward to seeing Luce each day. He is handsome, still, but he challenges me, and he pushes me, and... *holy shit, am I getting a crush on my grim reaper?*

No. I reassure myself. *Not a crush.* Maybe a Stockholm Syndrome-type thing?

"I want to ask you a question," Luce says, and I gesture for him to continue. "Did Olivia ever apologise?"

"No. Not in words, no." I pause. "The last time I saw her, she gave me a hug, and she said she would miss me. But she didn't apologise."

"Did you want her to?"

"I mean, sure. She called me a faggot. I was 14 and my world was falling apart, and my brain was messed up, and she piled onto it because I had hurt her. Y'know, I don't think she was homophobic, I just think she wanted to hurt me, too. And that's okay, that she wanted to hurt me. But I was hurting enough already."

"So I guess being gay wasn't good for you?"

I laugh. There's not really a good way to respond to that. "Being gay has never hurt someone. It's the rest of the world that hurts you because you're gay."

"If the world is hurting you because you're gay, why would you want to go back to that world?"

I smile and exhale, looking up at Luce, who is smirking like a shark. "Luce," I say, "Being gay is the best thing that ever happened to me. Without gay, there is no Abbas. Without Abbas, there is no me."

B.

The Ballad of a Lion

"Two young lovers lying in an orchard would have read the story of our love;

Would have known the legend of my passion, known the bitter secret of my heart,

Kissed as we have kissed, but never parted as we two are fated now to part."

—Oscar Wilde, *Flower of Love*

XII

The Butterflies

"So we know how you met him. In your sixth form classroom on the first day. We're dying to know what happens next." Luce speaks like a teenage girl at a sleepover and, honestly? I'm here for it.

"After we met, I spent the rest of my day hanging with various groups of people: the girls who had sat in front of me in form, and then a guy I met in the biology classroom we had both mistakenly entered thinking it was our history class, and then a boyfriend-and-girlfriend duo who were inseparable and gave off painful "looking-for-a-third" vibes that I was keen to escape. In my final class of the day, English Literature, I had strategically picked a seat far from the door in the hopes that people wouldn't want to sit next to me. I was drained, and really not in the mood to talk to any more strangers.

"My decision to study Lit was a last-minute one. I changed it on the day of my GCSE results from maths. I hadn't received a terrible grade in my Lit GCSE, but it hadn't been outstanding. I just didn't enjoy reading until that summer. I had always been a big politics and history fan, so maths seemed like it would round out my application nicely, but when I handed the form in, I snatched it back and scribbled out maths to print 'English Literature' in bold type, to my dad's confusion.

"'You don't even like reading,' he said, and I shrugged it off, saying I just wanted something different, and I did like reading. I'd read all those books he'd got me. I didn't mention Lois."

***

The Lit classroom was not a pretty one. It had holes in the walls from years of Blu Tack ripping away yellow paint and plaster. It had the most dreadful year seven artwork depicting Lady Macbeth, and it had a board listing fun adjectives. 'Fun' was not the adjective I would use to describe it.

Our Lit teacher was a young man with an acne-riddled forehead and glasses with a thin, wiry frame that highlighted a surprisingly thick head of hair for someone who looked like he was suffering from scurvy. He had the energy and enthusiasm of someone not yet disaffected by the long hours and low pay of public sector teaching. He matched his classroom, and I smiled awkwardly at his grin when he welcomed his first-ever A Level students.

As he finished introducing himself as Mr Wilson—"Yes, like the Dennis the Menace character," he laughed to a room of blank faces. The door swung open, and a head popped round.

"Is this English Lit?" Abbas asked, scanning the room with his piercing eyes. He didn't look at me.

"It sure is!" Mr Wilson clapped his hands together in glee.

"Sorry I'm late. My timetable still had physics on it. I only switched to English last week." *Ahhh, a fellow impulsive.*

"That's no problem at all! I'm Mr Wilson." He didn't repeat the cartoon anecdote.

"Abbas," he replied, strolling into the room with his hand outstretched to our teacher, who hastily flung his arm out and gripped Abbas's in a firm shake.

There were a few empty seats around the classroom, and definitely some closer to the door Abbas had walked in through, so I was surprised when he made a beeline for the chair next to me, and sat down, swinging his rucksack down beside him, and pulling out a fresh spiral-bound notebook and the book we had been assigned for our first term: *Jane Eyre*.

Mr Wilson had moved onto providing us an overview of the course on a bland monochrome slideshow that didn't match his effusive personality. The words began to blur into one another as I stared pointedly at the pen I was fidgeting with in my hands. I begged for Abbas not to notice me. Too much time had passed for me to look at him. This was our reality now. We were the people who didn't acknowledge each other until an educator mandated it. This was hell.

"Hey," he said, and I looked over. He was smiling at me. "We met in form, right?"

I nodded and smiled slightly, introducing myself again.

"I know, I remember!" He looked pleased with himself. His teeth were so white and symmetrical and perfect. This wasn't hell anymore.

I smiled back at him, but flicked my eyes back to my pen as soon as I could without being rude. It was a biro that I had been using for two months. I never lost a pen, and I used them until the ink ran out before buying another. I looked at the pen so hard it would have burst into flames if it could have. My heart was pounding in my chest, and I forced myself not to glance back across at Abbas. I daren't even view him peripherally.

There was a tap on my shoulder, and an electric jolt shocked through my body. *Fuck me.* I looked at Abbas, who was still smiling. "Hey, can I borrow a pen?"

My mind raced. It was my only pen, but I wasn't actually using it right now. But what if I needed to use it and he was using it? Were we going to share pens? Were we going to be the people that shared a single pen between them? That would be weird. But I couldn't deny him a pen, could I? That would be weirder. I stared at my pen. Things were getting weird already.

"Sure," I cracked half a smile, and handed my pen over, his

fingers grazing mine as he took it with a 'thank you'. Another electric shock. My skin tingled where we had touched.

"And so, guys, turn to your partner and tell them two interesting things about you, and then they will have to share those two things with the group." Mr Wilson's voice popped back into my consciousness in the most unpleasant way.

The room waited a beat and then erupted in polite chatter. There were about 12 of us in the class, and Abbas and I, with another boy called Tony, were drastically outnumbered by girls. At least Tony was paired with a girl. I was stranded with the most beautiful man in existence, and desperately trying to hide it from him.

Abbas turned his body to face me and grinned widely, again. It was like looking at the Joker, if the Joker had also been devastatingly attractive. *Well, eye of the beholder and all that.*

"I hate these things," I said, returning an awkward smile. Abbas wasn't phased.

"I know, right? This is 100% not how humans were made to interact. It's like all of a sudden, if it's a first day, we have to act like robots and not people in order to get to know each other." He laughed. "Weird, right?"

I chucked in response. "So do you have two fun facts?" Abbas laughed heartily, rolling his head back and his curly black hair bounced as he did so. I'm not sure what was so funny.

"I don't think there's even one fun fact I could tell you," I told him, trying to alleviate the awkwardness that so completely permeated me.

"Ah, I'm sure that's not true!" He replied earnestly, his wide eyes looking at me, sparkling. "But I guess I'll have to find out for myself if you're not going to tell me." He winked. I blushed on the outside and died on the inside.

"Okay, great guys, come on back!" Mr Wilson beckoned, and the class turned to face him, Abbas included.

"Wait, we don't have any facts!" I hissed at the boy, and he winked back, killing me again.

"Who wants to be the first to share their partner's fun facts?" Mr Wilson beamed.

Abbas raised his hand, and I sank into my chair.

Mr Wilson was thrilled. "Great! Why don't you introduce yourself, and your partner, and tell us your fun facts?"

We didn't have any fun facts! My brain raced in desperation. I was already humiliated sitting next to Abbas, and now my hole was being dug even deeper.

"Hi, my name's Abbas," he said, looking around. The room was captivated. He introduced me and I could feel my cheeks flame red again. "His fun facts were that when he was seven, his dad took him to Antarctica to study polar bears for six months, and that he once met the Queen in a pub in Scotland."

Mr Wilson gasped in amazement. I was speechless. *What the fuck?* The teacher turned to me, and nodded with a wide grin and raised eyebrows, waiting for me to share fun facts about Abbas.

"Hi everyone," I began, and somehow words started pouring out of my mouth before I could register what I was saying. "Abbas's fun facts were that his first words were 'Diet Coke' and he owns a cat called Snake."

Abbas winked at me a third time as Mr Wilson moved on, and I shook my head at him disapprovingly, mouthing 'I hate you'.

The next day, as I walked into form for registration, Abbas was waiting for me, and called my name as soon as I stepped through the door. He beckoned me over to where he was sitting on a table with Tom, Alonso, Lukas, and Liam around him. The quintet were an English town's answer for jocks. They were sporty, good looking, and instantly popular, and I absolutely would not fit in. I cursed Abbas internally for forcing me to join them. As I reached them at the opposite side of the classroom, Alonso was arguing with Tom about the proper pronunciation of 'scone'. An age-old debate, for sure, but not one I felt compelled to enter into, even though Tom was quite clearly wrong. It's easy to argue about things that don't matter, I guess. Lukas and Liam were watching from the sidelines, laughing, but Abbas's eyes were fixed on me.

"How are we feeling about our second day?" Abbas asked me, and my brain, again, stopped working. Evidently the pause as I formulated a response had strayed too far, and Abbas filled the silence with his own answer: "I hate the beginning of things, where it's all about 'what is maths?' and not about actually learning anything."

I nodded in agreement and commented that we had spent the whole of our Lit class yesterday talking about the importance of first sentences. That was an hour that wouldn't help us pass an exam. Abbas laughed and patted my shoulder with a grin. My stomach exploded into a flurry of butterflies.

"That's what we were saying," he gestured at Tom, whose wild eyes were still fired from the heat of debate.

"What?" Tom said, looking questioningly at Abbas, his mouth agape.

"I was saying that we were talking about how the first lessons are always a waste of time," Abbas replied.

"Oh, right, yeah," Tom said with a definitive nod before turning back into the ring with Alonso. Tom was slightly shorter than me, and paler, but he was wide with muscle and even broader with confidence. He didn't seem afraid of causing a scene and, indeed, most of the room was engaged in the performance he was putting on with Alonso.

Alonso was far taller and had stubble that looked like he had neatly trimmed that morning. The lack of patchiness made him look older than his 16 years, and his eyes were creased in laughter as Tom became more and more agitated in his defence of rhyming 'scone' with 'gone'. Lukas commented that they had been arguing about this since primary school, and Abbas shook his head with a chuckle.

There was a pause, and I felt obliged to patch it, as Abbas had done to the last one. "So you're doing English and maths?"

Abbas nodded, "And biology, yeah."

"Oh, how come?"

"My parents had always wanted me to study science and everything, and I like science, but I wanted to do English. I love reading. So I rang the school last week and asked if I could switch from physics, and they said I could."

"Yeah, I switched from maths to take English on results day, too." I nodded to reassure myself that my attempt at conversation wasn't pitiful.

"I just think that, sure, you can do science and those sorts of things, but English you won't really get a chance to properly learn it at university. You'll be stuck doing whatever subject you study, and you won't get a chance to read. I wanted to do it while I still could, y'know?" Abbas spoke quickly but smoothly. It didn't feel rushed or anxiety-inducing.

I nodded politely, clawing at my brain to come up with another thing to say, but it drew a blank. Abbas didn't seem phased.

"So you're doing English and...?" He asked, his gaze wrapping around me like a blanket.

"And history and politics."

"Nice." He folded his arms in front of him, the polyester of the cheap school shirt stretching under his muscles. He opened his mouth to say something, but then Mr Nathwani swung the door open, and slammed a stack of yellow exercise books onto his desk which was already piled high with books, papers, and discarded cups of mostly-drunk coffee. With half a smile, I waved a silent 'goodbye' to Abbas, who lifted his hand in a loose salute. I'm not sure how he pulled it off, but he did.

The days passed quickly, but each moment felt achingly long

until I saw Abbas again. Politics, my favourite subject, became a tortuous hour before English came around. Mr Whyssler had favourites, and it showed. I was one of them, as a result of my dad introducing me to him on results day and telling him of my "obsession" with politics, which pleased Mr Whyssler immensely. In discussions of Parliamentary Sovereignty, interspersed with barbs thrown at the succession of Prime Ministers we had thrust upon us, Mr Whyssler asked my opinion pretty relentlessly. Under ordinary circumstances, I would have relished the opportunity to share my thoughts on the role of the Privileges and Liaison Committees—Lord knows I had subjected my family to enough of them—but these were not ordinary circumstances. I was infatuated. How could I possibly focus on something as trivial as holding our government to account when the thought of Abbas fluttered around my mind like a butterfly, with only the slightest breeze sending it back into frenzied flight?

In my free periods, which never coincided with Abbas's, I started sitting in the common room with Alonso and Tom, while Abbas, Lukas and Liam had their science classes. I adored them both, and they never seemed to tire of winding each other up. Every hour eventually descended into a chaotic argument, a chase around the cluttered room, leaping across chairs and bean bags, until Alonso finally retrieved what Tom had inevitably stolen from him. If they weren't so rigidly heterosexual, it would have been adorable. No. It was still adorable.

Alonso was Argentinian, but his family had moved here when he was four years old for reasons he professed to still not understand. He regaled us with stories of cooking empanadas with his aunts and cousins, of dodging the annoyed swipes of his uncles when playing soldiers with his older brother, and of long days spent in the bustling streets and markets of Buenos Aires as his mother wrestled through tourists to get to work. Tom was a Yorkshire native, something he claimed was just as exotic as Argentina, though he lacked the accent. Always holding a cherry-flavoured Pepsi Max he bought every day from the common room vending machine, he was viciously sarcastic and endlessly enthusiastic about football, something Alonso and he could never see eye-to-eye on. His blond hair he fiddled with while staring blankly at an open textbook in a rare moment of silence which would, of course, be interrupted by an outburst on an unrelated thought that had just occurred to him, which would, in turn, antagonise Alonso. For a room consistently referred to by our teachers as a 'study room', very little studying took place there.

As the free periods came to an end, I would hang a little later, feigning difficulty in packing my books into my backpack, so I could cross paths with Abbas as he came in with Lukas and Liam and I left for history class. The lunchtimes and breaks we spent together were insufficient. I needed to see him like I needed to breathe.

English, of course, was my favourite hour of the day. With four classes every week, even Mr Wilson's painful enthusiasm couldn't put me off. Ms Robertson, a middle-aged woman who bore an uncanny resemblance to Dawn French, taught half our lessons—the ones on Civil Rights literature—while Mr Wilson taught us *Jane Eyre*, Shakespeare, and poetry. Though Ms Robertson was objectively the better—and less irritating—teacher, Mr Wilson's classes involved more partner discussion, and thus more time talking to Abbas.

My desperate attempts at jokes were completely ignored by the object of my affections, who remained singularly focussed on the questions raised by our teacher. Whether it was an analysis of the Red Room imagery or a criticism of Mr Rochester's personality, Abbas's love for literature knew no bounds. While in conversation, his eyes would be fixed on you. When he started talking about books, his eyes would flit around in space as his hands made sweeping gestures to illustrate his points. It was hard to focus on his words when he was so captivatingly lost in what he was saying, but every monologue would end with him asking my thoughts, and he was easily frustrated if I hadn't been listening intently and formulating my own response. A one-word response was never satisfactory. He would demand an answer as in-depth as his own, and he would scowl and probe if I agreed with him. When Mr Wilson would call the class back to attention, Abbas was always first to offer his comments, and his analysis was always sharper, more refined, and more comprehensive than anything the rest of us could offer. We often didn't bother, despite Abbas's insistence that we contribute. He acted more the teacher than Mr Wilson did.

Sitting next to him for four hours a week in class allowed me to study the boy beside me. His hands were large and veiny, with callouses he confessed were due to his poor attempts at playing the guitar, and his strong arms dusted in dark hairs. He seemed older than his 16 years, with his received pronunciation and poetic manner of speaking more like a man than a boy. He also didn't laugh as the rest of us did as Mr Wilson dived into the explicit sexual imagery of Rossetti's *Goblin Market*. When discussing the manner in which characters' names reflected their personalities in one class with Mr Wilson, the conversation floated onto our own names. I was ignorant of the meaning of mine, but Abbas told me his meant 'lion'. It suited him, though I wouldn't know how much until later.

He was easily lost in his own thoughts, coming back to reality with a jolt when someone called his name, and as his mind wandered, his fingers would absent-mindedly play with his lips. I would practically salivate watching him. The rest of the class adored him as much as I did, laughing with his jokes and greeting him enthusiastically as he arrived to every class a minute late, without fail. In my jealousy, I wouldn't join with the chorus that would welcome him, with Mr Wilson not starting the class until Abbas had arrived, but instead would wait until he was seated to say my own hello, which he would return with a crooked smile of white and perfectly-in-line teeth.

And so, English class became my oasis. I waited, watched intently, for my feelings to wane or for Abbas to repulse me in some way from which my crush could never recover. But he remained as frustratingly perfect as he did the moment I met him. And I hated myself for it.

***

"Does your face hurt?" Luce's questions are sometimes unexpected.

"Excuse me?"

"You haven't stopped smiling since you started talking."

"Ah. Yes."

"Did he know you were gay?"

"I don't think so. Not at first."

"Did you tell anyone that you had a crush on him?"

"I told my dad after a few months. He said the same thing as you, that I hadn't stopped smiling, and he asked why. I told him that I was just in a good mood, but he probed and prodded until I confessed it all in a dump of embarrassment and awkwardness." I chuckle, remembering the scene, and my dad's broad grin in response.

"So, he was happy for you?"

"Yeah, definitely. He was happy I was happy."

"And were you happy?"

I laugh. "Of course!"

"You're using a lot of negative words for someone who was so happy. You just said you hated yourself."

"Yeah, but not in that way. In the way that it was so..." I gesture like I'm stuck in a straitjacket. "It was a lot."

Luce is sitting with his arms crossed and his legs spread wide on the bench opposite me. He's wearing a dark grey pinstripe suit with a white shirt and open collar. I'm still wearing my hoodie and joggers, but it doesn't feel unequal. I guess we're just both wearing what we like. And it suits him. Over time, his handsomeness has faded somewhat to me, though I still find myself admiring him as he talks. It's his confidence and his ease that I'm most attracted to now, and the way he holds himself like he holds all the power, but wouldn't be threatened by someone trying to take it away.

The concept of the 'choice' that hangs over us is no longer the focus of my mind. I look forward to talking to Luce. I feel like it's helping clear my mind, sorting through the clutter that's built up over the 18 years I've been around. Almost 18, anyway. The thought that whenever this ends, we will have to decide whether I live or die seems less daunting than it was. Plus, I can never tire of talking about Abbas.

Luce smiles at me. He smiles like Abbas does, sort of wonkily in the most adorable way. "So, did you tell your mum about Abbas, too?"

XIII

The Lion in the Room

My mother looked at me across the table. The smell of smoke was hanging in the air like a film that suffocated us, though no one mentioned it. Her parents lived in a village about a 45-minute drive from our town, in a small house with low ceilings and abundant natural light that poured in from the array of windows onto old wooden furniture and dusty paperbacks on bookshelves. In keeping with the cottage-core theme, every surface was doused in houseplants.

It was the third time I had seen her that year. My sister was already in the garden gazing at the pond and making absent-minded small talk next to Gran as their old bulldog, Basil, snored on the grass. Grandad was upstairs and the floorboards creaked as he shuffled around, going about his business. My mother was still looking at me.

"How's your dad?" Her voice was quiet and soft.

"He's good." I didn't tell her about Lois. She had left now anyway. Mum hadn't been in another relationship since the divorce, and I didn't want to ask her about it. Penny and Gran were laughing at something, and I stared through the window at them, desperate to join them, but stuck in place. Every room my mother entered, the mood slowly died, like she was Miss Havisham from *Great Expectations*. I pitied her, and I hated her for it.

"How's school?" She sipped the lemon tea in front of her

from the delicate China teacup blooming with daffodils. Dad hated the smell of the stuff, so it was banished from our house. At least she had that.

"Good, thanks." I paused awkwardly. "I'm enjoying A levels a lot more than GCSEs. They go into more depth so you feel like you're learning stuff, rather than just reciting facts."

"How's Olivia?" The question was uncomfortable.

"I haven't spoken to her in a while. She moved away a few months ago."

"Oh, that's a shame. She was nice." It was disingenuous. My mother disliked Olivia for basically the whole time we were dating. "Is there anyone new on the scene?" Her thin lips curled into a feeble smile.

"Well..." My stomach curled and the back door opened, letting the warm autumn breeze into the room and swirling the dust particles up into the air. Penny walked in with Gran a step behind her, chatting about the painting she had been working on. An avid Monet fan, Gran spent hours painting in the small room next to the utility room, which was empty other than an easel and a poorly varnished console table stacked with oil paints. She was currently working on painting the pond, which Grandad had carefully crafted to resemble Monet's Water Lily Pond, minus the bridge.

Mum's smile had faded, but she painted it back on for Penny, who beamed back. "What are we talking about?" my sister asked, plonking herself down at the dining room table in between Mum and I. She had grown a lot in the last few years, and now towered over our mother, who was a little over five foot.

"I was just asking your brother about girlfriends."

Penny's eyes flicked to me and I grimaced. We had never told her about why Olivia and I broke up, and, over time, forgot to mention the news about my sexuality. Mum rarely asked personal questions, and so the topic had faded. I guess, to a point, Penny and I both assumed she knew.

"Oh, right," Penny said, looking at the table, nodding slowly with wide eyes.

"Actually, Mum," I said, slowly, praying the courage would find me along the way. "I'm gay."

"Oh," my mother replied. The syllable hung in the air like a noose.

Gran had returned with a plate of chocolate wafer biscuits—Penny's favourite. I loathed the things. My grandparents made no secret of who their favourite was, even though they professed to love us both equally.

I stared at my mother. She stared at the plate of biscuits. Penny stared at me. Gran sneezed into her monogrammed handkerchief. Basil wandered into the room as well but, sensing the atmosphere, immediately turned and ambled back out to the garden.

"I'm sorry. I didn't know," my mother said. It didn't help the situation.

"You don't have to apologise," I replied with a poor attempt at a smile.

"Does your father know?" Mum hated to be the last one to know things in our family. She hated it before the divorce, and she hated it even more since.

"Yeah," I said, then hastily followed it with, "But I only told him recently." It was a lie, but it wouldn't hurt anyone. "I just wanted to tell you in person."

"Right, well. Thank you."

Gran sneezed again. I'm not sure she was even paying attention as she thumbed through a newspaper, unhygienically licking her finger before turning each page.

There was another uncomfortable silence, and I was eager to fill it with something, but Penny beat me to the chase.

"He has a boyfriend, though," she said in a sing-song voice, taunting me. I was furious with her.

"He's not my boyfriend, Penelope," I snarled. Hearing people talk about Abbas infuriated me. I wanted him all to myself, even the knowledge of him.

"Who's this?" Mum asked, blinking.

"It's nothing, Mum," I replied.

"It's not nothing. He never stops talking about him."

"Shut up, Penelope," I snapped back. She hated it when I used her full name.

"Oh, well, I want to hear about him," my mother chimed in, barely concealing her desperation to be part of the in-crowd.

"He's just a friend, Mum."

"What's this, dear?" Gran asked, looking up from the obituary section over her wide-rimmed silver glasses.

Penny repeated the slander that I had a boyfriend, and Gran pursed her lips. "A boy," she said, looking over at me. I closed my eyes for a second. "That's nice, dear." She returned to her paper. The danger of homophobia had passed.

"Who is he?" Mum asked again.

"His name's Abbas," I relented, "And he's just a friend."

"Oh, please." I was delighted with Penny's contributions to this conversation. "They spend every waking moment together."

"We're just good friends," I shook my head, as if that would make the lie a truth.

I mean, the truth was that Abbas and I were good friends, and not boyfriends. I didn't even know if he was gay, or bi, or pan or anything. We'd never talked about that. But the thought that we *could* be boyfriends and weren't hurt like a bitch.

"Well, I'd love to meet him," Mum said, smiling weakly again. I didn't appreciate the sentiment.

The day eventually drew to a close, and thankfully, neither Mum nor Penny mentioned Abbas again. Dad came by to pick us up at seven, parking his newly cleaned Mercedes in front of the lush, manicured lawn, and waiting by the front door. In a carefully choreographed routine, Mum said her goodbyes minutes before he arrived and politely excused herself with a made-up story about needing to sort something in her bedroom at the back of the house. Dad made polite small talk with his former mother-in-law, and Grandad slipped battered old five pound notes into mine and Penny's hands as he hugged us goodbye. In the fresh air of the outside, freed from the smoke of the house, I looked up at the fading sunlight and a sky freckled with clouds and flocks of starlings, and felt a peculiar melancholy wash over me.

I had thought telling Mum I was gay would be freeing, or that it might reset our relationship that had been stalled by their divorce. But instead, it was just added to the pile of ways in which Mum felt left out, and I felt guilty for continuing to live a life with her not in it. I breathed in deeply and looked back to the house. As children, we spent hours playing in the landscaped gardens, and hiding in the nooks and crannies of nineteenth century architecture. Not just me and Penny, but Mum and Dad too, and Gran and Grandad. I missed those days. I missed us.

But now the house was just a reminder of Mum's misery, and I was glad to see the back of it.

***

At the beach with Rebecca, I'm free to reflect. I'm not sure if it's real, or if it's just an illusion like the rest of this place, but the salt air and cold sand feel real enough. Rebecca has slowly begun telling me more and more about what brought her here, but I still feel far from the full story. I hadn't seen her for a while before she brought me back here, and I had begun to miss her.

It turns out she grew up not far from where I lived—just a couple of towns over—and she knows a lot of the same places I do. We talk about the ice cream from the shop owned by the old man on the high street, and the different hats that would appear on the statue of an old explorer (read: coloniser) throughout the year, from a fluffy red Santa hat in December to a summery bonnet in June. No one knew who was putting the hats on, but the tradition was long-standing, and as much a part of the fabric of the town as the library both our parents dragged us to for each summer's 'Reading Challenge', where generations of kids would be forced to read as many books as they could stomach over the holidays for a measly five pound book voucher reward for the winner in each age range.

I'm surprised we knew none of the same people, and I quiz her endlessly for a mutual connection, to no avail, and to her irritation. She eventually begs me to stop, and instead she tries to teach me how to cartwheel, which leaves my leg throbbing and my self-esteem in tatters, as she dances around me in delight at one failed attempt after another.

Rebecca is also in the ICU, she tells me, but she can't remember what brought her there. Maybe we're in beds next to each other, I muse with a smile and laugh at the idea we would be friends back home. She's an eight-year-old girl who loved daisy chains and ponies, and I was a seventeen-year-old boy who was hopelessly in love with the boy I sat next to in English. And yet, here we are, she's my only friend in the Interlife.

I try not to think too much about what she told me. The thought makes my blood boil and my stomach nauseated, and I feel weak and powerless and pathetic. When I bring it up to Luce with regularity, he reminds me that Rebecca is safe here. It's hard to believe him, though. How can she be safe when her father is still out there? How can she be safe when she's had those things done to her? I feel sick again in the knowledge that there's fuck all I can do.

"Do you know when you're going to make a decision?" she asks while braiding strands of grass together.

I shake my head. "I don't think for a while yet."

"Do you know how time works here?" Her questions sure do test me.

I shake my head again and ponder the question. "Do you think that this is all like a second back home, or do you think every minute here is a minute back there?"

Rebecca doesn't know for sure, but she says she thinks time works the same. "I was here for a long time before I met you, and it feels just as long as it would have if I were home."

I make a mental note to ask Luce when I see him next. I watch as Rebecca finishes her braid—a stunningly neat end-product—and she hands it to me. I finger the tiny rope absent-mindedly.

"Have you spoken to anyone else here?" The question has been gnawing at me for a while.

"No," she replies simply, plucking new blades of long grass to be made into another braid. "I tried to at the start, when I first got here, but people didn't talk to me, so eventually I stopped trying."

"How come you spoke to me?"

"I told you. You're important."

The refrain is irritating.

***

When we got home from Mum's, I sat in the car for a minute before going into the house. Penny and Dad didn't seem to notice, but I was grateful for the breather. My leg had been hurting a lot recently, and I knew I needed to see the doctor again about my medication dosage—it needed to be assessed regularly as I grew up—but the thought of waiting in a doctor's office for hours just to be poked and prodded and treated like a zoo animal was nauseating. I crammed the pain back into its tiny box in my mind, and swung my limbs out of the car, closing the door behind me a little too loudly for my dad's tastes.

Inside, Penny had immediately run to her room, leaving Dad and me alone in the living room. He was flicking through some post, disregarding most as bills and junk, before tossing the rest on the coffee table, and leaning back with a sigh. I sat in the chair next to the sofa he was on and nervously pawed the worn fabric.

"Dad?" I said, and his eyes opened wearily. He smiled at me softly. "I told Mum I'm gay."

He sat up straighter and rubbed his jawline with his hand. "That's good, right?"

I nodded slowly. "I guess so."

"How did she take it?"

"She was fine, I guess. She didn't really say anything."

"Did you want her to?"

I sighed. "I don't know."

He coughed quietly and leaned forward, resting his elbows on his thighs. "Your mum loves you very much, kiddo. We both do. You being gay isn't going to change that. Nothing will."

I nodded again, trying to digest the message.

"How are things with you and that boy?" I looked at Dad, and he had a cheeky glint in his eye. Penny had clearly been talking.

"There's nothing going on, Dad. I don't know what Penny has been telling you," I sigh, collapsing back and slouching down.

"Penny's said nothing, kid. I'm just saying. The walls in this house aren't that thick. I can hear you talking to him all hours of the night."

It's true. Abbas and I video-chatted almost every evening, and our conversations often stretched into the early hours. I still knew practically nothing about him, except that he plays guitar—badly, he still professed, and refused to demonstrate—and that he lived with his aunt. I didn't know where his parents were, and I didn't want to ask too much and put him off.

Abbas was a closed book masquerading as open. He brushed off any unwanted questions with a laugh and a shake of his head. He asked plenty of questions himself, though, and I found myself pouring out my life story as he listened intently. Naturally, I minimised the Olivia-Marcus storyline as much as possible, and glossed over Lewis entirely, but I found that coming out to Abbas didn't feel like coming out to my mum. I'd never really denied my sexuality to myself. I'd known I was gay since I was first old enough to think about girls and boys. I just denied it to everyone else. Coming out to Abbas felt like coming out to myself: natural and seamless and right.

He didn't even say anything in response. He just nodded, and listened, like he always did. The only thing that gets him talking is literature, and I relish the moments when I get him all to myself as he rants about the latest stupid thing Tony had contributed to the class discussion, or why *From The Antique* by Rossetti was the perfect parallel to *Jane Eyre*. He once spoke for an hour straight about a feminist critique of *Romeo and Juliet* we hadn't even been asked to read, but that he had found and devoured, anyway.

I loved reading, and I adored *Jane Eyre*, but his passion for literature dwarfed mine. Ordinarily, I would feel threatened by an encroachment on such a fundamental part of me—the woman who kept me alive—but Abbas's knowledge far surpassed anything I could know about Jane or the Brontës, and listening to him was vindication of my love for the book. My love for any book. It was the most stunning defence of artistic expression mankind could offer, and it was for my ears only.

Abbas told me, in a slip-up he instantly regretted, that he learned English by watching pirated adaptations of classic works after his aunt had bought the box set of an old aristocratic TV drama. When I asked what his first language was, or how old he was when he started learning English, he clammed straight back up, and left me out in the cold.

XIV

The Trash

"That's you."

Abbas was pointing to a gruesome and creepily drawn diagram of the musculoskeletal system in his biology textbook. The intact eyeballs were a particularly uncomfortable highlight. He looked at me with a grin plastered on his face and a cheeky glint in his dark eyes that sent goosebumps rippling across my skin. I narrowed my eyes at him in a disapproving scowl, to his obvious delight.

Snatching the book from him, I thumbed through the pages until I found a suitably disgusting photograph of a dissected frog. "And that's you," I sneered.

He laughed and pulled the textbook back to his side of the desk. We were in my bedroom, with him perched on a chair "borrowed" from my sister's room, and me in my black computer chair as I scrolled through Google Scholar looking for someone who conveniently agreed with my hypothesis that the Treaty of Versailles was a fair bargain between the French, British and American positions. As with most A Level essays, I chose the position that struck a perfect balance between getting marks and being easy to write. Abbas was writing out notes on... Well, I guess, muscles? Some music played in the background, but we had to turn it down because Abbas couldn't focus with it too loud. Still, he had been humming along with the song under his breath.

"Okay, okay," Abbas chuckled, burying his head back into the dullest pages humanity could have mustered. "I'm the dead frog. You're the flayed human." His face dropped as he said it, and he hardened his stare on the page of words. An uncomfortable silence followed.

Abbas coming over to study had become somewhat of a regular occurrence. The first time, he had perched stiffly on the edge of the sofa as we listened to my dad talk about the last week of work (he had just come back from a three-day conference in Edinburgh on planning permission for on-shore wind farms—thrilling, I know), and spoken quietly when asked for a reply. My sister introduced herself briefly, with a giggle and a smile directed at me, before rushing upstairs to her room where she spent most of her time doing God-only-knows-what. My dad had thrown in some oven pizzas, apologising to Abbas that we lived in a dead-zone where the only food we could get delivered was a dodgy curry house with a reputation for rodents, before slapping the finished and slightly burned product onto plates for us to take upstairs to my room. When Mum was around, we were never allowed to eat upstairs, but seeing as Dad spent most of his time working or away, we'd let some rules slide.

Balancing his glass of water on the side of the plate, with his textbooks slung under the other hand, Abbas finally relaxed when we got to my room. He looked around at the walls covered with posters that varied from bands I was obsessed with to bands I had listened to once or twice, along with the odd movie poster, but he quickly gravitated to studying the volumes on my bookshelf, and nodding appreciatively when he came across one he liked.

He pointed at one that Lois had left me—one of the fateful 'gay' books. "I don't like this one."

The words stung and my cheeks reddened. "Oh. How come?"

"It's too sad. Needlessly. I think that sometimes love stories like to wallow in their own misery and tell us that love only comes from sadness. I don't think that's true."

"But isn't that part of the fun of it, when you get to feel these highest highs and lowest lows? I think that's the point of love. It opens you up to being happier than you've ever been, and being hurt more than you ever could be." He raises his eyebrows slightly, not taking his eyes off the book. I clench my jaw. I really shouldn't have been taking this so personally.

That was the last time we had discussed the book, though he made his disapproval of my literature known in other ways. Saying 'this is something you should really enjoy' as he loaned me a pristine paperback, with every margin filled with his careful, methodical annotations, as if the things I had been enjoying thus far were things I shouldn't have enjoyed.

But in the weeks since that first time he came, Abbas had grown accustomed to studying at my house most days after school. As we walked home from the bus stop together, he would be excitingly telling me about the things they had studied in biology or maths that day, his eyes wide, and his gestures growing bigger and bigger. He would throw a greeting to my sister, who yelled back from behind her bedroom door, and ask my dad about his day when he was home. The atmosphere was pleasant, like my whole body was slowly filling up.

My heart had never stopped fluttering around him, though, and each second with him in my room was torture, especially with the bed mere feet away. As he hugged me goodbye—the only person he did that to—my heart would leap into my throat, and that was definitely not the only muscle reacting to the touch. Talk about biology.

These thoughts streamed through my mind as I gazed blindly at the computer screen, hearing Abbas hum softly to the music. I knew he was musical, however much he professed to be "lame" at playing the guitar, but hearing him hum only made me want him to sing. Nothing he did was ever enough.

I prayed for a bottle of vodka to ease the tension, but unfortunately, our house was fit for 1920s America, minus the moonshine.

***

"Didn't a bottle of vodka get you into the mess in the first place with Marcus?" Luce smirks, with an eyebrow cocked like a shotgun.

"Ha."

"Can we skip ahead to the good part?"

"Patience is a virtue."

***

The good part was every tortuous moment spent with Abbas, whether we were studying side-by-side, or sat feet apart on my bed watching some sitcom or another on the TV propped on top of the drawers on the opposite wall. You could close your eyes and bask in his presence, or watch his eyes intently fixed on the screen as I introduced him to a new quirky set of twenty-something friends in New York or L.A. he had somehow never seen before, and for which I had to explain the slang as we went along.

After Lewis, I had been so intent on avoiding men, and somehow I found the perfect one was now an arm's-length away in my room. But, as Luce so kindly reminds me, I was paralysed. Abbas would turn his head away when I was stripping off my school shirt and throwing on a hoodie or tee, no matter how much I wanted him to steal a glance. His hugs never lingered too long, and I held my breath when we touched in the deluded hope that he wouldn't feel my heart beating faster and faster.

That was the good part, I promise.

But the best part came one night when the sun had set long ago, and Dad was away inspecting a new turbine or something or other. Penny was in her room, as always, and Abbas and I were lounging on my bed, watching the antics the comedy archetypes had got themselves into in these twenty minutes.

"That's you," he grinned, pointing at the screen where a man had fallen into a pile of rubbish after a poorly executed escape from seeing his ex.

A person crawled out from between the bags and told the man it was his spot. "That's you, asshole," I laughed.

"I'm the man in the trash. You are the trash," Abbas countered with a conspiratorial wink.

I pushed his shoulder lightly, and he grabbed my hand as I recoiled. His eyes were looking into mine. Our smiles faded.

Slowly, he dropped my hand, crawling over to me. He never broke our gaze. My heart was pounding.

He was on top of me as I lay with my shoulders propped up on the pillows. Suddenly, I was very aware of where my hands were meant to be. I kept them loosely by my sides, and my palms sweated.

"I'm your trash," I whispered with a smile that never actually materialised. The corners of his lips curled upwards, and I panicked that I had ruined the moment.

His lips were soft and full, pressing lightly down onto mine. I squeezed my eyes closed, begging my stupid, stupid brain to remember this moment. He pulled away, and I opened my eyes to see his were still closed. My breathing was shaky. *Please God, don't let him regret this. Please don't. Please.*

He opened his eyes and it was like I was swimming in them.

"Hey," he said, his voice barely a whisper.

"Hey."

He raised his right hand and touched my left cheek, his thumb brushing over my skin. "You're my trash," he said, and winked.

I burst out into an embarrassed laugh, which he silenced as

his thumb grazed my lip. His smile slowly faded, and he leant in for another kiss. I could feel my dick pressing into his leg. I begged him not to notice.

His kisses were soft. Perfect. It wasn't like fireworks. It was like being enveloped in chocolate, or the moment you step into a bath, or slowly falling asleep in the middle of the afternoon with your sunburn keeping you warm on holiday. It was bliss. My heart ached when he pulled away. I could feel his hot breath on my skin, but it wasn't enough. I fell in love with Abbas in all the ways that seem too mundane to put into words: the way he furrowed his brow as he read a book, or how he played with the buttons on his shirt absent-mindedly, or how in the silence we spent together, I had never felt so at peace and alive.

I felt the pressure lift off the mattress and opened my eyes to see him sitting on the edge of the bed, rubbing his jaw with his head pointed towards the ground.

"Are you okay?" I asked, terrified I had done something wrong. That I had fucked this up already.

He turned his head and looked at me over his hunched shoulders. "I'm good," he replied, with a half-smile.

I sat up, cross-legged on the bed, staring at his back. The millions of ways this could all go horribly wrong swarmed through my mind in a frenzy. In the heat of the moment, I decided to go for broke. Everything to lose. Everything to gain.

"I like you, Abbas." The words felt like they were falling from foreign lips. He turned to face me again, and looked at me through his long, black eyelashes and heavy lids.

"I like you too." The words surged through my heart like a shot of adrenaline. "I really do." He smiled. "My trash."

XV

The King of Misery

"When did you start cutting yourself?"

Oh, for fuck's sake. I loved Jo, I did. I enjoyed speaking to her, and I actually did look forward to our sessions. Mostly because I think I had already bored Penny's ears off with my gushing about Abbas, and at least Jo was duty bound to listen. The Hippocratic oath was a very useful thing. To be fair, though, she shouldn't start every session with a 'What's been on your mind?' when she knows that the only thing that's been on my mind is a certain 5'11 God of a human being with bronzed skin, biceps that could strangle a lion, and a butt that would make a Greek sculptor bashful.

"Why are you asking?" I scowled playfully, hoping we could jump over the hiccup she was putting in my road to full-on delusion.

"Well, you're here to talk to me because you're not happy," she replied, smiling softly.

"I am happy. That was the old me that did... that. The new me is happy."

"Because of Abbas?" she asked.

"Yeah. Because of Abbas."

"Do you ever think that maybe staking your happiness on one person is, firstly, a lot of pressure to put on them, and secondly, quite an unstable foundation to build it on?" Jo was something of a pessimist, I decided.

We were in a different room today. This one had a boarded-up fireplace hidden behind a dusty plastic floral arrangement, and a window overlooking the car park and the opposite DIY shop hidden behind cheap netted curtains. It was pure National Health Service-tackiness. Glorious. The sessions used to be on a Thursday afternoon, but I had convinced (read: *begged*) Jo to move me to a Friday morning for two reasons: firstly, I had two free periods on a Friday morning, so I wouldn't have to miss and then catch up on any class; secondly, because Thursday afternoon I had an English class, and I would rather never come to therapy again than miss an hour sitting next to Abbas.

He wasn't my boyfriend, per se, but he kissed me like I was. As soon as we got back to mine after school, the second my bedroom door clicked shut, his lips would be on mine with a hunger that could barely be contained. Honestly, I'm not sure I was the best kisser. I was only 16, and I knew I had a lot of catching up to do in that department, but who was I to complain? I was kissing Abbas. I had nothing to complain about.

My mind had wandered, and Jo lassoed it back to the present with a repetition of her unwelcome question.

"Oh, Jo," I sighed. "Do we have to talk about this today? That's not what's on my mind."

"I've noticed that your mind has seemed very singular for the last few weeks." She raised her eyebrows, her forehead wrinkling. "But answer the question. Quit dancing around it."

I sighed again and rolled my eyes to drive the point home. "The first time was maybe when I was 12. A few months after I started dating Olivia, I guess."

"What made you do it the first time?"

"I was just curious. I wasn't even sad. I wanted to see what it felt like."

"And what did it feel like?"

"Weird. It was painful. But I liked it. It felt... real." I twisted my mouth to one side and avoided Jo's knowing stare. I was weirdly proud of the fact that I had never cried in therapy. It was the saddest badge of honour I could wear, but at least I could wear it.

"Why did you like it?"

"It was a good kind of pain. Like when you stretch and feel your spine crack. Or when you've just done a workout." I made the last point up. I'd never done a workout beyond a few pitiful push-ups on my bedroom floor.

"And then?"

"Well, then I started doing it more. I started doing it every night, so that it would scab up and heal while I was asleep."

Jo nodded and made a note. *What I wouldn't give to see what she was writing all the time.*

I continued: "I used to get blood on my bedsheets sometimes, and I'd worry my parents would see, but I think by that point they were arguing so much, I could have stuck a dead rabbit in the laundry and they wouldn't have noticed.

"Then I started doing it every morning, too, because I was so nervous to go to school and spend the whole day with Olivia and everyone, and have to see Marcus, that I needed a little pick-me-up to force back the nerves." What a fucking morbid thing to say—'*a little pick-me-up*'. I shudder, replaying it in my head.

Jo was still looking at me, twiddling her perennial blue biro between her fingers. She was left-handed. Quirky. I looked out the window—what little you could see through the disgusting white sheet obscuring it—and forced myself to carry on in the most matter-of-fact tone I could, as if I would get another prize for being a masochist.

"It got to the point where I don't even know if I was doing it because I was sad or anxious or whatever, I was just doing it out of habit more than anything. Like brushing my teeth. I tried to be as careful as possible, cleaning the cuts with soap and hot water, and then with some alcohol that I found in an old first aid kit in the back of the bathroom cabinet.

"I think that's what made Dad maddest when he found out what I was doing: the fact that I thought I was being sensible about it. He started yelling at me, saying there's nothing smart or responsible about mutilating myself."

"How did you feel about what he said?"

"About me mutilating myself?" Jo nodded in reply. "It made me feel sick. He was so disgusted by me. It sucked to see how I see myself reflected in someone else. It feels so different from the kind of hate you have for yourself. It's so much worse. You can excuse hating yourself. You can't hide from someone hating you."

"Did he hate you?"

"He said he hated what I was doing."

"Is that hating you?"

I chewed on my bottom lip, pulling off the skin with my teeth. It was a tic I didn't even know I had until my lip was seemingly always bleeding. "This is where we always disagree, Jo." I forced an awkward and heartless smile. "If someone hates part of you, they might as well hate all of you. You can't separate people into the good and bad as you like."

"What do you think of the phrase 'hate the sin, love the sinner'?" Jo had flipped onto a new page of her notebook without breaking eye contact.

"It's fucked up." Jo exhaled through her nose sharply, her shoulders jolting in a minute laugh. I didn't usually swear around her; for some reason it felt like I shouldn't. She always laughed when I finally did. The first time I swore, I immediately apologised, and she told me I could swear as much as I wanted to within these four walls.

"Why do you think that?"

"People use it to justify homophobia, but that's the same thing as trying to separate one aspect of a person because that's the part you don't like."

"What do you mean by that?" I felt like I was being crystal clear, but here came another one of my patented analogies.

"Well, imagine you're, like, a puzzle; you've got all these pieces that make up the whole picture. Now imagine that one of those pieces is the bit you don't like, because that's the piece with a Pride flag on, or that's the bit with the scars on, and you hate that puzzle piece. You can remove it, but then you no longer have the whole picture. You've got something broken. That means you don't love the whole picture, you like the way you've broken it. That gives people a sense of power and control over you, because they think they can be the one to mould you into their own vision of what you should be. That's not love."

"Do you know what love is?"

"I want you to show me."

It took a second, but her poker-face cracked into a smile. "Hilarious." I knew it was. "But do you ever think that maybe your dad said those things just because he was so scared of you hurting yourself, and he hated the idea that you were hurting yourself?"

"I know my dad loves me. He's a great dad, I love him. But if he thought I was hurting, I don't think him hurting me more is the right answer."

"Do parents always have the right answer?"

"Yeah, I know. They're people too. But I'm a kid. I shouldn't have to realise that."

"Why not?"

"Being a kid is so complicated. You have to see the world in all these shades of grey when you've just spent the first decade being told everything is black-and-white. Good and bad. Right and wrong. Sometimes you just wanna see the world as it was."

"And what did you want to see?"

"I was hurting. I was hurting so, so bad." I was talking as

if it was many years ago, and not just a handful of months. "I wanted him to fix it. Parents are supposed to fix things for you."

"Can your dad fix you?"

"I don't know." My tone was getting a bit stroppy. "I'm not the king of misery."

Jo laughed. "What are you then?"

"One of his subjects."

The hour was done, and I was released back into my world that revolved around Abbas.

On my return to school, I found that Abbas was also missing that Friday morning. Usually, we would catch up during break time, holding hands behind our friends' backs and stealing furtive glances at each other. Real smooth criminals. But when I walked into the art classroom we hung out in—Alonso was the artist of the group, and a fucking phenomenal one at that—our four friends were sitting without Abbas. I was disappointed.

"Hey, guys." I swung my backpack onto the table by the door, and walked over to where they sat. "Where's Abbas?"

"I think he had an appointment or something. That's what Mr Nathwani said," Alonso replied without looking up from his painting. It was another stunning creation of what looked like wine pouring from a bottle. The dark grape tones and streaks of white highlight genuinely made it look as if it was rippling and dripping down the canvas. The way Alonso painted was an oxymoron. His deliberate strokes were so delicately applied, but he wielded the paintbrush like a weapon, as if with one flick, he could slay us all, and with an intensity that I had never seen in an artist. The rest of us could spend a lifetime looking for that same gift, and never find it.

Alonso and Tom weren't bickering for once. It was in these moments, when Alonso was so caught up in his craft, that Tom knew to bide his time until he was finished before winding him right back up again. I sometimes thought if Alonso wore a blood-pressure monitor, it would read like a perfect up-and-down oscillation, which the doctors could easily ascribe to Tom, and Tom-free moments. Tom's blood-pressure monitor would just be a constant peak. How he hadn't crashed under the weight of his own energy was a mystery.

Lukas and Liam were quiet, scrolling through their phones. They weren't the chattiest duo, Liam especially, but I knew that the four of them had been hanging around since primary school, and so they had settled into their equilibrium long ago, until Abbas and I intruded on their little group.

I drifted over to the window overlooking the quad, where some much-envied teachers parked their cars and where a flagpole which had long since lost its flag stood lonely, surrounded by small bushes and bedraggled flowers. At the end of the stumpy road leading into the school, I could see Abbas standing by the gate talking to a stranger. I knew from the photos he had shown me what his aunt looked like, and this woman, aside from definitely not being Arabic, was certainly not her. She was short with what still looked like baby fat that hadn't burned off, wore her cropped blonde hair in a manner that resembled a sports commentator Lukas was fond of sending me clips of, and wore a stylish grey suit. They looked as though they were arguing, with Abbas towering over the woman and, for the first time I had ever seen him, looking every bit the 16-year-old kid he was.

The woman put a hand on his arm, and he shuffled awkwardly, before turning and walking back to the school building with his head firmly down. At that moment, the bell rang, and the teacher who was walking past Abbas by coincidence—a shrill little twat called Mr Kerr (or Mr Wan-Kerr to the rest of us)—snapped at Abbas, probably telling him to get to his next class. Abbas waited until Mr Wanker's back was turned before flipping him the finger.

I dragged my backpack on and joined Liam to head towards history class. Still another hour stood between me and seeing Abbas. *Disaster.*

***

Luce smells like pomegranate shampoo. I'm not sure why I haven't noticed before, but the scent of it lingers in the air when he leaves the room, thinking that was the perfect place to end the session. I'm not sure if he gets jealous when I talk about Jo—I mean, why would he? He's an immortal God-like being, I guess, but to me they play relatively the same function: asking lots of questions with the end goal of me deciding whether to live or to die. It's just Luce wants me dead, and Jo wanted me alive… I assume.

I sit for a minute in the Commons and look around, feeling more of a sense of peace than I have since I got here. Talking about Abbas is my safe space, especially in the happy years—well, *year*—and getting to relive it all again relaxes me, but the anxiety of knowing what comes next still gnaws away at my stomach and my heart, like a moth on an old cardigan that someone had left in their closet for too many years. Schrödinger's cardigan—you don't know how much has been eaten until you put it on.

My dad always used to say I'd end up here, in the Commons, and for a long time I believed him. I'm not sure I quite pictured myself in a coma fighting for my life and just imagining I'm here, but beggars can't be choosers. When I was growing up, still with Olivia, I would watch PMQs every Wednesday evening and watch them rip each other to shreds. There was something about the smarmy, righteous way they spoke, the glint in their eye as their voice thundered out one canned rebuttal after another. It was as infuriating as it was compelling.

Mum always hated me watching it. She never voted, because she loathed every single one of the 650 people in that chamber, and thought that each one managed to be worse than the one before. Dad voted out of principle, saying it was his civic duty to do so, but I don't think he ever voted for someone as long as I knew him; he'd only vote against the alternative.

But aside from the rough and tumble of dirty politics and stale rhetoric, this was where lives were changed forever. It was what they decided in this House that would mean someone could eat that night, or someone could not; that someone could grow up or not at all; that some would live while others died.

Luce asked me early on in our time together why I chose the House of Commons. That is why.

And for every moment I spent with Abbas, I wanted more and more to be here, to be in this room, and to fight for him. For us.

But this isn't how I thought I would end up sitting on this long green bench. I always thought my family rows would take me to Ms Badden's debate club, which would take me to university, which would take me to Parliament. But, when I think about it more closely, when Ms Badden set up the debate club at school, she didn't do it because of me. She did so because Lukas fell in love.

XVI

Kiss Her, You Fool

Cath was a goddess. She was tall, with waves of blonde hair flowing to the floor, piercing blue eyes the colour of the sea, and an unblemished complexion dusted with light freckles. She didn't walk around the school; she strutted. She didn't dance like nobody was watching, she knew we all were. She didn't study. That's it; she just didn't study. But, hey, even goddesses can't be everything.

Lukas was transfixed from the moment he saw her walking across the hall, and his obsession with her conveniently distracted from mine with Abbas. The more he talked about her, especially to Liam, the more we would laugh and groan, and goad him on. "You have no chance," we told him, and he would shake his head with a lovesick grin.

"It's insane," Lukas said one lunchtime, as we sat in the art classroom, with Alonso sketching a banana with photorealistic accuracy. "How can one person be so fucking gorgeous? I genuinely think I've gone insane."

"You have, mate," Tom replied, fidgeting with his watch.

"She was on the way to yoga at lunchtime yesterday, and those yoga pants... *Man*." He whined out the last word like a toddler being denied a sweet.

"You haven't even spoken to her," Liam muttered, loud enough for us all to hear it. He pretended to be introverted, but he loved nothing more than stirring the pot.

"I have, you twat," Lukas hissed back. "She dropped her sports textbook the other day, and I handed it to her."

"I'm not sure mumbling some gibberish crap and turning bright red counts as talking," Liam winked back, and we laughed as Lukas's face burned scarlet again. The smell of Ms Badden's blue cheese salad dressing wafted over to us, and our noses wrinkled. We had long since known not to mention it, though.

"Irregardless…" Lukas began, before Liam interrupted.

"Not a word."

"Irregardless," Lukas stared daggers at Liam, whose face was buried in his folded arms. "She knows I exist."

Lukas wasn't an unattractive guy by any stretch of the imagination. Proudly and vocally half-Portuguese and half-Polish, Liam had christened him with the nickname 'Pee Pee', which Lukas would only ever permit Liam to use—anyone else who uttered the word would be thumped. Lukas was always in some form of trouble. But even with my homosexual gaze, I could see that Lukas was not in the same league as Cath. Not even slightly.

Cath was one of the most popular girls who was above any interaction with mortal men, and she wouldn't have done anything more than glance at Lukas even if he had the abs he was constantly aiming for. While they were both in the same sports science class, they sat at opposite ends of the room, and Cath likely didn't even know Lukas's name. It was a sore spot for him.

"Have you tried doing more press-ups? I think that might fix it," Abbas sniggered, and Lukas turned even redder.

"You guys are absolute... Fuck off." He folded his arms in a huff. "I just don't get why you can't support me on this."

Alonso looked up from his drawing and started sharpening his pencil. "It's like we learned in psychology: you shouldn't indulge people's psychoses. It's not healthy for them."

"See, man?" Abbas patted Lukas on the shoulder in sympathy. "We only want what's best for you."

Lukas called us twats again as the bell rang. We gathered our things, and Abbas and I headed to Lit.

"Kids are stupid. They're reckless, and they can't be trusted to fall in love." It was a good thing that Ms Robertson wasn't teaching us *Romeo and Juliet* if this was the scathing criticism she meted out to the protagonist of a mid-twentieth-century novel.

Abbas winked at me, and I hid my grin under my hand. The class laughed good-naturedly at another one of the teacher's off-topic but entertaining rants.

Civil rights literature wasn't always the most uplifting writing, but Ms Robertson was keen for us to look at it through a 21st century lens, with the hindsight we had been given by history. For our coursework topics, I had selected a mundane (to everyone else) question comparing the role of the government in queer literature, from the poetry of Oscar Wilde, which Abbas had suggested, to *Red, White and Royal Blue*. Abbas, with a poet's heart, was considering the portrayal of love and relationships against the backdrop of racist lynchings and discriminatory abuse, from *The Colour Purple* to *Giovanni's Room*. It was his coursework that was currently the focus of conversation.

My boyfriend—*I had begun calling him this in my head, if not out loud*—fervently disagreed with the woman's proposition.

"Just because someone is young doesn't make their love any less real. You can't just invalidate the experiences of people when what they lack in years they make up for in feeling," Abbas protested.

Ms Robertson chuckled. "I used to think the same, Mr Rahim, but when you get to an old age, like me, you might not be so naive."

Abbas shook his head. "Never."

The class moved on, and I poked Abbas in the arm. He looked over at me, his thick eyebrows furrowed.

"Hey," I said. I didn't have anything to say, I just wanted to say something to him. His eyes narrowed.

"What?"

"Nothing," I said with a goofy grin. I was like a lovesick puppy. *Disgusting*, Luce groans.

"Get back to work," Abbas hissed, scowling, but following it quickly with an air kiss which reassured me that he hadn't started to hate me in the last five seconds.

Abbas was highlighting the pages of his book, and cramming progressively smaller handwriting into the margins as he annotated what I always thought was the most mundane passage, but he had a knack for whipping beauty out of the ordinary that I just could never do. His head was inches from his page, and his knuckles white on his pencil as he concentrated on forcing words into infinitesimal spaces. I didn't have the same concern for my books—scrawling messy pen and folding down the corners of pages to mark my place. The first thing I did when I opened a new book was break the spine, and Abbas would shudder, glaring at me disapprovingly as he managed to dissect every line in his without a single mistake, blemish, or crack in the spine. The tension between our two styles could be cut with a knife.

"Something on your mind?" The suddenness of Ms Robertson appearing over my shoulder made me jump.

"Fuck." The word slipped out.

"No, thank you. Just focus on your work."

I had been staring at Abbas for God-knows-how-long, and I panicked momentarily that someone had noticed me. The panic subsided when I remembered that everyone knew I was gay here. I no longer had a closet to feel guilty in.

I had come out in the first month or so, when Lukas, in one of his dopey rants about Cath, asked me if I had a girlfriend.

The rest of the group had confessed to their singleness, and I was the only one remaining.

"Ummm..." I paused, considering my prior commitment to myself not to lie about this anymore. "Uh, no. I'm gay, actually."

"Oh, nice," Lukas replied with an appreciative nod.

"Congrats," and "Good for you, bro," Alonso and Tom chimed in. Liam wasn't there that day, but he was filled in shortly after, I assumed.

Only Abbas had been silent, scanning the boys' faces. He didn't acknowledge my confession.

Then the conversation resumed, debating whether Lukas had a chance with Cath. Lukas asked me for validation that he was an attractive guy, which he was, but he didn't need the ego-boost. Abbas had flipped open a book—one I didn't recognise from class—and was deep in thought, staring at a page.

***

"Did you think he might be homophobic?" Luce asks.

The question takes me by surprise. "I mean, that's always a worry, isn't it? Not to profile or anything, but he was Middle Eastern. They haven't always been the kindest cultures to queer people."

"So when he didn't acknowledge you coming out, did you worry?"

"Yeah, of course. I was obsessed with him. I thought about him every second I was awake, and I dreamt about him most nights. Fuck knows what I would have done if it had turned out he was a raging bigot." I chew my lip, considering the thought. "But, anyway, that's not what we're talking about."

"It is now."

"Oh, fuck off," I say as Luce chuckles and waves me on. "We're talking about Cath."

"Yeah, why are we doing that again?" Luce asks, leaning

forward as if my answer would be the most interesting thing he has heard all week.

"Because the story of Cath and Lukas is the story of how Ms Badden started the debate club. And the story of the debate club is the story of Abbas and me."

Luce leans back in weariness.

"Hey, this whole thing was your idea," I call at him.

***

But the story of Lukas and Cath was quickly going to take a turn for what she would have considered the worst, and what he considered the best.

It was a Wednesday afternoon, and I remember that distinctly because Mr Wilson was ill, and so Abbas and I could finally spend a free period together. He called it our first date, but it was rudely interrupted when Lukas abruptly looked up.

"What are you two doing?"

I looked down and saw that Abbas's hand was resting on my thigh, as my head rested on his shoulder. Shit.

Lukas's eyes widened to the size of plates. "Are you guys... like... *together*?"

Abbas squeezed my leg and laughed. "Cat's out the bag, babe." He nuzzled his nose into my ear.

I laughed, not sure if he was doing it for show, or if this was genuinely how we were telling our friends.

"Are you guys serious?" Tom looked furious.

The common room had gone silent, and I could feel everyone's eyes on us. I looked with panic at Abbas, who was grinning in his casual, devastatingly attractive manner that made my stomach swirl. My heart was pounding with anxiety that was completely unwarranted.

Abbas nodded and looked around at our four friends, ignoring the silent crowd around the room.

"Oh. My. Fucking. God." Tom leapt out of his seat and wrapped his arms around the two of us. I felt Alonso clap us on the back and Liam whistle appreciatively. There was half-hearted clapping from our fellow sixth form audience, those of whom that were semi-invested, whereas the others just wanted the scoop before they could return to their own conversations.

I beamed a smile that was crushed between Tom's chest and Abbas's shoulder, and when the boy finally released us, I saw Lukas sitting, mouth agape, opposite us. He hadn't moved a muscle.

"You okay, bro?" Abbas asked, cocking his right eyebrow. His tone was playful. His face, a warning.

"I just..." Lukas panted, "I don't get why you guys get to be all happy and cutesy, and I'm just..." he waved his hand in the general direction of where Cath was sitting, headphones in and social media open.

"No one likes a Bitter Betty, Lukas," Tom cautioned, before turning back to his psychology textbook, working on his essay that was due last week.

"You both have sports science together. Why don't you just talk to her, Pee Pee?" Tom asked.

"If only it were that simple, Tommy," Lukas replied sadly.

Tom took Lukas's face between his hands and squeezed his cheeks. "Promise me this, Lukas. You will talk to her in your next class."

Lukas wriggled out of Tom's embrace. "Fine, fine. Just fuck off first."

He recounted the story the next day before we were registered in form like it was one of the epics: *The Odyssey*, *War and Peace*, and *Lukas Spoke to Cath*.

"So there we were, on opposite sides of the class, and yet closer than we've ever been. Winstow asked us to find a partner, and I saw that Naomi wasn't in, so I flew from my seat, dodged around Crystal and George, practically had to tackle Jack, that horny bastard, but I made it. And I asked her."

"To marry you?"

Lukas punched Tom in the arm. "If she wanted to work on the project with me."

"And what did she say?" Abbas stared at Lukas with his intense brown eyes.

"She said, 'Yes, yes, a thousand times, yes'." We laughed at his imitation of a blushing bride.

"Nah, in all seriousness, I'm proud of you, man," Alonso said, tousling Lukas's crisp, blond hair. "So, what's the project?"

"Fuck knows. I was so nervous about sitting next to Cath I forgot to listen for the rest of the lesson." *Classic Lukas.*

"You've spoken to Cath, haven't you?" Lukas slammed his rucksack down on the table in the art room, and marched towards Abbas, who had been talking quietly to me about how his English coursework was going. I did not welcome the interruption, but I said nothing.

"Yeah, we sit on the same table in bio," Abbas replied, brushing a curl of hair out of his eye as he turned to look at Lukas.

"You have to tell me everything you know about her."

"Trouble in paradise?" Abbas grinned.

"I just realised I know nothing about this girl. You gotta tell me something, anything. She's coming round tonight to work on this project with me, and I don't know what the fuck to do." Lukas's eyes were wide with fear.

"I'm not your spy, Lukas," Abbas chuckled, his pearly white teeth showing.

"This is nothing to do with that. This is to do with us being friends and one friend asking another friend for help."

"I'm not going to give you a secret briefing, bro. That's creepy. Just relax, talk to her, get to know her yourself. That's it. She'll grow to love you like we did."

"Some of us have still got a bit of growing to do," Tom

muttered with a devious smirk.

Lukas ignored him. "What the fuck do I say to her?"

"You know how to talk to girls," Abbas soothed.

"No, he doesn't." Tom now earned a glare from Lukas. Liam sniggered.

"Girls are people, Lukas. Just talk to her like you would talk to us. Ask her questions. You know, like humans do?"

The next day at lunch, we got the debrief from a buzzing Lukas. The project was moving along smoothly—that was Alonso's first question, which he asked with mock sincerity—but more importantly, Lukas had got to know Cath.

"She's not just beautiful, guys. She's smart. She's savvy..."

"She's got what it takes to go all the way?" Tom quipped.

"What did you get to know about her?" Abbas asked. His eyes were heavy lidded, and he was quieter than usual.

"All sorts. We talked for hours."

"Just give us the highlights," Abbas yawned, covering his mouth with his hand and dropping mine in the process.

"I mean, we knew she dances, but I didn't know she was applying to dance schools for university. She was telling me all about them. This one in London she really wants has all these great teachers who have worked on the West End and in ballets and shit like that. She likes the same kind of music I do, and no, not trash," Lukas silenced Tom's opened mouth, "And she likes the same movies. We talked about our families. She told me about her sister, who was her brother, but now they're trans." Lukas looked at Abbas and me for approval, as though he had earned another allyship point. I ignored him. "She was telling me about how hard it is for them to get treatment, and how she had to move schools because a parent found out and started fucking bullying the teachers into not letting them use the girls' toilets."

"Yeah, shit's fucked with trans people," Liam noted sadly, and the six of us were silent for a moment.

"Yeah, man, I had no idea. It's so unfair." Lukas started reeling off these statistics from a night of reading up on the subject to impress Cath the next time they spoke. "And don't get me started on the fucking government."

"Mate, we didn't get you started on any of this." Alonso audibly sighed.

"Can we not talk about depressing shit at lunch? I'm trying to eat my sandwich. I don't wanna hear about trans suicide statistics while I'm eating my ham sandwich," Liam asked, presenting his half-eaten lunch to the group as evidence of his predicament.

"Well, I'm sorry reality is too hard for you guys to face," Lukas looked around at each of us. "People like Cath can't just ignore this because it's unpleasant at lunchtime."

"No one's giving you an award for your allyship, man, so just give it a rest right now," Tom sighed. Abbas and I were inconspicuously quiet. I had very strong opinions, naturally, but I didn't know these guys well enough to voice them. Plus, I told myself, it shouldn't be for the gays to be the voice for the whole community. It was a noble excuse for my dereliction of queer duty.

Ms Badden clicked her Tupperware closed in the awkward silence as Lukas glared at us all. You would've been able to hear a pin drop, but instead you heard a box being fastened. Luckily, the blue cheese aroma was being swept out of the window by an increasingly cool autumn breeze.

"When would be convenient for you guys to discuss trans rights, then? I'd hate for it to be a bother to you all." Lukas pursed his lips. Abbas stared down at his hands. I stared at Abbas. We were all silent.

"If you boys want to discuss something, maybe some kind of debate club would be a good idea?" Ms Badden's voice snapped the tension in the room like a rubber band recoiling. We turned to face the woman, who was such a quiet, ubiquitous presence in the art room that we often forgot she was there.

"What, miss?" Liam asked. Alonso was the only one here who actually studied art, and Liam was always nervous that we were overstaying our welcome. Until now, Ms Badden had held her tongue in our conversations.

"If you boys want to have an argument, maybe we should start a debate club?" she repeated, peering over the stack of art portfolios teetering on the edge of her desk.

"Oh, Miss, we didn't mean like that," Lukas tripped over his words as he tried to get out of a potential new commitment. The guy's distaste for school was perpetually a sour grape in the bunch of our happy sixth form. "And we wouldn't want to add to your workload, for sure," he continued in one run-on sentence after another. Ms Badden stared at him through heavily lidded eyes.

"I was thinking of setting up a debate club, anyway. But we would need buy-in by the sixth formers. Otherwise it'll just be me and a bunch of twelve-year-olds." Her face twisted in disgust.

Lukas began lathering on compliments in a desperate attempt to remedy the damage he thought he had done.

"So, you wouldn't come to a debate club?" Ms Badden interrupted Lukas. An awkward silence ensued.

"I would?" I said, raising my hand for some reason. Abbas looked at me with raised eyebrows and the ghost of a smile. The rest stared at me. "I like debating and politics and stuff. Plus, it's something else to put on my uni applications, isn't it?"

"Oh yeah, cause the wonderchild who's acing his A levels is going to be scraping the bottom of the barrel for a degree," Lukas said sarcastically.

I ignored him.

"That's great," Ms Badden replied, also ignoring Lukas, "I'll set something up."

"See?" Alonso said to Lukas as Ms Badden shuffled out of

the room. "See what happens when you talk?"

Lukas pouted and we laughed.

***

"So you got the debate club," Luce concludes, and I nod with an awkward smile, the kind English guys do when they see someone they sort of know, but not well enough to say hello. "And this relates to Abbas how?"

"For fuck's sake," I laugh, "I'm getting there. If I'm fighting for my life, I'm going to do it properly. I might never get a chance to tell this story again."

"What happened to Lukas and Cath?" Luce asks, leaning forward, as though he was finally going to engage in the conversation.

"Oh, they started dating soon after that, sort of out of the blue. We were at someone's party, I think it was Tom's, and they came out of the house into the back garden holding hands and smiling like the village idiots they were, and announced it to the group. Then Alonso yelled, 'Kiss her, you fool' and they kissed. Happily ever after." I smile, remembering the moment. A cute little heterosexual love story.

"You know, I think they're going to stay together for a long time.

XVII

Missing Pieces

Rebecca reminds me a lot of Penny when she was that age. There's something so innocent, and so pure, about a little kid who isn't afraid not to grow up. At that age—hell, even until she was 12—Penny was still playing with Barbies and obsessed with Disney Princesses, to the extent that I knew all the songs to most of the films, against my every intention to never watch them in the first place. It was a big about-turn when she started to dress solely in hoodies and jeans.

Penny was everything a little sister should be: rude, annoying, a complete and utter bitch, and one of my best friends. When I had that... breakdown with Lois, my sister avoided me for a week. Her room was down the hall from mine, a weird little cave with posters of Jacen Taylor plastered on the pink walls (a legacy from her princess-obsessed childhood), and yes, I was the classic gay kid with the same celebrity crush as his younger sister and his first girlfriend. After a week had gone by of barely seeing her face as she left for primary school and I left for secondary, I finally worked up the courage to knock on her door. The classic 'Do Not Disturb' sign nailed to her door swung a little as I rapped my knuckles against it. She grunted a 'come in' from inside.

***

I creaked the door open, and saw her lying on her bed, her feet on the wall above the pillow in a pair of the fluffy socks Dad always bought her for Christmas, and her hip-length brown hair sprawled across the pink patterned duvet. She was scrolling on her phone and watched me enter in her periphery.

"What?" she barked, her voice rough and deep. You'd think a girl who had grown up drowning in pink would have the most angelic voice, but God gave her a demon's instead.

"Hey, I just," I stood awkwardly, wringing my hands. "I just haven't seen you in a while."

She was silent, and resumed her scrolling, liking every other post in a pattern so methodical she can't have been concentrating.

"I don't know if you've spoken to Dad or Lois, but..." I trailed off again, praying that the ends of my sentences were better than the starts.

"What?" she said. I guess the public speaking-genes weren't split evenly between my sibling and me.

"Well, I didn't know if you wanted to talk or something?" My brain was swimming with the desire to go back to my room. I don't know why I bothered with this in the first place. I was about to turn around and click the door shut behind me, pretending I was never there in the first place, when she closed her phone and dropped it on the bed beside her. Penny sat up and looked at me with her dark brown eyes.

She said my name. She never called me by my name. She called me 'stupid' and 'bro', but never by my name. I stared at her, my hands still wringing.

"I just don't know why you didn't tell me," Penny said, flicking her eyes to the floor.

"Tell you what?" *The self-harm, the depression, the gay? What?*

"Any of it."

"I didn't tell anyone, Penny," I said. Tears prickled my eyes.

She was silent for a few moments. "You told Lois." Her

voice cracked a little.

"I mean, yeah. Eventually."

"Why Lois, though? Why not me, or Dad or Mum?"

My heart sank, and I felt shittier than I had the whole week.

Penny continued: "You chose her over us. She's not even part of the family."

"I didn't choose her, Penny," I croaked. A tear strolled down my cheek and I hated the bastard.

"I'm your sister. We're meant to talk about this kind of stuff. We're family."

I nodded slowly and walked out of the room without another word. The weight of the world pushed my shoulders onto my bed, and I went to sleep, crying. I hated them all.

***

Rebecca asks me how things are going in my 'sessions' with Luce, and I realise I've been staring at her face this whole time, deep in thought. She's been sitting next to me on my favourite bench on the third floor for a while, but we haven't said anything since 'Hey'.

"Good, I guess."

"What have you been talking about?" she asks.

"Are you allowed to ask me that?" I laugh.

"I can tell you what I talk about," she counters, matter-of-factly in the oh-so-annoying way she does sometimes.

My mind flashes back to the scary-as-fuck images that I have been trying to block out since she told me about her father. I swallow nervously.

"I'm telling him about my boyfriend," I say with a forced half-smile. "Well, ex-boyfriend, I guess? I don't know."

"My friend James has two dads," she says, looking up at me and flashing a toothy smile. "I don't like James. He's always so mean to me."

I laugh. "I think that's probably unrelated, but I get you."

"When are you going to make your decision?" Rebecca asks, her wide brown eyes staring up at me like a puppy. I miss my dogs.

"I don't know, Rebecca." I shrug. She asks me this every time I see her, and I always answer the same way.

"Luce told me when I got here that everything here is like a story. It has a beginning, a middle, and then an end. But he says that with every story, the person writing it has to decide when it ends. He says that otherwise a book will go on forever. So when you're telling the story of you, you need to decide when it ends." She says it while tracing a flower in the pattern of her skirt.

"What do you mean 'decide when it ends'?" I ask.

"Well, the whole point of us being here is to make our decision, so by the time you get to the end of the story, you need to know what your decision is, and you only know what your decision is when you get to the end of your story." She speaks like the fucking Riddler sometimes, I swear.

"So, I have to make my choice when I get to the end of my story?" It seems logical, but also, I was hit by a car when I was a few weeks shy of my eighteenth birthday, and in my story, I'm now halfway to seventeen. The thought hits me like a punch in the gut. I guess you can't put off death forever. Thank fuck I can talk about Abbas until the cows go home.

"So where are you at with your story? The beginning, the middle, or the end?" Rebecca asks, and I want to smack her for a second. I shake the thought from my mind. *I'm not a bad person. Who can honestly say they've never wanted to smack a kid?*

"I mean, it's not that easy. I have to go back and fill in some of the gaps, and, like, the last few years are the most important, so..." I trail off hopelessly.

"So, you're pretty near the end?"

Ughhhhhhhhhhh.

"I guess."

"Do you think the rest of your family felt the same way?" Luce asks. I don't like the question. I don't particularly like Luce right now.

"Felt the same way about what?"

"Well, your sister, Penny, she seemed upset that you told Lois first about everything. I mean, that's a lot to dump on someone who had been dating your dad for like six months. It's understandable she'd feel a little betrayed, right?"

I groan. "If anything, it's a compliment. It's like coming out. I mean, it was coming out. I had all these big things to tell someone and it was going to burst open eventually, and I didn't want to tell my dad or my mum or my sister, because they're family. They matter, you know? If their opinion of me changes, then that's sort of fucked everything, hasn't it? Whereas if I tell Lois, who cares what she thinks? She just left anyway, so no harm, no foul, really."

"So... Lois didn't matter?"

Sometimes when Luce asks a question, you can just feel the smugness radiating off of him.

"Obviously that's not what I meant. Lois mattered a lot to me. It means something when you feel safe enough to tell them that kind of shit. But when it's someone who isn't family, or someone who isn't irremovably (*I'm sure it's a real word*) part of your life, it's like a safety rail. It's like if they take it badly, which she did, then life can still go on, even if it's a bit emptier than before."

"Why are you so obsessed with the idea that Lois took this whole thing badly?" Luce seems exasperated, and it's kind of fun to see him lose his cool a bit. The dude is unflappable. It's nice to see him flap.

"Look at the evidence." I count on my fingers. "Number one: she left. Number two: she told my dad. Number three: she barely spoke to me again." I really thought I had more numbers to go through.

"Okay, and what if she left because her relationship with your dad had run out of steam? And if she told your dad in the first place because you were a fucking safeguarding issue? And if she barely spoke to you again because she just didn't have anything to say to you, kiddo." His tone turns soft towards the end, and his black eyes look weary.

"I guess we'll never know."

Luce sits down, shrugging. "Here's what we do know: you have a very cavalier attitude toward your life."

"What?" My face breaks into a befuddled expression.

"Let's look at the evidence." I don't appreciate his callback. "You cut yourself every which way to hell every morning and night for a year. You spend half your time in here talking about a boy when you're supposed to be making a decision. And you have one bad day and throw yourself in front of the nearest van."

"What?"

I still didn't remember that day. I still didn't remember the van. I didn't remember why it happened.

"Forget it."

"No. You said that I had a bad day and threw myself in front of a van." I glare at him. I feel the blood pounding in my veins. "I don't remember that."

"You will." Luce leaves.

XVIII

Whatever Happened to David and Jonathan?

Texting Abbas was like texting my grandmother. The dead one. He had no idea how to use emojis, or how to punctuate in anything but perfect grammar. It was painful. Whenever he sent me a text, it was like Jane Austen had drafted it at her bureau with a quill, and he would always follow up with a puzzled, crazed selfie when I would question what the actual fuck he meant.

"You can't put an ellipsis and just the basic smiling face," I told him, laughing down the phone. His face was blurry and pixelated, but it was still the only one I was looking at, when on every other video call, I would be checking my own mug out.

"I don't get why not. That's what I'm doing: pausing and smiling."

"You're like my grandma."

I cackled as he blustered in offence. He eventually calmed down and looked at me intensely with a smile that could stop traffic. "I'm your grandma. You're my baby."

I groaned. "You disgust me."

"Your grandma, my baby," he repeated, looking at me grinning like a devil. His dark brows and deep eyes were practically hidden by a combination of the awful lighting in his bedroom, the pixelation, and his impeccable bone structure.

"How's home?" I asked, knowing I wouldn't get a proper response anytime soon. Abbas was suspiciously closed off about his personal life. Even with me.

"Oh, you know." He nodded, as if I actually knew. "Can't complain."

"Can't explain," I muttered in reply.

He heard it and called me a twat.

I countered with a wicked smile and, "Your twat. My grandma."

When the disgusted laughter died, I put on my best serious face, paired with my sweetest smile. "So when am I actually ever going to come to yours?"

"What do you mean?"

The question was pretty self-explanatory. "Well, you've come to my house a bunch. You've met my dad and my sister, and my dogs, and I've never even seen your house. I don't even know where you live. For all I know, your aunt could be an old white guy with a beer belly and a swastika tattoo."

"Oh, fuck, how did you know?" He laughed, but he wasn't wriggling away from it that easily, the snake.

"Come on, babe, you know what I mean." The 'babe' was one of the few hangovers from my relationship with Olivia. "We've been dating a few months now, and I've known you for about six, so it's only reasonable that I'd want to get to know you a bit better. You know everything about me."

"All in good time." He blew me a kiss. I stuck my middle finger up at him. "You'll meet her soon enough, but it's really nothing special. It's just a flat, and she's just your average Arabic aunt."

"Triple A," I replied. I don't know why.

"Triple A," he confirmed. I don't know why again.

"Well, put it on the record that I would like to meet your aunt," I ordered, and he dutifully threw me a thumbs up.

"So, how's debate going?" That conversation had clearly ended.

I ended up dragging Tom to debate, and I think Alonso

was relieved by the respite. Lukas and Liam refused to join, and Alonso needed to finish the painting he had been working on for months that looked pretty finished to the rest of us, but we had learned long ago not to question his methods. He was the virtuoso, after all. Tom was reluctant, but his interest was easy to pique, as was his penchant for drawing people into ridiculous discussions, and Ms Badden found herself flummoxed at the topics we would find ourselves discussing, having completely disregarded the set question at the beginning of the Tuesday-lunchtime session. That day, Tom had diverted our conversation from the institution of the monarchy to the extent to which the story of One Direction was an allegory for the Cold War. For a straight guy, he knew a suspicious amount about the boy band. Intellectually, I'm a Harry stan. Biologically, I'm all for Liam.

Abbas maintained a polite curiosity about our debate club, although he was clearly a bit put out by the fact I had abandoned him for one lunchtime a week. When I reminded him that he kept mysteriously sneaking off for an hour in Friday second period, only to return at the beginning of third, he smiled coyly, and abruptly moved the conversation on again. A master of the pivot, my lion.

It wasn't long before he questioned why I never turned up to Friday first period, meaning that we missed each other until lunchtime on Fridays, and, in the spirit of honesty, I told him that I went to therapy. He was quiet.

"Why?"

"Oh, I went through a bad period a few years ago, and my dad makes me keep going just in case."

"Do you like it?" he asked, glancing up at me from the biology textbook he was examining on my bed one Friday evening. A half-eaten pizza sat between us. I never liked to eat in front of Abbas, and while he usually hoovered up whatever food was in front of him, he had only picked at the pepperoni slices and had left his crusts on the plate.

"I mean, I don't dislike it. It's helpful sometimes, you know, getting your mind all sorted out, and it's nice to have a place to vent about shit and not have to worry about the consequences."

"Do you talk about me?" His dark eyes looked deeper than they ever had, and my heart panged for a reason I didn't fully understand. For *him*.

"I mean, sure, babe. You're an important part of my life."

"Do you vent about me?"

I laugh and tousle his thick black locks of hair. "Of course not. What could I possibly have to complain about?"

He took my hand in his and kissed the top of it like I was his prince. It was moments like these that it hit me how fucking lucky I was to have him. For months I had fawned and obsessed over him like he was a celebrity that would never know I existed. I dreamt about him and fantasised about him, and now I have him. He always had me, and now I have him. This is fucking bliss.

Bliss that I was willing to sabotage to meet his aunt.

It took a lot of convincing, nagging, and complaining, but finally, Abbas relented and let me visit his home. We had been dating for four months, since January, and both were very thankful that AS exams had been done away with, so at least we had May to enjoy (aside from the coursework we were drowning in finalising). We took the bus to the next town over, and walked down a street where all the houses looked the same, except the lawns. Some were overgrown with grasses and wild bushes, whereas others were perfectly manicured and tastefully decorated. Of course, in any English town, there was the one house whose owner went overboard with the statues of rabbits and gnomes, and who had a weirdly ornate fake well as its centrepiece. The concept always freaked me out.

The building in which lay Abbas's flat was identical to the

others that lined both sides of the street: a faded cream paint interspersed with exposed brickwork and concrete in an attempt to convey style that ended ultimately in eclectic blandness. He held a fob to the keypad, and the door buzzed threateningly as it unlocked. Abbas shot me an apologetic smile.

Inside, the air was humid from the heat outside and some unknown source of moisture. A small window at the back of the foyer was cracked open, but it was no match for the swamp that had been created. The lift had a dusty out-of-order sign taped askew on its door, and I followed Abbas as he ascended the dark stairwell, illuminated by fluorescent lights that flicked on as we reached each floor. The distinct smell of barbeque hung in the air, but with the humidity and the small plants growing through cracks in the concrete steps, it was not appetising. On reaching the fourth floor, Abbas opened a cream-coloured door with a flickering fire-escape light overhead, and held it open for me as I followed him through. We stopped at the first door on the left, marked with the number 24 in an elegant script, and Abbas slid a key into the lock and cracked it to the right.

Abbas's flat was decidedly average. I'm not sure why I had expected something extraordinary, but I was disappointed by its normality, nonetheless. A large cabinet filled with odd china cups, a dazzling topaz teapot, and various books and knick-knacks blocked the light from pouring into the hall, and there was the overpowering smell of cheap air freshener. On the left was a small kitchen with a humming refrigerator, and on the right, a small corridor leading to three closed doors. Immediately in front of us was a doorway draped in a wooden beaded curtain that led into the living room. A bubbling fish tank in which huge—like, *unrealistically* big—goldfish swam leisurely around live plants and a decorative castle. A piano stood alongside it, but Abbas assured me he didn't play.

"My aunt's," he said with an apologetic nod.

Pushing aside the beads, I was immediately accosted by the coos and greetings of three elderly women surrounding a circular wooden table covered with cards. Abbas, following me with his hand on the small of my back, introduced them to me.

"This is Pamela." He gestured at a woman grinning widely with braided hair, "Charlie," the lady in a bright floral blouse waved her hand, "and my Auntie Nafisah." The smallest of the trio stood up and walked up to me with wide eyes and a toothy smile. She took both my hands and squeezed them in hers. Abbas then introduced me to them all, and they repeated my name in a chorus.

"So handsome," Pamela purred, and my face turned bright red, to their delight.

Abbas's aunt welcomed me to her home and offered me some iced tea, which I politely declined. I told her it was lovely to meet her, and thanked her for letting me in her home, which she waved away dismissively.

"Nonsense!" she laughed. "I've been hearing so much about you from this one." She pointed at Abbas, whose turn it was to blush. "It's so lovely to meet you." She spoke with a light accent, unlike Abbas, whose voice was completely unaffected, as if he had been born into the landed gentry. Even I had a Midlands twang.

Abbas made a feeble excuse before dragging me down the hall to his room. It was smaller than mine, but I wasn't sure whether that was just the fact he had a double bed and mine was only a single. His room was relatively bare, except for a neat stack of paperbacks on every available surface. His windows were wide open, and a light breeze flowed into the room, drawing my eyes to the guitar in the corner, which I immediately went to.

"I told you, I'm not very good," Abbas protested, but I reminded him that everyone who plays a guitar says that. I handed it to him and he took it awkwardly, holding it suspended for a few moments before he replaced it on its small stand, shaking his head with joking disapproval.

He sat on the bed and gestured for me to join him. Kicking off my shoes by the door, I crawled across the sheet and lay with my head on his shoulder. He wrapped his arms around me and pecked my forehead gently, and we started talking about random, irrelevant crap, from coursework to debate club to why he refused to play his guitar for me. Before we knew it, the sun was beginning to set, and we had done little more than entangle the other in our limbs, our kisses, and our conversation. After a discussion of the latest season of a reality show we were both addicted to and had binged the past fourteen seasons of together because even when we were procrastinating, it felt like it was meant to be, Abbas relented and picked up his guitar with a nervous laugh and a playful scowl with me. He plucked the strings clumsily and made me watch in anticipation as he adjusted the tuning with an app on his phone.

Abbas looked up at me nervously and swallowed as he started to strum, his long fingers moving around the frets as he started to play a song I recognised from one of our first nights together.

It was about two months or so into our dating, and as my father was away on site inspections and my sister had burrowed away in her room, Abbas had agreed to stay the night, even as he dwarfed my tiny twin bed, but even though I was not small—average, I reminded Tom when he teased me, though Tom was merely a half-inch taller—my head slotted comfortably on his chest under his chin, and our legs interlaced like a rope, bound together. He insisted we close the window, and though I usually struggled to sleep without the crisp night air on my face, I surrendered to bathing in his heat and aura. As we drifted to sleep, Abbas flicked through the songs on my phone, playing soft melodies one after the other, and muttering quiet conversation on the pillow we were sharing.

The song was the only song of this artist's I knew, with distinctive vocals layered over a surprisingly gentle tune, the singer professed her love for a boy who was to modernity what she was to the classics, yet both of them could outlast anything else.

He had whispered the lyrics in my ear, and I had laughed, and kissed his lips gently as my eyes closed and I fell into a deep sleep.

Abbas was playing that same song in his bedroom. He wasn't lying when he said he wasn't the best at the guitar, and I didn't doubt that he wouldn't be winning any awards for his fingering—*not in that sense, anyway*—but his voice stopped my heart from beating. It was hauntingly beautiful; so gentle but with a soft growl that underlay the smooth tone of his voice. His eyes were fixed on his hands, as he stumbled over a few chords, but never losing the melody, and I was transfixed, frozen in time as the words washed over me, pricking my skin into goosebumps and sending an electric shiver down my spine.

Abbas ended abruptly, swinging a final downward strum with a muffled chord, and, fiddling with the leather strap that was tied by frayed string to the instrument, he looked sheepishly up at me, my mouth agape. *Fuck me.*

"So...?" he said, his eyes flicking between me and the guitar.

"Fuck me."

And he did.

***

"What? No juicy details or sordid scenes?" Luce laughs.

"Ahhh, a gentleman doesn't kiss and tell," I reply with a chuckle, my face flushing nonetheless.

"Let me ask you something, though," Luce says, remaining seated on his green bench, reclining onto the headboard.

"Shoot." I stay standing, my hands stuffed uncomfortably into my trouser pockets.

"How did you find it?"

My face turns a deeper shade of red. I find myself permanently embarrassed by my own life story. "Well, it was good. He was gentle and sweet, and he stopped every few moments and asked if I was okay. He held me in his arms, and our breaths fell into sync, and it was uncomfortable, obviously, and, you know, a little sweaty and messy, but it was good."

"Are you glad it happened?"

I pause. "Yes."

"Did it come at the right time?"

I shrug, pulling my hands out of my pockets for theatrical effect. "It doesn't matter when it happens, it just matters that it was right."

I don't like Luce's questions. The sex was good. It was with Abbas. It was good. There's no need to try to undermine it. The questioning felt eerily familiar, and a sense of foreboding was pulled over me. As Luce leaves, throwing his hand up in a 'goodbye', I sit in front of my despatch box, and swing my legs in front of me. They're not long enough to reach the table, and they fall back with a painful jolt. Rebecca's voice frustrates me as it plays in my head. There's a little over a year of my life left to tell, plus a whole host of gaps to fill in along the way, and then... what? I have to make a choice? I have to decide whether to live or die? It seems unfair. A lot of pressure to put on a kid who isn't even mature enough for a shag, apparently.

But then again, Rebecca is so much younger than I am, and she's been here an unspecified amount of time longer than I have been, and she is still here. I don't know why she gets to hang around while I'm rushed into making a decision based solely on chronology.

My feelings about the girl are complex. Like an older brother, who sees so much of his sister in her, I want to protect her from the evil that I know has touched her. Like an older brother, I want to slap her. But she still feels like a stranger. She's not a friend—I don't think you can have friends in the Interlife—but aside from Luce, she's all I have here.

Too many thoughts for one day, I tell myself, and I turn to leave the Commons.

XIX

An Aftermath I Didn't Even Know Had Math'd

Jo looked at me over the rims of glasses I hadn't seen her wear before. She was not pleased. I shifted uncomfortably in my seat, wishing for the air to cool so I could stop feeling the drips of sweat bead on my forehead. She tapped the tip of her pen on her notebook, leaving little dots of ink haphazardly across the lines. I looked around the room awkwardly, but I kept coming back to her stare.

"I'm sorry." I grin awkwardly, my eyes remaining unmoved, and she tilted her head back slightly in dismissal.

"Why are you sorry?" she asked.

"Well, you're not happy with me," I replied, and she scrawled a quick note on her page.

"I'm not unhappy with you," she said, using my name in a way that made me tense. "I want to talk about why you did it."

After weeks and weeks of me spending my hour gushing over Abbas, the tone marked an unwelcome shift in our conversations. I knew intellectually that therapists weren't personally involved in the lives of their patients, and that it was just as unhealthy to aim to please her as to aim to please anyone else, but I couldn't help it. I had come to think of Jo as a friend; yes, a friend the NHS paid money to listen to me every week, but a friend nonetheless, and I hated the idea that I was letting her down.

I fiddled with the cuffs of my long tee and continued to

sweat in the still air of the office. The sun beamed through the window and I begged that I could turn it off.

"The same reasons," I whispered, and Jo asked me to repeat myself louder, so I did.

"What are those reasons?"

"I'm feeling out of control again."

"What do you feel out of control of?"

I hated her clinical questioning. I hated her passive detachment.

"Everything," I shrugged, looking pleadingly out the window in the hopes that some better answer would come flying into the glass like a kamikaze sparrow.

"What's going on?" Jo asked, and I felt my heart beat faster and faster. I was going to be sick, and I sweated more.

Abbas hadn't replied to me in a week, and I spent my spare time staring at my phone, waiting in vain for it to light up with his name and photo. I didn't know what I had done wrong. Nothing had changed, and I had wracked my brain for hours and hours non-stop to think of something, anything, that could have turned him away, but nothing. Like a lovesick puppy, I threw myself listlessly from one depressive spiral to another. It was the beginning of the summer holidays, and I didn't have any coursework to force my brain to switch off from the obsessive thoughts about Abbas, nor did I have any debate club to perfect a speech for.

The last time I had seen Abbas was Friday lunchtime. In our usual pattern, we had missed each other while I was at therapy and he disappeared to wherever he went on Friday mornings. It was the Friday lunchtime of the last day of year 12, and Abbas gave me a quick, tight hug as he walked into the hall where I was sitting on the edge of the stage with Tom, and he took his seat in the front row next to Alonso, Lukas and Liam, who greeted him enthusiastically, despite having seen him the period before in biology class.

Tom peppered me with questions, to which I remained stoically nonchalant. Ms Badden had somehow convinced the school it was a good idea for the debate club to put on a 'show' debate for the rest of the school one lunchtime and, predictably, turnout was low. Aside from the nerds who would have otherwise spent the last day of term in the library, the audience was made up solely of the friends of the participants. I led my team, tasked with making the closing statement, and Tom led my opposition, hence his distracting tactics. I had spent hours writing and rewriting my speech, painstakingly tailoring the arguments to perfect the balance between theory and practice, logic and rhetoric, and slowly but methodically ripping the arguments of the opposition to shreds.

We had, of course, protested when Ms Badden wrote the motion on the board. Tom described it as being a "pseudo-fascist piece of political pageantry", but our objections were overruled. She reminded us that these were the terms on which the politics of the day were being decided, and what is a debate club if not an opportunity to reflect society back onto ourselves? We had relented, but the objections resurfaced when our teacher revealed that we were to perform this for the school. Again, we were overruled, with Tom only agreeing to participate if he could lead the opposition to the motion.

"This House will make turning back the small boats the main focus of its domestic and foreign policy."

It was broad, intentionally so, but boiled down to the basic arguments and tensions between asylum and immigration, economics and diplomacy, and right and wrong. Unfortunately, I was leading the wrong, but, as my father reminded me, I had a knack for arguing for something I didn't believe in.

The lights turned on, and the audience were shrouded in darkness. I had purposefully refused to tell Abbas the motion to be debated, no matter how much he tickled my ribs in the way he knew would crumple me. I muffled the sounds of the speakers going back and forth and reread my speech, making the odd final amendment when I heard a particularly good point I had to rebut with the rhetorical flourish my father was so irritated by in our bickering around the kitchen table. He said I could weave a tapestry out of toilet paper. I took it as the compliment I doubt it was intended as.

Tom's closing speech was predictably long, and Ms Badden had to ask him twice to wrap it up. His face turned red as he made repeated jabs at not only our arguments, but ourselves. He called Lydia an arrogant wanna-be dictator, Anne-Marie was the reincarnation of Enoch Powell, and he labelled Sachin an authoritarian piece of crap (the last one Ms Badden chastised him for, despite the amusement of the audience). I smirked along, grateful that he preceded me and so had no ammunition to throw my way.

Ms Badden called my name, and I stood, walking to the podium in the centre, and throwing a wink at Tom, who grinned back.

My speech wasn't the one I was proudest of, given the subject matter, but I had worked my arse off on it, and I hope it showed. I pointed out the necessity of secure borders and effective immigration controls to everything from economic forecasting to foreign policy. To make the argument more palatable, I argued for greater foreign aid for the originating countries of the migrants—always migrants, never refugees—to increase economic opportunity which would remove the incentive to travel. I reiterated the importance of safe routes to the UK, and the need to deter criminal smugglers and dangerous journeys. If we were to invest in our asylum and immigration systems, we could clear the backlog and begin properly processing new claims. If we renew our relationship with Europe, we can ensure that the UK is taking its fair share of migrants, but our public services, our housing market, and our workforce won't be, can't be, and shouldn't be overwhelmed by influxes of migrants as a result of instability in their home countries. Our priority should be making sure people can come to the UK for a better life if they so choose, but not as their first resort when things get tough. A progressive's approach to authoritarianism.

The words slipped out of my mouth like caramel, sweet and sickly, and my team and I ended up winning the debate. I assured the audience with a laugh that I didn't believe any of the crap I had said, but when the house lights came on, Abbas had gone. Reuniting with the gang, who fiercely congratulated Tom and me on our efforts, and we reconciled with a rough hug, I asked Alonso where Abbas had gone; a question which received a shrug in reply.

"He left after you finished speaking, said he had forgotten some English work or something, I don't know," the boy said, and I stared at him quizzically.

"We didn't have any English work?" It is a statement, but it comes out as a question, and Alonso is ill-equipped to reassure me.

"I don't know, man, that's just what he said."

I shrug it off, and assume I will see him in the form time we had before the dreaded end-of-year assembly, that the four of them left me no doubt would be even worse than they could possibly describe. But when we arrived at our form room, we were greeted only with Mr Nathwani's ruddy cheeks hiding behind an ever-bushier beard, and an empty seat where Abbas should have been. I shoot him a text:

`Hey babe, what did you think?`

The second tick never appears. He didn't get the message. Over the next few days, I message him more and more:

`Hey? You okay?`

```
Abbas?
You good?
Are we good?
```

But eventually, the messages taper out to nothing. I have no more questions to ask. It is clear he doesn't want to reply. Winning isn't worth it if you're the only one celebrating.

"So to answer you, Jo, that's why I feel out of control."

She looked at me with a curious eye and made another note on her pad. I wanted to break the pen. "You feel out of control because he isn't replying to you?"

I nodded.

"Is that something you could ever be able to control?"

"I mean, not unless I locked him up in a room somewhere and held a gun to his head, but then I guess I wouldn't need him to message me then."

"So if this is something you wouldn't be able to control, why does feeling out of control of it make you want to self-harm?" I felt the cuts burn on my forearm when she mentioned it.

I sighed and tried to piece together the right words. "I don't need him to reply. I mean, I want him to reply, you know? But I need to know what I did wrong. That's what's bothering me. The sense of complete helplessness that somehow I fucked up, and now the guy I'm in love with won't even tell me how. That's the powerlessness. If I knew, I could fix it, or at least make peace with it, but..."

Jo interjected, "Could you make peace with it?"

I chewed the question over in my mind. "I don't know." That was the honest answer. "Maybe eventually? I don't know." The thought of having to come to terms with Abbas, my boyfriend, never speaking to me again, was too devastating to consider for any longer. "No."

"What about now?" I look up. Luce is looking at me. "Could

you make peace with that now?"

The answer is the same: "No."

"So really nothing has changed since then? When was this, a year ago?"

"Yeah, I guess a year ago. But things did change. Even if the answer is the same."

"Ultimately, they didn't." Luce's tone is sympathetic, like Jo's was. "Then, and now: you still can't imagine a life without Abbas."

He replied eventually. I considered going over to his house a dozen times, but dreaded what I would find there. I couldn't put myself in a situation I couldn't control like that. If he was going to break me, it would have to be on my own turf. Lukas, Alonso, Tom and Liam all told me they hadn't heard from him either, but they didn't seem worried. I thought they might have been lying to me, but I couldn't look them in the eye. Every day I grew more suspicious, more self-loathing, and more miserable.

But he replied eventually.

```
Hey. Sorry for the late reply.
```

The message was short and abrupt and stabbed me in the heart with each full stop. I hated Abbas, and I hated myself for the fact that I didn't hate him even a little bit. I had taken to leaving my phone in my desk drawer so I didn't have to look at it. I would walk the five minutes over fallen logs and random rocks to my clearing, with the knowledge that not even Abbas could penetrate here, not if I left my phone at home.

I sat in the clearing, on the grass that was still a little dewy from a summer's midnight rain, and breathed in deeply. The air was gently humid, and a light breeze ruffled the grass blades like a caress. I watched a pair of sparrows dart across the grassy patch that felt so much smaller than it did when I was a child—I practically could reach from one end to the other if I laid out flat—and twitched my lips into a smile at their playful antics. There were a few dandelions in the grass that I poked at, dying to rip them from the roots, but letting them rest, and I let the morning pass.

Though I wished time would stand still when I was in the clearing, when I returned, over an hour had passed, and I rewarded myself with a glimpse of my phone. After I had dismissed my low battery warning, Abbas's name crept up on the screen, and my heart stopped.

`Hey. Sorry for the late reply.`

Even at the best of times—and any time with Abbas was the best of times—I struggled to interpret his messaging style. No emojis, proper punctuation, no feeling. I wasn't sure whether describing it as a "late reply" properly reflected the crime that had been committed: six days with no message, no response, no answer. That wasn't a late reply. That was wilful ignoring. I hated Abbas. *No, I didn't.*

I didn't open the message. I just stared at it hovering on my screen like a storm cloud, as my heart restarted at a ferocious rate. Boys were so complicated; put two together, and any equation was unsolvable.

After an indeterminable length of time spent pacing across my floor, clawing at my skin in the hopes that everything that was inside of me would crawl out of the red stripes my fingernails left in the wake, I opened the message. Read receipts. Now I had to come up with a reply. It was another age before I started typing, slowly. I wasn't going to make the mistake of fingers moving faster than my brain. I couldn't risk a reply sent by accident.

`Hey. That's no worries. Hope you're okay? :)`

It was casual. It was cool. It wasn't needy, or stressy, or too... *me*. It had been several hours since Abbas's original text, but I needed him to reply instantly, and so I stared at that watched pot until it boiled. Eventually it did. My phone buzzed with a startling beep—for some reason I had turned the volume up, as if I would have missed a reply if I blinked—and Abbas's name and picture flashed up. His profile photo was quintessentially Abbas—incredibly manicured, but not staged, in a fashionable shirt, with the chain necklace he always wore around his neck, smiling warmly at some character off-screen. It had been taken somewhere I didn't recognise—it looked hot though, and I think there was a pool or a lake in the blurry background. My heart bled.

Abbas's reply was alarming:

`I think we should talk. Did you want to come over?`

XX

Compulsion

Abbas's flat still smelled like cheap air freshener. His shoes were still kicked in a pile by the cabinet in the hall. His guitar was still in the corner, and his bed was still immaculately made. The last time I was here, we had... *you know.* That left like a lifetime ago, as I sat on the edge of his bed, staring awkwardly at the floor while he offered me a glass of water, which I politely declined.

His aunt was gone for the day, he told me, visiting friends by the coast. But he thought we should talk. I knew that. That was what he had messaged me. Frankly, aside from letting me know when I could come over, it was the only thing he had said to me in over a week.

He sat on the end of the bed, and we were facing away from each other almost perpendicular. It was uncomfortable. I dared not look at him though, out of a paralysing fear that if I did, I would see the truth that he no longer loved me, he didn't even like me, and he didn't want to see me anymore. Jo's question clutched at my thoughts. His window was open, and I could hear some birds bickering outside. I wanted to go outside. I didn't want to be in that room. I didn't want to be part of the end of my own relationship. I cursed myself for letting him drag me here, when if he wanted to end it, he should've had the guts to do it at my house, on my terms. My weakness disgusted me, but no more so than the fear that drowned me.

"So..." Abbas sighed, and I could feel him looking at me from the side of his eyes. He wasn't even brave enough to face me. He was going to break my heart without even a look. "I think I should tell you what's been going on."

"Sure," I shrugged. *I was so good at playing it cool.* I didn't look at him either.

"The last time I saw you was at the debate, right?"

"Right."

"You spoke well, by the way."

"Thank you."

"You're welcome."

Goddamn stilted conversation.

"But I had to leave before the end. I didn't get to see who the winner was, but I heard from the guys that you won. Congratulations."

"Thanks."

"So I want to tell you why I left."

"You don't have to do that."

He called me by my name, and I twisted my neck to see him looking at me, the sun bouncing off his caramel irises that melted like honey in the blaze. When the light hit his eyes, they turned from almost black to the most beautiful shades of chocolate, of maroon, of mahogany, that you could ever imagine.

"I want to," he said.

XXI

A Lion's Pride

Abbas was born on the 17th of February, 2002, to Shabaz and Fatima Rahim in a small town about 80 kilometres from Aleppo, in a house with mountain views and a thick grove of olive trees they would harvest at the end of every summer. Shabaz had inherited a fair sum from his own father, who had served in an indistinct civil service role until his untimely death from a heart attack at 48, but rather than climbing the public sector ladder in his father's wake, Shabaz and his mother moved out of the city to the house with the olive grove. The town wasn't rich, and Shabaz was able to use his comfortable lifestyle to pay a handsome dowry for the beautiful daughter of a local farmer, who mixed his cow milk with honey and sold it across the region. Shabaz and Fatima married in what they thought was an extravagant ceremony, but what the photographs showed was a relatively modest affair, and she moved into the house.

Eventually, though, the money ran out, and Shabaz found his olive grove was insufficient to pay the bills, especially as they faced infertility that his mother blamed on God for a sin Shabaz was yet to decipher. She was losing her mind, he told himself, and he returned to Aleppo, leaving his young wife with his allegedly senile mother so he could make his fortune. With a degree in economics, he quickly found himself in middle-management at a bank that was desperately trying to entice investment into Syria with little to show for it thus far. As a subsidiary of a subsidiary of a subsidiary, the bank was well-funded, somehow, and Shabaz began to travel across the region, and later the world, representing his company at conferences and in boardrooms, and his quick tongue and charming good looks won him a great deal of admirers. He was offered more than once to leave Syria and bring his family to Dubai, to Frankfurt, to London, and even to New York, but each time, he declined politely, saying he couldn't possibly leave his wife and his home until he had started a family. The others would laugh, and applaud his family ethic, playfully declaring that when he had a kid, Shabaz wouldn't have an excuse anymore.

And that kid came along in 1994 when Suhail was born, but Shabaz wanted a daughter too. With another round of IVF that didn't take, and then another that did, Jamila was born in 1998. An heir and a spare, his mother joked when Shabaz and Fatima announced their third pregnancy three years later: a beautiful baby boy they would name Abbas. Lion.

With his father away on business for most of his childhood, Abbas was close to his mother: a tall and graceful woman who would sit for hours on the terrace overlooking the valley with her potting wheel, and stroke the clay into vases and bowls that she would stain and fire in a kiln before they would emerge reborn in bright sapphires and deep jades. Abbas would watch his mother as she threw a lump onto the wheel, and within seconds, her creation was taking form. He thought she was like God.

Shabaz and Fatima tried for another baby, twice, but eventually Fatima refused to try anymore, and the five of them settled into a quiet domestic life. Mornings would be spent eating fresh fruit and running through the twisted trunks of the olive trees, dodging the farmhands their father employed as they swiped at the laughing children. In the afternoons, they would play with their soldiers in the living room, imagining the expansive carpet was the desert, and their toys were fighting an intense battle that none of them really knew what it was for. Jamila would cry when Suhail and Abbas broke her dolls, claiming they were casualties in a war that knew no bounds, but they would make it up to her by carefully glueing them back together and setting them up in makeshift wards in the kitchen. Five times a day, the family would pray, at peace in the knowledge that, wherever Shabaz was, he would be doing the same. The world seemed simple. Right.

When Abbas started school, two things happened. Firstly, he was plunged into a world where he could ask questions, make sense of things, discover new ideas, and read. He read, for sure. It started as just whatever old books the school had lying around in its relatively meagre library, but soon he was begging Shabaz to bring new books home from his trips, and he devoured one novel after another, graduating from simple fairy tales into explosions of love, war, pain, and beauty. Abbas read, and read, and read. He read so much, his parents would chide him for having his head in between the pages of a book at the dinner table, for eschewing his evening prayers for just one more chapter, for bumping into furniture because he refused to put a novel down. Abbas never argued, but when his mother started to sort the books into ones she no longer wanted, he stood guard, growling with the piles behind him, refusing to let anyone any closer until he knew the books would be safe. Abbas read so much that he almost didn't notice when his father died.

That was the second thing. A year or so after he started school, he came home one day to find his mother weeping on the terrace overlooking the olive grove and the mountains, clutching the landline phone that had delivered the fatal news. Abbas cried too, not because he missed his father—he didn't really see a difference between him dead or alive—but because he hated to see his mother, his sister, and his brother cry. The funeral, he could barely remember. A hazy white shroud covering his father's body, some music, and it was the first time he had met his aunt, his father's sister: Nafisah.

Unlike the rest of his extended family, who were in slick suits, robes, and beautiful silken scarves, Nafisah wore a simple dress, with a bulky jade necklace dangling awkwardly from her thin neck. Nafisah took him aside as he sweated in the burning heat inside his crisp new clothes and held his hand.

She told Abbas to be strong, to be brave. He nodded, but he didn't really understand. There were a lot of things he didn't understand about his life, which is why it was so much easier to spend it with his head in a book. He didn't understand the arguments raging between his mother and her in-laws. He didn't understand why his brother, even at the same age, had been teasing girls and talking about kissing them. He didn't understand why, no matter how much he read, he couldn't find a boy kissing a boy. Nafisah moved into the house shortly after the funeral—another thing that was never explained to Abbas—and his mother, after meeting a lot of old men in suits, donned her own sleek pantsuit and followed them out of the house one day. She barely said goodbye; she just left. But Abbas never saw her cry after that, so whatever had happened mustn't have been bad.

Nafisah and his grandmother, who Abbas only called Gidda, ruled the house in Fatima's absence. When she returned, only sparingly, the only thing Abbas would care about was the book she would leave on his shelf for him when he woke. Every time, it was a different volume, a different adventure, and a different world. She no longer made her pottery. She barely even looked at her children.

As they grew older, Abbas and his family spent less and less time together. He would spend his afternoons in the olive grove, hiding from the heat of the desert sun beneath their branches thick with fruit, while his sister would study, and his brother did more and more reckless things. First, it was pranks, then tricks, then Suhail conducted what could only be described as full-on heists.

Every time he came home, escorted by the furious victim of his hijinks, Gidda would smack his head and drag him by the ear to his bedroom, where he would be forced to spend the rest of the evening without dinner. Abbas could hear how, as he grew, Suhail's protests turned from mournful wails to furious diatribes against his grandmother's autocracy. It was no bother to Abbas. As long as he had his books, he was happy.

For his ninth birthday, Abbas's mother—though she was not present—bought him a DVD player, and a selection of films ranging from goofy animated romps to action-packed killing bonanzas. His aunt, who usually never participated in such trivial celebrations, seemed pleased when he opened her gift, the season of what appeared to be a relatively new release: a drama of an old English aristocratic family adjusting to the modern world. To his aunt's disappointment, he eschewed the banalities of rich white people for the excitement of less-rich white people, and for a while, the books took a back seat.

It wasn't long, however, before reality caught up with the family. His mother came home one morning, stressed and frantic, screaming in a language Abbas didn't understand down the phone to a muffled voice. The family was gathered in the sitting room and were told in stark terms that Syria was in crisis. From Abbas's understanding, which was limited, people were protesting against the Government in cities, demanding something that Abbas didn't quite comprehend. That night, they huddled around the television and watched the President give a speech. Abbas didn't know what was happening, but he knew it was serious. The President was worried, his mother said, and Gidda and Nafisah nodded gravely in reply.

The next day at school, their teacher told all the students that they were confident the crisis wouldn't reach their town. It was too small, too unimportant. But they should pray for their family and pray for their country. Abbas did both dutifully. Every night for weeks, Nafisah, Fatima, Gidda, Jamila, and Abbas would crowd around the television as they ate their dinner and watch as bombs went off, guns were fired, and people screamed. It was just like the movies, but instead of his family smiling in awe, they stared with greyed complexions at the scenes before them. Abbas didn't understand that either. It was just like the films, he told them, but they shushed him, chided him, and eventually ignored him.

Some nights, Abbas would lie awake and hear planes howling overhead. He knew they were going to the cities, and he knew they were going there to kill people, but he didn't know why. His mother and the President told him that people were rioting and they were breaking the law, but he didn't understand why that meant they should be blown up. He couldn't sleep not knowing such things, but when he went to ask someone, he found his aunt curled on the sofa in darkness, illuminated only by the bright screen of the television, as a family dressed in odd clothes with odd voices spoke to each other over a decadent dining table, with people standing behind them dressed just as fancily. Nafisah didn't want to answer questions, she told him, but she wrapped Abbas in her arms, tucking his head under her chin, and holding him against her breast. Together, they would watch this family do strange things, meet stranger people, and argue about the strangest topics. His aunt would summarise for him when there was a pause in what seemed like never ending dialogue, but as this became a nightly ritual, which Nafisah assured him would not end soon given the length of the war that was raging over the mountains, and given the back-catalogue of seasons they had to catch up on, Abbas soon began to pick up certain words and phrases. He learned from watching them what they were talking about, and associated the images he saw before him with the conversations accompanying them.

As a result of this nontraditional approach to learning, Abbas's first knowledge of the English language was incredibly formal, aged, and stilted. But the more he watched, the more he learned, and soon his aunt would introduce him to new programs and films, and he fell in love with them more and more. The way they looked at each other, with each glance holding more meaning than all the words Abbas could put together in English and Arabic combined; the way they touched each other, with every brush of hands sparking fires like the ones that lit the cloudy nights over the mountains with burning embers.

Suhail was in that city on the other side of the mountains—the one that seemed to perpetually burn. Abbas remembered how his mother would phone him and beg him to come home, but Suhail refused every time, and she would never tell Abbas why. The last time they had seen each other—Suhail and Abbas—was about a month before the country had gone to shit. Suhail seemed happy, with wild eyes and big hands that he would gesticulate energetically with as he told his younger brother all about his life studying international relations. He told Abbas that one day he would be a leader of their country; he would be representing Syria on the world stage and show everyone else what a beautiful place it was, and how much it had to offer.

Suhail told his brother a lot of things, and Abbas would lie awake as his brother spoke, weaving one tale after another into a huge tapestry that hung over the pair and fuelled Abbas's imagination of what life would be like when he was a grownup too. Abbas wanted to be like his brother: a revolutionary, a leader. Abbas didn't understand any of it, but he knew he loved his brother, and he knew he loved his country, and so he believed that the two went hand-in-hand in the uncomplicated way children can view the world before they get corrupted by everyone else's intolerances.

The next time Abbas saw Suhail was almost six months after the bombings began. Food was beginning to become scarce, and Abbas would cry in his bed after having to skip dinner so they would have enough food for breakfast. His mother, aunt, and Gidda would desperately barter with the other people in the town—people with guns whom Abbas would stare at through the window of the car—but they didn't have anything either. His family were richer than everyone else in the village, but they couldn't pay hunger to go away. They hadn't heard from Suhail in about six months, and Abbas wasn't quite sure whether the gaunt look on his mother's face was from the slow starvation or the worry that she couldn't mask with a weak smile anymore.

Fatima had stopped travelling for work, but Abbas wasn't sure that was such a good thing. For one, she had stopped bringing him books, and the books he did have she burnt in a pile one morning along with the carcasses of cows they had stripped clean of any muscle or fat, not that there was much to begin with. The family stopped shouting when they argued, but instead would hiss increasingly vitriolic words across the room, their backs arched and hackles raised like the stray cats that were picked off one by one by the hungry villagers. One such argument between his mother and aunt ended with them both whispering through tears over Nafisah's refusal to burn her DVD collection. Electricity was pretty intermittent, but they had enough fuel in the generator to keep their mobile phones charged, the news channel on, and the refrigerator running, but Abbas quickly surmised it wasn't the availability of power that was the issue. Like the bonfire of his books, Abbas knew anything Western was to be destroyed. His mother had ordered it for reasons that Abbas didn't understand but still complied with, but Nafisah was clinging tightly to a stack of discs, swearing that she would not get rid of them on pain of death.

"Death?" Abbas's mother barked. "It will be so much worse than death, Nafisah."

Abbas didn't know what she meant, but knew it was bad. He didn't know how bad it was until Suhail came home.

After six months of radio silence, Abbas awoke one morning to his mother's screams being hushed by Gidda and Nafisah. He ran from his room, rubbing the sleep from his eyes, and saw the three women huddled over an object on the porch. Abbas didn't recognise it at first. At first he thought it was a zombie from one of the comics he had read occasionally as a kid, and then he thought it was a sack of rubbish, but on closer inspection, as he edged closer to the door, he made out the eyes of his brother.

Suhail was lying crumpled on the floor, his face gaunt and skeletal. His sharp cheekbones, the same as his father's, jutted out like ridges in a mountain above his cratered cheeks. He smelt bad, Abbas remembers, like shit and death. His naked body was almost entirely blue, purple and black with bruises, and festering wounds oozed yellowish pus. You could have counted the vertebrae in his spine, or run your finger over every rib like braille. But that was not the worst part of it.

Where Suhail's right hand should have been was a bloody stump, partly scabbed over, but part of it was still weeping blood so dark it looked black. It had been haphazardly wrapped in a dirty rag, but that didn't prevent the stench of rotting flesh from making Abbas sick. That was the last time Abbas cried in many, many years.

***

I felt sick just listening to the story, but Abbas remained stony-faced. His voice was monotone as he recounted his past, and I spent every second watching his face as he stared at the floor, not making eye-contact with me. The thought of what I had said at the debate still hung over me, but obscured by how utterly speechless I was at that moment. That's a problem I perpetually suffered from: an inability to speak without preparing thoroughly in advance.

"I'm so sorry," I said, my voice coming out as a hoarse whisper. Abbas didn't look at me still. My heart tugged at my chest, dying to wrap myself in his arms and block out the horror story that was coming from his lips, but I stayed where I sat, a few feet away from him on his bed, and listened.

XXII

Like a Whisper

In fact, it was his whispers of revolution that had lost Suhail his hand, several of his teeth, and broken a number of his bones. His cautionary tale burned through the village like a wildfire, and to spare the rumours at school, Fatima sat her two youngest children down to tell them, matter-of-factly, what had happened.

Suhail, in his pursuit of an international relations degree in the exotic metropolis on the other side of the mountain, had involved himself with some radical elements. He aligned himself with—and Fatima grimaced when she uttered the words—Christians and secularists, and got involved with a bad crowd who had begun agitating against the state, against the President, who had given this family so much. Suhail, in his youthful ignorance, had allowed himself to be indoctrinated by radicals who believed that the President should be overthrown, his family executed, and Islamic law abandoned in the pursuit of 'democracy'.

He had begun attending these meetings about a year prior, after his friends from class had told him about a group they had joined who read extremist literature and shared treacherous ideas, and he had joined the protests which had sprung up from nowhere the year before in cities across Syria. Not only had he joined these people, but from what Suhail had told Fatima prior to his disappearance, he was organising students, inciting them to join the riots, paint graffiti criticising the President, and commit crimes designed to weaken the Government. Even when his friends were killed—Fatima didn't say by whom—Suhail refused her pleas to come home, to stop his madness. From what she could understand from Suhail, who was still isolated in his blacked-out bedroom suffering from a fever and chills, he had been awoken in the middle of the night by a group of armed men who had pulled a black bag over his head, tied his hands behind his back, while beating him with their fists, their heavy boots, and their batons, and they dragged him from his bed to a van waiting outside his apartment building in the student-dominated street of the city.

For three months—while Fatima had called him every day to no avail and while Nafisah had spent hours on the phone to local hospitals and morgues—Suhail had been beaten, starved, electrocuted, thrown against concrete walls, and been kept in a cramped box. For three months, they had ordered him to renounce his crazy ideas, his treason, and for three months he had refused.

Abbas would later be told by his brother, for whom the ordeal remained like a scarlet letter emblazoned on his chest, that he had begun to crave the interrogations. They were the only time he was permitted out of his cell, and the only taste he got of fresh air, and the only glimpse he got of sunlight. For three months, Suhail endured torture that neither Abbas—nor I—could ever imagine, and for three months, he had refused to break.

The men at first had told Suhail that his father was a good citizen, his mother had been strong; they had both been loyal to the president, and that is why they had not killed him yet. The men told him that his family needn't suffer his loss if he would just admit he was wrong. But when Suhail had remained defiantly silent in their faces, after three months, they sat Suhail down on a metal chair in the middle of a dark room illuminated by a single flickering exposed bulb dangling precariously from the ceiling, and the men told Suhail that because he had not bent to their will, they would kill his family. They would drag Fatima, Nafisah, his Gidda, Jamila and his nine-year-old brother Abbas down to the same prison they were holding Suhail in, and they would, one-by-one, torture them to death in front of him. They slapped onto the table photographs of other people who had met this fate—the bloated bodies of pre-pubescent boys and girls, swollen from internal bleeding and their faces unrecognisable, the crumpled figures of elderly men and women whose brittle bones had been cracked and splintered—and Suhail vomited down himself, the sick mixed with scarlet streams of blood.

It was when Suhail was staring at these pictures with tears burning his eyes that he finally relented. He apologised, repented, and renounced everything that he had done. He swore his loyalty to the President, to Islam, to prayer, and he begged for forgiveness and mercy for his family.

As Suhail wept in hacking sobs that wracked his pained body, the men had looked at each other with solemn acceptance, before wrenching Suhail's hand onto the table still littered with the pictures of death. They uncurled his broken fingers so they lay flat on the surface, and in one swift machete swing, they severed the hand from his arm. Suhail told Abbas that he didn't realise at first that the sounds he heard were coming from him. It wasn't a scream, it was a deep howl, a wail punctuated by sobs. They cauterised the wound with a blowtorch that rendered Suhail unconscious, and they wrapped his naked body in a light cloth, and the next thing he remembers is seeing his little brother's face staring at him in horror as he lay broken on the porch.

Abbas hated his brother after that. He hated looking at him and seeing the death of a soul that permeated every fibre of his broken body. He hated the smell that he could remember every time he was in the room with Suhail. He hated the idea that his brother had done this to himself, when he could have stopped it so much earlier, when he could have saved himself by never getting involved in the first place. Abbas believed his mother to be right, and therefore, in the diametrically opposed binary logic of the times, he believed his brother to be wrong.

Gone were the days of playing together in the olive grove, of winding up their sister, of watching sports and racing around the village on their bikes. Now, all Suhail did was lie in his bed and stare at the ceiling, and all Abbas did was avoid his older brother.

Every day and night, the family, in silence, could hear the planes overhead, and the distant sound of explosions. The sharp patter of gunfire would ricochet across the valley, but their town lacked strategic importance. They were too close to regime-controlled cities and towns to be a viable conquest for the revolution, and they were too far from the universities or metropolitan elites to be considered a viable threat to the government. But that is not to say that they were untouched by the war entirely. Food continued to be scarce, and the family had long since eaten every scrap of meat they could find lazing in the sunshine of their house, from their cows and chickens to their cat and its feral kittens.

The President had stopped his appearances on the news, and any information was hard to come by. The internet was spotty at the best of times, and relatives from across Syria had long since been killed, died, or fled across the borders to Turkey, Lebanon or Jordan. Slowly, the people in the village also began to leave. The school stopped running classes, and the small clinic shuttered as the doctor fled to join family in Palestine. All Abbas and his family knew was what they experienced themselves: hunger, failing electricity, and dread. Even Fatima, in her stony loyalty to the regime, stopped calling it an insurrection. There was no way for them to know who was firing the guns at the backs of children, dropping bombs on schools and hospitals, or gassing entire villages of people.

Gidda died in 2013, two years into the war, when she got a viral infection of some sorts, and there were no medicines to help her, no matter how much Nafisah pleaded with the soldiers permanently stationed at what used to be the local government offices, but was now a half-destroyed shell of a building after a stray bomb was dropped next to it one morning, killing the three people inside, and permanently disfiguring two more. Abbas didn't cry then. Since Suhail came home, Abbas had lost the ability to shed any more tears. What was the point? Instead, as they covered the body in curtains and unceremoniously dropped it in a pit with dozens of others—the graveyard had been overflowing for months with casualties from the front line—Abbas wandered back to the olive grove, and sat in the shade of their twisted and scarred trunks which were bare with leaves in the winter. Abbas wrapped his arms around himself, cradling his legs for warmth, and stared at the cracked ground.

Nafisah left soon after that, in the spring, when the ground had softened a little and the risk of hypothermia had passed. She had wanted to train as a doctor, but there were no formal opportunities, and she had run out of whatever energy she had somehow had left after all this time. She said her goodbyes—there was no use trying to convince Fatima to leave—and hitched a ride to Turkey with one of the few remaining families in the town. Before she left, she had pulled Abbas into her room, where her clothes and photographs had been crammed into a single suitcase, and she pressed into his hand a hardback book with a ripped dust jacket. She made Abbas swear not to tell anyone about it, and Abbas duly swore. Nafisah had heard rumours, she said, and seen things online suggesting there was this new group in the West who were more strict than the Government. She warned Abbas that, should these people come to their village, he would need to protect his family. Abbas was only 11, but he said he would. And he would need to hide this book—the only one that Nafisah had saved from Fatima's bonfire—somewhere nobody could ever find it. Abbas promised, and Nafisah kissed him on the forehead and left.

***

"So my auntie went to Turkey, and there she managed to get across to Greece, then Austria and Germany, then France where she paid a smuggler to bring her across the Channel to England," Abbas said, flicking a stray piece of hair from his eye. He looked at me for the first time since this story had begun, and I looked straight back at him in a desperate attempt to show him that I wouldn't hide from the reality of his life.

"Thank you for telling me," I mumbled. "I'm so sorry for what I said during the debate, but you know I don't actually believe that shit—that was just saying a position, you know? It wasn't actually what I believe."

"You said it very convincingly."

I felt guilty, as if for a second I wasn't sure whether I believed the xenophobic crap that I had spewed during the debate. "I know," I laughed half-heartedly but stopped immediately when I saw the humour wasn't at all reciprocated in the boy sitting opposite me. "It's just a debate. I just had to argue a position the best I could. You don't get to pick what you argue about."

He said my name, and I fell silent into a pool of my own self-loathing. "Even if you don't believe that stuff, you still said it, and you still said things that weren't true. Things that fuck with the lives of people, you know."

"I know, I get that, and I'm so sorry, Abbas." I said his name, hoping it would convey my sincerity, but I don't think he was receptive. "But thank you for telling me this. I didn't realise what your family had been through, and I'll do better in the future." There was an awkward pause where I had expected, or hoped rather, that Abbas would reassure me that it was water under the bridge, but he didn't. "How is your aunt now?"

"She's good, you saw. She got granted asylum eventually, and now she's studying to become a nurse."

"That's amazing."

Abbas nodded. I desperately wanted to reach out to him, but how could I when I wasn't sure whether he would explode, collapse, or something completely different? I stayed sat where I was, fiddling with my hands. *He hates me*, I told myself over and over again. I've fucked it, and now he hates me. My arms itched with the urge to cut them open and bleed out the pain. But there was one last question I wanted to ask him before he left me forever.

"What was the book?"

"Huh?" Abbas looked at me with his brows furrowed over his dark eyes.

"You said your aunt gave you a book before she left. What was the book?" I gestured weakly towards one of the many stacks of novels that lined the room.

"Oh, yeah." He twisted his body to pull open the drawer of his bedside table, almost knocking over a glass of water but managing to contain it to a single drop that spilled over the edge onto the floor. He cursed under his breath and pulled a book out of the drawer. He handed it to me gingerly, as if afraid I would break it somehow. I looked at the cover, which still had a rip down the edge that Abbas, I assumed, had patched with a careful strip of tape.

"Oscar Wilde," I whispered, unsure why I felt I needed to keep it a secret.

***

Luce's head tilts to one side, and he looks at me quizzically. I look back at him, unsure of what the fuck is going to come out of his mouth next. He has an unpleasant habit of surprising me. But he stays silent, and I feel that sickening compulsion to fill the pause.

"So that's the story of how I fucked up by joining a debate team," I say awkwardly, attempting a smile.

"You said the story of the debate club was the story of you and Abbas?" Luce asks, kissing his teeth with a click.

"Well, yeah. It's the story of how I found out about his family and his past, and... well..." I look around as if the words are floating just above my head for me to put into the sentence.

Luce nods encouragingly.

"Well, I guess a lot more of it comes later on, when I find out about the lady he kept meeting after school."

"For fuck's sake, kiddo," Luce laughs. "How long does this story go on for?"

"I can talk about Abbas for ages," I reply with a smile.

"Is this just putting off the inevitable?"

"Isn't everything you do in life just putting off the inevitable?"

"Touché, kiddo. Touché."

***

Rebecca is smiling when she walks over to me. For some unknown reason, she has an amazing ability to find me, but I can never find her when I go looking. It's unnerving.

"Hello," she says with a wave of her tiny hand.

"Hello," I reply, returning the wave. Why is it then when you're with a child, all the normal rules of society go out the window, and you follow their weird little alien ways, like waving at your friend as if you're stuck behind the window of a train that's pulling away from the platform?

“I have news,” Rebecca announces, and I nod questioningly, gesturing for her to proceed.

“Luce says he thinks I’m almost ready to make my decision.”

My stomach sinks and the smile drops from my face. “What do you mean? I thought you were waiting for me to decide?”

“I know, and I still will, but he says you’re almost ready too.” My stomach sinks deeper. “Are you okay?” she asks, putting a hand on my shoulder.

“Yeah, yeah, I’m fine.” I shrug her off. “I just didn’t expect this, I guess.”

“Well, you knew we had to make a decision, didn’t you?” I nod. “And you knew I’ve been here longer than you?” I nod again. “So what didn’t you expect?” Her way of talking like a 90-year-old is unpleasant at this moment.

“I know all that, I just... Do you think you’re ready?”

“I’m ready when you are,” she replies, and I want to punch her a little bit, but she’s a child, and this is one rule of society you cannot throw out the window. *I assume.*

Rebecca sits down beside me and takes my hand in hers. My long fingers dwarf her hand, but she doesn’t seem to mind. I guess it feels good to have something so much bigger encase you, like a hug from a bear. She points at the scars criss-crossing my arm, and asks, “What are these?”

The first time I cut myself, like I told Jo, was a few months after I started dating Olivia. I knew I was gay, of course I did, but I had pushed myself into this corner, and I was desperate for a way out. Olivia was a good person. She had baggage, like we all did, but she didn’t deserve a boyfriend who was incapable of loving her the way she wanted to be loved.

It’s crazy, I always think, how the drive for self-preservation—the drive to stay in the closet—can force you into self-destruction. The brain wasn’t built for the 21st century. Maybe things would make more sense if we were back in cavemen times, but then at least we have electricity and running water.

Grass is always greener, ey?

When I confessed—if confession is the right word here—to Lois, I wasn't suicidal. I knew that. I knew myself. But it scared my dad so much that I was put on a suicide watch that I never needed. But before you ask whether I have ever been suicidal, the answer is yes. I think everyone has, maybe to varying degrees, but I think that everyone is capable of killing themselves, even if they try to convince themselves that they're not.

When self-harm becomes as much a ritual as it is a coping mechanism, it feeds that part of you that craves continuity and begs for stability when your brain is constantly in fight-or-flight mode because you're so deep in the closet you might bump into the Minotaur. I never tried to kill myself over Olivia, or Marcus. That summer, when I was lying in the clearing and staring up at the sky, I would beg for something to kill me, whether a falling tree or a lightning bolt, but I didn't want to kill myself.

"Why didn't you?" Luce asks.

I look up at him. "I mean, first of all, I never had the opportunity. When everyone was out of lockdown, I was still in the quarantine imposed by my father, and so I never had unsupervised access to anything even remotely dangerous, unless my method of suicide would be to choke on the sweetcorn at dinner. But I guess a part of me thought that, however unceremoniously it had occurred, I was now out of the closet, and there was that bit of me that saw a tiny glimmer of rainbow-infused hope that maybe this would be the thing that changed everything."

"And did it?"

"No. Just because everyone knew I liked boys didn't mean that anything else had changed. I was still in a situation with no friends, no boyfriend, no... *anyone*."

"So why weren't you suicidal?"

"Don't sound so disappointed." I laugh heart-heartedly, and Luce winks back at me. "I don't know why I wasn't suicidal."

"So when were you suicidal?" Luce asks.

"I... don't know."

"You don't know?"

"I mean, I know, I just... can't remember properly?" I shake my head, as if the answer would come tumbling out of one ear. It didn't.

Luce stands up and straightens his jacket. "You'll remember soon, don't worry."

It feels like a threat, but he's gone before I can ask.

XXIII

The Patron Saint of Falling in Love

After I had handed the book of poetry back to Abbas as gently as he had given it to me, we curled up on his bed, him kissing my forehead gently and running his fingers through my hair, and we watched some crap on TV. All was forgiven, and my heart, which had been screaming in panic that everything had been lost, eventually calmed in his embrace.

And—after the (what I had prayed was just the) initial hiccup—thus began the summer of love. With coursework and mock exams out of the way, Abbas and I were inseparable. I'm not sure whether my family or his was becoming more irritated at the other's perpetual presence as we stuck to each other like tattoos or shadows, but frankly, I didn't give a shit. I was with the most beautiful boy in the world, and I wasn't going to let anything get in the way of that. I was so lovesick that even a night out of his arms felt like torture (although the memory of Abbas's brother quickly stuffed that thought into a dark pit), and waking up next to his body made me finally understand all the heteronormative crap society feeds gay kids. I understood the feeling of watching someone sleep with your heart brimming with adoration; I felt my heart skip beats and burst into song when his sleepy eyes drifted open to look into mine; I knew what it was like to be drawn to someone with all the magnetic force of every fibre of your body dying to be close to them.

Even though Abbas was ridiculously good looking—with

pecs that made me salivate, thighs that could crush coconuts, and a smile that felt like God was pouring pure happiness into my soul—spending that summer with Abbas showed me the perfection of mundanity with the love of your life. Whether we were walking to the shop together to pick up a carton of milk, or folding laundry in an attempt to make ourselves less of a burden at the other's home, or even just sitting next to each other scrolling on our phones and sending memes without a word spoken, time with Abbas was like a drug whose addiction I couldn't shake, and nor would I want to.

"Would you call it an obsession?" Luce asks.

The dictionary defines 'obsession' as "an idea or thought that continually preoccupies or intrudes on a person's mind", and the thought of Abbas definitely continually preoccupied my mind. I would be thinking about him even when I was staring at him, my brain reeling with every aspect of him that I would lap up like I had been deprived of him for years. Carly Rae Jepson was right when she said, 'Before you came into my life, I missed you so bad.'

"Because," I tell Luce, "you have no idea how lonely it feels to grow up gay. It's not a community you're born into. My parents were—are—straight, my grandparents, also straight. My sister, presumptively straight. The vast majority of the people around you are straight, or closeted, and you feel like you're the only person in the world who is the same as you, and you don't even know that you're gay, you just know that something about you doesn't add up, and when you finally figure out that the whole thing is just that you like boys, it's anticlimactic, because that's never going to make you the 'Chosen One' in a young-adult fantasy book series, and it feels like the most natural, normal, beautiful thing in the world, and yet you have to hide it, and you don't know why, you just know that you do.

"Abbas was the first person I could love completely and

freely and openly and who loved me back, and when you give all that to a kid who has never had it before, it's such a fundamental, primal need, that I could only imagine it's like when you've been stuck in the desert for days without water, and you finally find some, and you drink it all then and there like a really thirsty fucking camel."

"That's not healthy," Luce says, and I roll my eyes.

"What's not healthy is the deprivation—you can't blame the kid who wants too much of something he's never been allowed to have before."

But the summer of love plodded on, and I was so blessed I might as well have been anointed and canonised. When my father handed us two train tickets and a stern warning not to get into any trouble, I'm not sure whether it was to reward us for our young love or to save himself the torture of sitting through another episode of a God-awful reality show that Abbas and I would binge in the living room. We knew better than to kill that particular curious cat, however, and took the tickets with profuse gratitude and a solemn vow not to take any unnecessary risks, and boarded the train destined for gay ol' Brighton.

It was Abbas's first time seeing the English coast, and he was—understandably—wistfully disappointed at what he saw, but the sad reality of sunburn, seagulls, and cigarettes was immediately plastered over with the horrific beauty of rainbows, love, and Pride.

I cough. I'm not sure why. "I think," I say, pausing to illustrate the fact that I'm thinking about it, "it's hard to describe Pride to people who haven't been.

"I know I said before that being gay comes out as a massive anti-climax, but then you go to Pride and you realise that the reason it feels like such an anti-climax is because you've been built up to think that everything is going to be a huge deal, because why would you keep something as mundane as who you fall in love with a secret? Not even that, but who you have sex with. And it's hard to understand because you're so confused as to why this is such a problem for everyone to deal with when it's something that comes so naturally. But then you go to Pride, and you realise. You realise that the reason it's been built up to be such a big deal is because the world hates you for it. Maybe not as much now, but they still hate you for it more than they hate you for being anything else that you are—and you realise that that..." I try not to repeat myself but no other word comes out, "That that realisation is the difference between life or death, because not saying it and not living it will drive you to die, and saying it and living it risks that you will be killed.

"They say Pride is a protest, and that's something I didn't understand until I went to Brighton with Abbas. I knew, of course, that it was a protest against homophobia and bigotry and hatred, and a protest against the way queer people are so mistreated and so oppressed, I knew that. I didn't know how going to Pride as a queer person, an openly gay person in a relationship, was the biggest protest of it all. It's not the signs or the flags or the provocative outfits or the rainbow makeup. It's not that at all. It's, in the face of everything else, the sheer audacity of seeing all this pain and all this hurt, and living all this shame and all this hatred, and being able to stare it in the eye and not blink. To confront the very worst that the world has to offer, and meet it on the battlefield, and not flinch.

"That summer with Abbas, that Pride with him... That's when I realised that being gay is the biggest gift I was ever given. I don't know if it's God or genetics or upbringing or a freak accident, but whatever the cause, that capacity that's inherent in all of us gay people to have all this fear and fucking do it, anyway. That's Pride."

I feel myself sweating as I work myself into a furore with the sheer excitement of my own homosexuality.

Luce smiles at me, his eyes glinting like they're on fire. "So, what happened at this Pride to make it so special?"

"I did not expect this," Abbas said, looking around in what I wasn't sure whether it was amazement, disbelief, or disappointment. I laughed.

The streets were teeming with people in garish and, naturally, rainbow-adorned outfits. The main thing I felt was how the natural colour of both Abbas and my hair set us apart immediately from the kaleidoscope of dye-jobs we saw in front of us. A couple walked past us, one wearing a cream-coloured mesh tank top and booty-shorts with a nose ring, and the other tall and tanned with his offensively perfect abs on full display, obscured only slightly by his body bag. They smiled at us, and we grinned back. The couple stopped, looking the pair of us up and down.

"Hey, there," the meshed boy said with a Liverpudlian twang. "What's youse names?"

Abbas extended his hand, and the couple chuckled. "I'm Abbas," he said with a keen smile, before introducing me.

"Pleasure," tanned said, pulling Abbas's hand up to peck it with his lips.

"I'm Ean-with-an-E, this is Matt," Mesh replied with a curtsey. Abbas laughed. "Is this your first Brighton Pride?"

"Yeah, yeah," I said, unsure of where the conversation was going to go, and feeling increasingly possessive of Abbas in this sea of twinks that made what I considered to be my unique boyish charm very... inferior.

"Are you going to Latex tonight?" Matt asked, with a smile almost as flawless as his torso. I hated him then and there. Our blank faces gave away our innocence. "It's a club," he clarified, stroking his perfectly manicured stubble. Everything I noticed about this man was deeply, deeply enviable and infuriating.

"Ohhh," Abbas laughed, "No, we're only 17." I didn't bother to correct him that I was still 16. I didn't want this Olympian God in front of us to think I was any less than I already felt like I was in his presence.

"Oh, my God," Ean cackled, "They're kids!"

"Pleasure to meet you," Matt laughed as Ean howled, dragging him away.

"So... Latex?" Abbas turned to me with a wink and I punched him on the shoulder.

The rest of Pride was pretty fucking gay: rainbow after rainbow; watching a parade of queer people walk past with cheers and cheesy music; and slowly digging down into the bottomless pit of my love for Abbas. He watched the events go on pretty silently, but with an ever-present smile on his face, brushing off the dozens and dozens and dozens of compliments he received by hugging me closer every time a new man approached him. The gesture was small, but very, very much appreciated, and quelled my jealousy somewhat. With no alcohol on our underage agenda, as the crowds dispersed to their parties and club nights, Abbas took my hand in his, and gently led me through the rainbow-strewn street as the last few NHS trusts filtered past with tired enthusiasm.

In our aimless wandering, we came across a bar stuffed in a back street that seemed deceptively wide thanks to the rainbow bunting and the throngs of people stuffed into it like messy, gay sardines. On a small stage that didn't look much bigger than an exam desk stood a drag queen in furs and a heavy wig, despite the scorching heat. She wasn't really doing much, other than bobbing her head around and clapping. We fought our way through to the bar and each ordered a Diet Coke, knowing we wouldn't be able to pass as 18, before squirming back out to the alley. The speakers were loud, and all you could hear was the music and the faint yelling of the assembled queers along to the lyrics of an early 2000s pop song that I hadn't heard in years, and yet still remembered like the back of my hand.

Taking Abbas's hand, with my drink in the other, I started dancing—not properly, just stepping back and forth and waving my arms rhythmically. Abbas laughed and danced along. We ducked down low as the song built up to its final chorus, our whispering of the lyrics growing to full out screaming as the drums heralded its arrival. Abbas didn't know the words but the rest of us were more than making it up for him, and though our hands were broken apart by the tidal movements of the crowd, they were quickly grabbed by strangers who twirled us around, laughing as we did so, and we fell into old women and young boys, spilling our drinks but I never missed a lyric, and Abbas never lost his grin.

The music faded as we walked back to the train station, careful not to miss the last train of the night, but you could sense that neither of us wanted the day to end. As we waited on the platform, Abbas wrapped his arm around my shoulder, pushing my face into his broad shoulders. I closed my eyes and sighed, breathing in the intoxicating mix of sweat, salt air, and his rustic aftershave.

"I didn't realise it would be like that," he said quietly, kissing my forehead through my mop of windswept hair.

"What do you mean?" I nuzzled into him.

"We didn't have Pride where I grew up. We didn't see anything like that. I didn't realise..." He paused, and I let the silence hang in the air for a moment. "I didn't realise how beautiful it could be."

I looked up and saw him staring off into the distance. Some fireworks were going off from the direction of the beach, and the muffled pops and bangs broke the relative quiet of the train station. I watched the explosions of light reflected in his mahogany eyes. Sensing me staring at him, he looked down at my face and a ghost of a smile washed across his peaceful expression. We kissed—slowly and gently, in the way where there is no lust or heat or passion, but the reassuring knowledge that you're wrapped completely in someone, and the earnest wish to never let that moment end.

***

"I've been thinking..."

"Oh, dear," I groaned, looking up from the book I was reading. Abbas was sitting on my bed, his arms wrapped around his legs in front of him as he leaned against the wall behind him.

He huffed playfully, shaking his head in disapproval. I laughed, and he smiled back sarcastically. He called me an arsehole, which I shrugged off with a wink and a blown kiss. "I've been thinking that maybe I should start to learn more about this stuff."

"What stuff?" I asked. We hadn't spoken in about an hour while we read side-by-side. Abbas had stayed at mine the night before when we finally got home from Brighton after delayed trains and almost two hours waiting in an uncomfortable drizzle at 1am. My dad wasn't pleased to pick us up when we managed to reach the closest station in the dead of night, but we were grateful for our knight in shining armour (or, at the very least, the warmth of the car). Warm showers and a lie-in were the perfect remedy.

"You know, being gay." Abbas looked at me and the smile dropped from my face. This was a serious discussion, and I rearranged my expression to reflect that.

"What do you mean?"

"Well, all of that stuff yesterday—I just wish I understood more about the history, and the culture, and all the references."

"The references?" I asked, with my eyebrow cocked.

He chuckled and my heart melted that little bit it always did when Abbas laughed. "The voguing, the music, the drag queens, the movies, the miners. I don't understand any of it."

"Oh, babe... You came to the right place."

The next weekend, when Liam finally managed to get an evening off from the shitty pub job we were all pretty confident was breaching a number of employment laws despite Liam's naive protestations that it was all above board, the gang settled in for the Education of Abbas.

It turned out, however, that the rest of the boys needed the education just as much as my boyfriend. Alonso knew Frida Kahlo, and, of course, we had all heard of Elton John, but aside from that, my friends were clueless.

We watched an episode of a drag competition show, followed by a documentary on ballroom culture—during which we found out that Lukas was weirdly good at voguing, despite having never danced in front of us before—and then a couple of the biggest gay movies and television shows of all time, with AIDS featuring prominently, of course. The sun was beginning to rise when we finally moved onto watching YouTube music videos by gay pop stars, trans rappers, and bisexual punk bands. The whole community was well represented in the collection I had spent hours carefully curating. By the end of it, despite being extremely sleep-deprived (thanks to Tom's valiant efforts to ensure we all remained constantly awake throughout the night), I clapped my hands together and declared my work complete.

Abbas gave me a kiss on the cheek and thanked me for my service. The boys heartedly, though exhaustedly, concurred.

"You know what I didn't realise?" Tom said, and we all groaned in despair. Tom's insights were usually fairly surface-level. "How fucking depressing it is to be gay."

Alonso threw his hands up. "What the fuck, man?"

"No, no, I'm not saying that being gay is bad, but all of these shows and movies and videos and everything, either they all end sadly, or the happy ending is a surprise because of how sad everything else was." Tom looked around earnestly, searching for our support.

"Shut the fuck up, Tom," Lukas sighed, rolling over to shove his face into the pillows of my bed (many of which I had stolen from my dad's room).

We sat in silence for a few moments, with Tom scrolling on his phone—no doubt to find something to vindicate his remarks. I looked around at the five boys in my room: Tom, Alonso, Lukas, Liam and, of course, Abbas.

"Hey, guys, I wanted to just..." I have a recurring problem where if I don't write down my sentences in advance, they never come out smoothly. "I wanted to say thanks for doing this. It's nice that you all care."

"Of course we care," Liam replied, and the rest nodded. "We're not gay"— he looked at Abbas—"Us four aren't gay, but this stuff is who you are. We love you guys, and it's not in spite of you being who you are, so why wouldn't we want to know more about you?"

Liam—the quiet one—was quite the wordsmith. My heart was fit to burst.

"Yeah, we're like..." Tom looked at Abbas and I. "We're your '*allies*'." His arms hadn't dropped from performing the air-quotes before three different pillows were thrown at him.

***

"I've been thinking," I said, and Abbas stuck his middle finger up at me. One of the things I loved about us is how mature and sensitive our relationship is.

"What's up, doc?" He asked with mock sincerity, and I returned the finger.

"The way you said you wanted to know more about being gay and gay culture and stuff, and then what the guys said about wanting to support us..."

Abbas nodded with an "Mhm."

"I want to know more about you. I know you told me about your family, and your brother and your aunt, but... I want to know more about you."

"What do you mean 'more about me'?" Abbas clicked his phone off and put it on the desk next to him. We were in his room this time, and I'd been staring in thought at the guitar propped up against a pile of books.

"Well, you told me why your aunt left Syria, but you didn't say why you left, and why your family didn't come with you, and... I don't know—the stories you told me were about your family, and then they ended before you finished, I feel." I thought the 'feel' at the end would soften the blow of me essentially being a nosy bastard. I'd watched too much therapy on TV and not been paying enough attention in my own sessions with Jo, who kept reminding me that I'm her patient, and we're not just there for a chat.

Abbas looked at his hands, rubbing his thumbs together in a little pattern I didn't understand. I felt an urge to keep talking but manage to restrain myself in the knowledge that I would surely end up with a foot in my mouth.

"Well, you know sometimes I miss a Friday morning at school?"

"Yeah?"

"And you said that you saw me one time with a lady?"

"Yeah?"

"That's Mary..."

XXIV

A Lion Hunted

"I feel like I need to remind you, again, that this is not meant to be all about Abbas." Luce shakes his head at me in despair again, and I laugh, again.

"I keep telling you, Luce: the story of me is the story of Abbas."

"Abbas is not the one whose life hangs in the balance here." Why he says these things, I'm not sure. Luce is looking at me with his head tilted slightly to one side. He's wearing a loose white t-shirt and jeans that hug his hips just right, and his forearms are heavy with bracelets like the ones Marcus used to wear, except not bought from tacky tourist shops in Marbella. I'm still in my t-shirt and joggers, and still in my socks without shoes. I wonder where his wardrobe is with these perennial outfit changes, while I'm stuck in the same clothes (plus socks!) that I turned up to the Interlife wearing.

I sigh. "Anyway..."

***

The chair I was sitting on was pretty uncomfortable, which felt a stark contrast to the pristine corporate-ness of the room. Across the table was a chest of drawers with labelless bottles of chilled water flanked by rows of glasses that completely outnumbered the capacity of this room, which could have sat six at most. A piece of nondescript artwork hung from the wall, with a TV behind me, and Abbas to my right. I had put on a shirt for the occasion, and wore my best chinos, but Abbas was in jeans and a tee with his new favourite artist (Jacen Taylor, unsurprisingly, queer education is not complete without the heterosexual heartthrobs) emblazoned on the front, flashing his literally award-winning smile. His trainers—an article I had come to know is very dear to his heart—were his favourites: white with electric blue stitches. My shoes were the smartest I owned.

Despite the air-con blasting down on us, I still sweated in anticipation of the arrival of the woman I had heard so very little about: Mary. She was a lawyer, that much I knew, and she worked for the semi-prestigious firm of Kirkham & Knight, which I had googled and studied the webpage of in advance of this moment. The firm specialised in two things: immigration and tax, which I believed to be as boring as they sounded, but their offices were good enough for me to realise that the tax money must be sufficient to make up for the fact that Abbas wasn't paying them a penny. He stressed this to me when I stepped in the lift and immediately queried how he could afford to hire a firm with an abstract sculpture entitled *Silent Justice* plopped in their lobby.

When Mary walked in, accompanied by a young, attractive woman who introduced herself as Chris, the first thing that struck me was how tired she looked. When she shook my hand with a firm grip and a smile, the bags under her eyes looked heavy enough to cost a hell of a lot extra on a Ryanair flight. As Mary sat herself down, dropping a folder onto the table and pulling out a chair, Chris was already typing furiously away on her laptop. I sat awkwardly in silence as Mary surveyed me with piercing green eyes, and Abbas stared at me from the side. Chris was still bashing her keyboard with a force that I'm surprised didn't dent the solid wood table.

"Thank you for agreeing to speak with us today," Mary said in a soft voice that made me lean forward to hear her properly. Her earrings looked to be diamond, and they caught the light from under her choppy blonde hair as she spoke.

"No problem," I replied, unsure of what the fuck I'd got myself into.

When Abbas had explained that he had a lawyer who was helping him with his immigration status, I had assumed that it would be paperwork and forms, so when he asked me to come in and meet his lawyer, I assumed that I would be needing to witness something and sign something to say I knew who Abbas was. How little I actually knew Abbas was about to become painfully apparent.

"Has Abbas explained to you the process we're going through here?" Mary asked, and I glanced over at Abbas, whose eyes were now fixed firmly on the glass of water in front of him. Mary clicked the cap off her pen and flicked it through her fingers menacingly.

"He said that you're helping him with his immigration, and you wanted to meet with me?" I ventured, and Mary looked over at Abbas, whose stare did not move from his glass.

"Yes, that's right. Abbas is applying for asylum, which is when..."

"I, uh... I know what asylum is," I interrupted, turning my head to look at my boyfriend, whose cheeks had reddened. Mine blazed scarlet too.

"So Abbas came to the UK because it wasn't safe for him in his home country," Mary continued. "And when you apply for asylum, you have to submit evidence of why it wasn't safe for you to stay where you were, and part of that evidence is talking to the people who know Abbas, and who can vouch for him and that what he's saying is truthful."

"Yeah, so, uh, I can sign something that says that, yeah," I nodded. "He's telling the truth." I'm not sure why I said this when he hadn't even told me he was applying for asylum. I guess I should have put two and two together when he told me the stories of his brother and the war, but I was never going to win an award for my detective skills, anyway.

"So what we need from you is a little more than just saying he's telling the truth. We need you to tell us more about your relationship with Abbas, so we can..." She glanced at Chris. "So we can prove to the Home Office that what Abbas is saying is the truth."

"My relationship?" I asked. My mouth was suddenly very dry. Why did this feel like being outed?

"Abbas is applying for asylum on the basis that it wouldn't be safe for him to stay in Syria because he's gay. When you apply for asylum because of your sexual orientation, the Home Office asks that you prove that you are gay." My mouth got even drier. "So we need to find as much evidence to support that Abbas is gay so that the Home Office believes him."

"But... he is gay?" My face burned red. I felt like I was missing something very obvious here.

"I know, but the Home Office requires him to prove that. It's not something they just take at face value, because they're worried that people will just say that they're gay so they can claim asylum and live in the UK, when they're not actually gay," Mary replied with a sympathetic nod. The room was silent except for the ticking of a clock that I couldn't actually see, and Chris's ferocious typing.

"But how do you prove you're gay?"

"Well, it's not as if they can make Abbas kiss you in front of them." She chuckled, but none of the rest of us joined her. "We just need to find as many ways we can show it as possible. We've got screenshots of Abbas's Instagram, and we've got a witness statement from his brother, and we've, of course, got Abbas's own story, but we'd also like to hear from you. The more we can show the Home Office, the more likely they are to believe that Abbas is telling the truth, and the more likely they are to grant him asylum so that he can stay in the UK."

"What happens if they don't grant him asylum?" I asked. I hadn't even considered the possibility that Abbas could ever leave.

"So, if they don't grant him asylum, he will have to go back."

"Oh." I replied. I didn't look at Abbas this time. I didn't want to think of a world where he wasn't by my side.

"But we can appeal before that happens. We're quite confident that he'll stay, no matter the outcome of this application. We'll do everything we can to make sure of it. So we've got some questions for you, and Chris here," Mary gestured at the woman who still didn't look up from her laptop, "will be taking a note so we can put it all in a witness statement for you to sign and then we can submit that with Abbas's application to the Home Office." She paused for a beat. "Is that all okay with you?"

I nodded, feeling sick to my stomach.

"Do you have any questions?" Mary asked, and I shook my head. "Okay, well, if you have any at any time, you can ask them, and we can also take a break whenever you need to, okay?" I nodded again.

"Has Abbas told you about his first boyfriend?"

"The answer was 'no'," I tell Luce, who doesn't seem particularly interested. He's not as invested in the great love story of Abbas and me as the rest of us, which disappoints me more than I thought it would. When you're fighting for your life, you hope the self-proclaimed judge would be a little interested in your defence, but I guess you can't be everyone's cup of tea.

"Weren't you his first boyfriend?" Luce asks.

"Apparently not," I reply, and Luce raises his eyebrows in mild surprise. "After I told Mary that I didn't know about that, she moved on with disinterested efficiency to the next question on her list, flicking over a page in her folder,"—I mime the gesture—"and started asking me to talk about how Abbas and I met, and our relationship and everything. I was probably in that room for about two and a half hours, which that Chris lady had condensed into eight pages of single-space size 12 font. Pretty ruthless, isn't it?"

"I wish you had given us the eight-page version, kiddo," Luce comments with a smirk, and I flip him off. Sometimes I forget that my conduct is hardly parliamentary, but given the distinct lack of a Speaker to enforce any rules, I figure I can get away with the odd lewd gesture.

"But when we got back to my house afterwards—it was about a 30-minute bus ride where we sat in absolute silence the whole way—Abbas sat me down on my bed, and told me the story. He said he didn't realise Mary would ask me about his first boyfriend, and he was sorry for not telling me earlier. I tried to brush it off and act like I wasn't disappointed or, for some weird fucking reason, betrayed by the fact I wasn't the first boy he'd ever loved, but I think he saw straight through that.

"So he told me about him and Kharouf."

***

The war in Syria, which had left Abbas's village relatively unscathed compared to the rest of the country, continued long after the television cameras and 'foreign' correspondents stopped standing and pointing in front of rubble and men with guns. It was increasingly hard to get reliable news, with internet so spotty his mother banned Abbas and his siblings from using it at all so she could protect her own connection to the rest of the world.

It was through word-of-mouth that the remaining villagers heard of new happenings in the Northwest: a new group—or not a group, actually, just a few guys—or a collective, no;

it was an army. This amorphous entity—ISIS, ISIL, Daesh, Islamic State, whatever—was, piece by piece, taking land from the government and from the rebels indiscriminately. Tariq, the surviving son of the shopkeeper, told Abbas and his family that these people had been killing everyone they came across: women, children, men. Anyone. And they draped their jet-black flag across the scorched earth that lay in their wake.

People had been steadily fleeing Syria for many years now, but all of a sudden it wasn't just a stream anymore, it was a flood, a tidal wave. Entire villages were deserted overnight, and those that remained survived only at the mercy of Daesh. That's when the Americans and the Europeans arrived with their drones and their bombs, levelling buildings to help Assad take back the territory he had raped and pillaged just months before. Thousands and thousands more were killed by explosions, with survivors maimed and disfigured beyond recognition.

Abbas told me once that the regime had killed over one hundred thousand civilians, compared to just five thousand killed by Daesh. He didn't call the Government a government: "A regime is just guns. No government."

When these fighters arrived in Abbas's village one morning, they heralded their arrival with the burning of the two regime soldiers at the stake. Basam and Naeem had been sitting outside the shack they used as a guard post, smoking cigarettes and flicking the glowing ashes into the endless dirt and sand that surrounded the village. For a people so used to death, Basam's death was not a big loss; he had lost the hearts of the people he was sworn to protect when he had raped Marya, a farmer's daughter, at gunpoint in broad daylight and when he had shot the farmer who rushed to his daughter's aid in the head mid-thrust. Basam deserved to die. Naeem, however, was a sweet boy who had lived in the village his whole life, with long skinny arms and legs, and a bright smile underneath a wispy moustache. He was only 17 when he was handed a gun and an old, bullet-riddled bullet-proof vest and ordered to shoot protestors on sight, though no one thought he had ever pulled that trigger in his life. For a people so used to death, they watched with quiet understanding as the flames crept up Basam's body and licked his neck as he howled like a lame dog. For a people so used to death, they somehow managed to shed a tear when sweet Naeem finally fell silent, too.

That is how Abbas was introduced to Daesh.

The transition was seamless, and his mother professed her gratitude to the men who finally brought food to their family after so many years of them wasting away. They started to fix up the broken town, starting with the mosque that had been damaged by a freak explosion two years prior, and suddenly Abbas and his brother were no longer the only two people praying there every morning. Abbas had always thought the enemy of your enemy was your friend, and so he had a sense of quiet relief when Daesh turned up that morning, knowing that they were fighting against the same regime that had treated his brother so cruelly, but Suhail spat at them behind closed doors, shouting at his brother in the quietest whisper he could that these men had betrayed Syria, betrayed Islam. Abbas didn't know what that meant, but he knew he loved his brother, and so he believed him.

What made Abbas hate Daesh was very simple. Although girls were not permitted to attend mosque, and were required to pray in private with their mothers, Jamila would wait outside to walk the 10 minutes up the hill to their home with her brothers. Jamila had suffered most by the war, Abbas thought. She had no education, and she was now forbidden from reading or speaking to men who were not her family. She was whipped for failing to properly cover her whole face, and was always the last to be provided with food. She survived—though she didn't live—without complaint, and Abbas's mother would comment frequently on what a good wife she would make one day. It was a far cry from her childhood of fighting with her brothers, but this was now all Jamila could ever be: a wife.

In October, Jamila was waiting outside the mosque with her mother, having just collected what little groceries they could—it turned out Daesh's bounty was not limitless—when a spray of bullets shot up from a few doors down. The pair of women ducked for cover behind a wall of what used to be the library, but now served as a shelter for a family of stray cats.

Abbas didn't go into detail about what happened next. He either didn't know, or he didn't want to say, and I wasn't going to press him for answers.

Jamila was raped by a man who held her mother back at gunpoint as her muffled sobs crept out from behind the veil she was forced to wear. Jamila didn't speak after that; not a word to her mother, her brothers, anyone. Suhail, when his mother told the brothers what had happened, was incensed: the fire in his eyes flickered alight for the first time since he had returned home from his detention, but missing one hand and in a village crawling with Daesh, there was nothing he could do from which he would have escaped with his life.

Abbas didn't react to the news, except for a slight furrowing of his brows as his brother raged around him, and his mother begged him to be quiet so his sister could rest in the next room. He hated the Government for what they had done to his brother, and he hated Daesh for what they had done to his sister. It was then that Abbas, with silent understanding, resigned himself to the truth that his country had been lost forever. No longer would he believe that one day the war would blow over and he could go back to reading under the shade of the olive trees. He didn't share his brother's militant belief that Syria could only be rescued by a secular revolution from below, nor did he believe his mother's ever contradictory proclamations and prayers that the President—who had given their family so much—would ride in on his white horse and save the nation from the riots and from the insurgents. In that evening, Abbas came to terms with the fact that Syria had been shattered and had nothing left to offer the world.

When the Government finally recaptured every inch of territory that had been stolen from them by the rebels and Daesh, the village was abandoned by the terrorists as they retreated further and further east. The peace that Fatima had yearned for arrived like a dust cloud, snatching the oxygen and the moisture that had cradled the breath of revolution, and leaving behind only a people entombed in their grief like a Middle Eastern Pompeii.

While fighting continued across the country between the rebels and the regime, Abbas's village was steadfast in its exhausted defeatism, and no help came from either side. The President, who had promised so much should ISIS be defeated, turned his sights back on the people who had defeated them with further bombardment that he blamed on the need to exterminate the terrorists he had already claimed were gone. His mother, still praying every day, no longer whispered the name of the man she had thanked every night since Shabaz had died, and instead prayed for the country—hope for which Abbas had long since abandoned.

Hope that not even Kharouf could rekindle.

XXV

Tale as Old as Sin

Kharouf was tall, thin, with a smooth face that his uncles would tease him for, and neatly trimmed short black hair above effortlessly shaped eyebrows and a bright smile. His outfit of choice consisted of a white linen shirt, grey shorts that hung low on his thin waist and bony hips, and an array of knock-off trainers, of which he was immensely proud. His eyes were deep brown but shone like amber in the desert sun, and his skin always glistened with sweat, but he was never sticky or wet. He smelt like the blossom that grew beyond the olive grove and Kharouf's trainer prints would remain in the cracked dirt long after the flowers had died of thirst.

Abbas doesn't remember the first time he saw him the same way I remember the first time I saw Abbas. He said that eventually, he just came to know that Kharouf would always be there—stalking the paths between the trees like a cat, effortlessly silent. Always alone, Kharouf would appear when Abbas walked through the town with his brother. After Jamila was raped, Abbas made an effort to glare at the ground while he walked. He had begun exercising in the house, with press-ups and sit-ups and chin-ups until he was down for the count, and his body had grown leaner and more muscular; the same muscles I would trace with my fingers as Abbas read beside me in bed. But Abbas did not want to make friends, particularly with any strange new boys that came into town.

Kharouf's parents had been killed during the war and he had been collected by his uncle who lived in Abbas's village, though there was very little binding anyone to the settlement anymore. There was no community, nor neighbours, nor friendships, and yet people would still cling to what little they had left, and so Kharouf's uncle had dragged his nephew one hundred miles north to their home. Fatima would talk about how Daesh had been forced out, but the truth was that one day, they were there, and the next, they were still there but without the black flag. The men of Daesh—those who remained—became part of the same group of people who lived in that part of the world, the same as Abbas and his family. Though Suhail had threatened to kill every single one of them after what they had done to his sister, the threats were empty and the anger dissipated into simmering resentment and disillusionment. Though Fatima still held out hope that the Government would rebuild what they had destroyed, there was no evidence that this would ever happen, and so Abbas had resigned himself to a life of repressed hatred. Who knew, maybe he would even join some militant group himself and get his limbs blown apart by a buried IED and bleed out by the side of the road?

But Kharouf spoke little of war and spoke little of his parents. When he spoke to Abbas, it was quiet and quick and Abbas found himself throwing glances at the boy lingering around him as he marched through the buildings and across the streets. His presence didn't irritate him, no matter how hard he tried to build up some bitterness to throw at his new shadow. Rather, Kharouf intrigued him. No one had shown Abbas such interest, such seeming fascination which swirled through Abbas's mind in confusion and bewilderment.

Kharouf was the first boy Abbas ever kissed. It happened late at night when Suhail had hiked up the nearby hill with morbid curiosity to watch the 'fireworks' of barrel bombs being dropped on the town across the valley, and Abbas, who had initially followed his brother up the path, turned back and walked home. Kharouf appeared by his side in the silent way that he did, and the pair walked in silence for a few hundred metres before Abbas stopped.

"What the fuck do you want?" Abbas hissed, screwing his face into an expression of contempt. "You're always fucking following me. Just fuck off."

But the anger didn't hold, no matter how many times Abbas tried to light the fuse. He stared into Kharouf's doe-like eyes that reflected the stars of the clear night sky, and Abbas found his stomach squirming inside himself.

"There was no way to look into those eyes and feel anger," Abbas told me. "I barely knew him, but his eyes... They made me want to protect him."

"I'm Kharouf," the boy said softly, unperturbed by Abbas's aggression.

"I know that," Abbas replied, trying to whip the resentment back into his voice and falling, instead sounding as innocent as Kharouf before him. "Why are you following me?"

"We're walking side-by-side." The answer was accurate, but it evaded the point of the question. *He's a bit like you in that way*, Abbas said to me.

"You know what I mean."

Kharouf stared at him, giving Abbas goosebumps that he blamed on the breeze that rustled the dry leaves of the olive trees. There were wildcats and wolves in these woods, but Abbas had been taught to fear the deer more. *Cats are cowards*, his grandfather would say, *but catch one of those deer on a bad day and you'll be gone*. The boy in front of him reached out, and Abbas's mind flinched, but his body remained steady. Kharouf took Abbas's hand in his own and a jolt of electricity surged from the touch. Abbas's heart pounded in his chest at the certainty of what was happening, and the complete uncertainty of what the fuck was happening. Staring into those big, deep brown eyes, Abbas's breathing grew shallower and breathier, until he closed his eyes softly and felt the boy's lips press onto his own.

Abbas had never kissed a boy; he had barely thought of one in that way. Nor had he really thought of girls. He grew up surrounded by war and violence with no room for love, not even to consider who he found attractive or who he wanted to touch. He thought after Jamila was raped that men were evil and he despised them, and he thought after his mother had continually defended the very country that had brutalised his brother that women had no purpose either. But when Kharouf kissed Abbas, the hate he felt for the world dissolved away, and the only thing he could focus on was the boy in front of him as Abbas slowly snaked his arm around Kharouf's slender hip and caressed the small of his back and Kharouf's hand slid into Abbas's curls before cradling his sharp jaw. The thunder of the bombs in the distance were dulled by the cool breeze that swept around the boys and Abbas's arm hairs pricked up in goosebumps feeling the warm body against his own.

For a boy who had spent the last fifteen years reading and being read to, Abbas had never found a word that could describe the feeling. When they separated, he found his eyes staying closed in the hopes that if he never opened them again, he would remain forever in this moment. Kharouf's lips were soft and warm and sweet, like breaking open a fig on the terrace at dusk and eating the flesh within. His body fit perfectly in the crevices of Abbas's growing muscles, like a puzzle piece that, once slotted together, would fuse and could never be removed. Wordlessly, he curled his fingers into a fist, grabbing a handful of Kharouf's white t-shirt, and pulled the boy back against his chest, and his lips back against his own.

***

“I have a question,” Luce interjects, his voice inquisitive but his eyes bored.

“Shoot,” I reply, waving him on.

“You told me before that you’d never fallen in love before Abbas,” Luce says, and I nod. “So how would you describe Olivia?”

I furrow my brows. “That wasn’t *real* love. That was... desperation that I could love her. Any girl, really. It was wishful thinking.”

“And Marcus?”

“A depression-induced infatuation.”

“And Lewis?”

I’m about to shoot off another quick reply, but the question throws me off. The pit in my stomach gapes open and my organs fall into it. I can feel my heart’s pace quicken and my leg bursts into pins-and-needles. My leg throbs.

“Lewis?”

“You mentioned him in passing.”

“I remember.” Of course I remember. I never mention him without knowing exactly what I’m doing. His name is like a bullet I have to load into the gun. I remember.

“So did you love Lewis?”

“I don’t want to talk about him.”

“You don’t have a choice.”

“I have a choice.”

“Not on this one, you don’t.”

Luce’s jaw is squeezed shut, and I’m not sure whether he hates where this conversation is going more than I do. I don’t know if I dreamed Luce up—if he were a figment of my imagination, it would explain a lot. Or if he was some kind of omniscient deity. Either way, I know Luce knows about Lewis, and I hope he feels the same when the name slips from his tongue. I hope he feels his throat close up and his palms start to sweat. I hope he feels the pain I feel. I hope everyone does.

I remember the day after the end with Lewis, when I walked around in a daze, going about my life with the sheer confusion hanging over me, with my mind holding back the truth like a dam that was bound to break and flood. How I hadn't survived the war, but rather died before the battle lines had even been drawn. How I surrendered in a way that broke every single cell in my body. How in a mind that couldn't block out Lewis, I could wrap myself in Abbas and pray he wouldn't find me.

When you have a reputation as the gay kid at school, however young and modern the rest of the world is, it's not easy to convince people that nothing has changed about you. And that was where I found myself: the gay kid who had forced himself out of the closet after a drunken mistake with the school staring at him.

In my last year of school, my attendance plummeted after I convinced my doctor to write me a sick note which my father gladly supported once Lois had left and he decided to travel less for work (a feat made easier by a pandemic that had forced him back into our house). We spent our days sitting silently in different rooms of the house, with all the doors open, and the dogs walking nervously from one of us to the other. When my sister returned home from school in the afternoons, life would be breathed back into the house like Persephone arriving from the Underworld, though it was a chore she didn't relish.

"Did you hate him?" Luce asks.

"What? Who?" I reply, confused.

"Your father."

"No?"

"He took your independence, your privacy, your personhood. He left you with nothing but a cold house to sit in while you wouldn't go to school."

"In an ideal world, sure, I would have spent my days in my clearing with no one around, with music or a book, and

I could've searched desperately for a meaning to a life that I didn't want anymore. Sure. But instead, I sat inside in silence with my father. He gave me space without setting me free to go and ruin my life. He gave me constancy when my head was anything but. He'd lost my mother, and he'd lost Lois, and he didn't want to lose me too. I can't hate him for that."

But the isolation gets to a person when your father lacks the words to sustain a conversation with a person he both loves and fears. Nor did I want him to speak to me; how could I ever begin to apologise for taking so much from him. He needed me just as much as I wished he didn't.

I once tried to convince my dad to let me go. When he drove me home from therapy, I turned off the music in the car and, with my adult voice on, I told him that I didn't want to be alive anymore. I didn't want to disappoint him or hurt him, but the kindest thing for him to do would be to let me die. That's what I wanted, and that's what I needed. However much it scared him, there was nothing scarier than what I was feeling in my life, and if he really did love me, he would give me his blessing.

My father, never the wordsmith when conversation veered from his stock sayings, replied "No" while looking steely ahead, flicked back on the music, and we drove home without another word. When I got to my room (without closing the door), I threw myself on my bed, landing uncomfortably on the book I had forgotten I'd left there, and began scrolling on my phone. My phone was the last vestige of my privacy, the one thing my dad didn't ask to look through.

With a knot in my stomach, I searched for the one app I knew I shouldn't be going on, and the orange icon flicked up on a black screen as it opened for the first time. Setting up a profile was easy when you weren't putting any information on it, just a picture of my jawline and collarbone that I thought would be far more alluring than one of my face. The profiles

I swiped through were bland and uninteresting: mostly middle-aged men who took better care of the dead fish in their profile pictures than they did of their own sense of style. I could practically smell the bait shop from my bed.

Which brings me to the biggest drawback of the countryside: there are far fewer people than in a city, and to get anywhere you have to drive. It would take me an hour's walking to meet with the closest person on this app, and I'd rather walk another hour to avoid meeting them. The man—my closest—had a profile that I struggled to believe could be attractive to anyone. His mouth was agape, like he was struggling to breathe, but his face was entirely relaxed. You could see the chip in his front tooth, and the scraggly beard scattered across his lower face, and his bio was equally off-putting: "`Be real. Not here for time wasters. Send xxx pic or blocked.`"

I looked at the copy of *Pride and Prejudice* I had got two chapters into before giving up, and wondered if Mr Darcy would have had a similar biography for a dating app. *Probably*, I concluded. A message popped up from the man and I opened it with a sense of dread unparalleled since I jumped out of the closet. Accompanied by a photo taken from the most distasteful angle of his erect penis buried underneath his furry potbelly was the message:

`Sexy. Wanna meet?`

I switched my phone off and threw it across the bed, praying to every God that the image would be cleansed from my mind and I would be reborn as I was a minute ago. If this was being gay, and if this was my first foray into gay dating, I might as well have never left the fucking closet in the first place.

When you're a horrendously depressed and recently out-and-single teenager, you get the same urges any teenage boy does, and when you've barely seen another human that wasn't your dad, your sister, or your middle-aged therapist Jo in weeks, you turn to the internet to satisfy your... *curiosity*.

I gingerly retrieved my phone, with the sad acknowledgement that I had to delete this app and never, ever open it again so long as people like that were allowed to send their willy out willy-nilly. As I closed my eyes to avoid reliving the experience of that photograph, a new message popped up from a profile that looked a lot more palatable to me.

`Heya :)`

The photo was of a young guy with a sharp jawline, hollow cheeks and moss-green eyes. The next few photos on his profile were him in various stages of undress, showing his skinny torso and defined abs with his phone covering his face in the mirror, but the last photo showed him lying on a park bench with a wide grin, shielding his eyes from the bright light. He was wearing a red and black plaid shirt with black skinny jeans and sleek trainers, and the sun glistened on his pale skin like an iridescent scale. His bio was to-the-point, like the other man's, with "Don't be creepy lol" followed by his age of 18 years and an arrow pointing up and down. It didn't take a cryptographer to decipher his meaning.

I replied:

`Hey, nice to meet you`

His next message asked me what I was on the app for, and I replied with a shrug emoji and a laughing face. Our conversation was pretty banal, just discussing our interests and the films we liked. I didn't mention my love for books in case it wasn't cool, and I inflated my love of old-school rock music just in case it was. As the discussion petered out, he sent a final message:

`Wanna talk somewhere else? You got socials?`

I did, and I told him as much. A few seconds later, a follow request popped up and I accepted and returned the favour. His social media was mostly your bland photos of sunsets, food and gigs, mixed in with one or two selfies that highlighted his abs and impeccable facial structure. His name was Lewis—I liked it and it suited him. He smiled in very few of his photos, just the last on his dating profile that I noticed was also posted a few months ago on his social media with a song lyric as the caption, but I liked his smile and the way his eyes crinkled and I imagined how his laugh would be harsh and rough, like a bark of unexpected joy. Somehow, so much time had passed just messaging this boy, this Lewis, and as I scrolled back further on his page, my sister was yelling my name for dinner. With a sigh, and an unexpected pit in my stomach, I tossed my phone onto the bedside table and went downstairs.

***

It became something of a ritual for Abbas. Every evening after he had finished his studies for the day—not that there was a formal school or anything to go to—he would grab his backpack, cram a couple of freshly baked flatbreads that his sister had prepared into it, and make a beeline down the valley to where a reservoir lay among the brush. Taking shade under a tree that had died many years ago but never fallen, Abbas would not have to wait long before Kharouf would appear beside him, throwing him a bottle of cold juice that he had swiped from his uncle's pantry along with a warm smile that melted the ventricles of Abbas's heart.

The boys would conduct a ritual before they would touch—pacing around the rim of the reservoir to ensure no one was hiding in the bushes or had fallen asleep under the pines. When they met back under the skeletal tree, Kharouf would be grinning with that adorably stupid little grin of his, and Abbas would be forced to break out laughing as he wrapped his arms around the boy's waist. They would kiss, softly at first and then harder and harder until they pulled apart, panting and sweating slightly under the hot sun. They would lie together, wrapped in each other's arms, taking dips in the reservoir when things got too hot, and then crawling back up the soft dirt under the tree to rest against its hollowed trunk and draw their fingers through each other's hair, across each other's bodies, tracing the muscles and the bones until each was a path well-worn that they could travel a billion times before becoming bored, if ever.

They would drink their juice and snack on the flatbreads until the sun drew down to an orange-pink haze behind the forested mountains. Under the cover of darkness, they would walk hand-in-hand back to the village, separating at every sound with a panicked gasp before giggling when they realised it was just an owl or a lizard. When they reached the edge of the first house, they would sneak a kiss if they could be sure that no one was watching, but otherwise they would part silently and quickly, Abbas running back up the path to his house while Kharouf watched his silhouette fade into shadows before heading to his home with his uncle.

Abbas found himself thinking about Kharouf constantly. His eyes, his hands, his shoulders and how his collar bone protruded from his slight frame, his black hair as soft as feathers, his long legs, his laugh that could only be described as a giggle. When they would lie together under the stars, Abbas would wrap his arms around the boy who rested his head on his chest and draw his fingers through his hair while Kharouf told him the stories his mother once told him when he was a child. Stories of princes and lions and beggars and maidens, of magic and moons and fires and rubies.

Most of them blurred together over the months, no matter how hard Abbas would listen with rapt attention, hanging on every word Kharouf said so he could replay them over and over in his voice at night when they couldn't be together. But one story stayed with Abbas, one that he would find himself thinking about in bored moments in class when his mind would wander, on walks back to his aunt's flat, and when he was fingering his guitar strings.

When Abbas gave me these examples, my heart ached knowing that another boy was on his mind.

The story was one of a wicked king who ruled over an evil empire that treated its people horribly. The king had inherited the throne from his father, who had ruled just as violently, if not more so, than his son. Over time, the king grew weary of his life, of the 'yes men' advisers who surrounded him, the scheming and feuding nobility in his kingdom, and of the fact that he went to bed in his opulent palace every night alone. One day, when he was meant to greet the Sultan of the neighbouring land he wished to conquer, instead he shaved his trademark beard and cut his long hair, took off his robes and his finery, dressing in the plain garb of his servants, and he walked out the front door without anybody recognising him.

He wandered the streets for hours on his own, confused by everything he saw: the people, his people, were miserable and tired. Everywhere he had been as a king had been draped in red and purple and golden sheets, with fresh paint and the finest jewels. Instead, here, he only saw people who didn't even look angry; they just looked hollow. When the clouds opened and the rain began to pour, the king took shelter in a merchant's shop. The merchant's daughter, a beautiful young woman, put a heavy and warm coat around his shoulders, ignoring his protests that he couldn't possibly pay for such a thing.

The king fell in love with the daughter, and they spent many days roaming the city and riding out into the countryside to see the beautiful rolling hills dappled with sunlight and the shimmering leaves of the forested peaks. After a while, the king began to wonder if anyone had even realised he was gone. He had heard nothing from anyone else that the king had disappeared, and he worried what it must mean for his people—the same people that had been mistreated by him and his family for generations—but the same people he had fallen in love with through the eyes of the merchant's daughter. One night, after gorging themselves on fruits and cheeses, the king confessed his identity to the daughter, who recoiled when she realised who her lover was. She screamed and cried at him, horrified that she had been so sweet to, and fallen in love with, a man who had done nothing but hurt people.

The king promised to her that he had never done anything—he had made no orders, no directions, no rules—that forced the abuse of his people. He wept as he told her he had simply sat by and done nothing while the regime was ruled instead by the doctrine of his dead father. He did not realise the extent to which people were hurt by him, and he promised her that in the morning he would return to the palace and he would take control of his government and restore the peace and hope to his country that her grandmother had once told her of. The merchant's daughter accepted his promise, and in return she swore that she would be by his side as he did as he had said.

The next morning, as he had promised, the king and the merchant's daughter walked hand in hand into the palace, where the king found his advisers in the throne room, standing around the empty chair and discussing their plots and misdeeds. The king told the men, who were all far older and wiser than he, that he had seen the harm done to his people, and he intended to stop the horrible things they were doing. Instead, the people would be free, and there would be no more war. The king introduced the merchant's daughter and proclaimed that he would marry her the next day to mark a new beginning for his reign and his country.

The advisers looked at each other with nasty grins and told the king that they would not permit him to do so. The king protested, reminding them that he was their ruler, and it was his decision that would be final. The advisers said in unison that they had kept the king's departure a secret from his people, and they had not noticed he was missing. The country could continue without its king, and they would be there to make sure it did so. The advisers gave the king a choice: he could return as king but he would not be permitted to make any changes and he would not be allowed to marry his lover, or he could leave with the merchant's daughter and never return to the palace. The king looked at his love and knew in that instant he could not survive without her beside him, as she had promised.

The king and the merchant's daughter left the palace and escaped to the countryside, where they set up a home among the rolling hills and swaying trees. The king forgot he was ever king, yet the merchant's daughter forever remembered his promise to her that he would change the way his kingdom was ruled. He had broken that promise, and though she loved him so, she could not allow the people to continue to be oppressed by their government. She gave her king an ultimatum that he could return as king and he could behead his advisers and he could bring peace to the nation, or he could stay in their home but without her.

Once again, the king knew he could not bear to live a day without her, and he promised to her that he would return the next day and he would take back his throne and bring about peace. The next morning, he rose with the merchant's daughter, donning the finest robes he had preserved when he fled the palace, and now with his beard and long hair regrown, the people gasped in astonishment as he rode through the streets of the city to the palace gates. He was greeted by the advisers who had chased him away with their threats the last time he was here. The men allowed the king to enter the grounds, but the merchant's daughter was not permitted to join him. He kissed her and promised her once again that he would rule with peace with her by his side.

Once in the palace, the advisers surrounded the king and, in one quick motion, they chopped off his head with a sword. As the king had no heir, they proclaimed to the kingdom that their king was dead and they would rule in his place. The merchant's daughter fell to her knees when she heard the news, and her father appeared next to her and dragged her as she sobbed back to their house where, until his death, he hid her away for fear that the advisers would kill her too.

Kharouf didn't remember what happened after that, but when he told Abbas the story one night as they lay under the tree, pointing up at the stars so far overhead, with Kharouf's head on Abbas's chest and Abbas's hands running through Kharouf's curls, Abbas felt his heart stop beating for a second. He knew that the boy lying next to him, lying on him, had so entangled himself in Abbas's heart that there would be no alternative for him. The pictures he had seen over the years flung through his head, with the brutality and atrocities he had seen during the wars, the deaths of his father and grandmother, how his aunt had fled the country, and how his sister had stopped speaking. He knew that the one he had fallen in love with, who had himself seen so much horror, would never be accepted by his country as his. Abbas, with a shiver of dread, pulled the boy closer and wrapped his arms around him, kissing him on his head, which brought a giggle from Kharouf.

Abbas took his phone out from his pocket and snapped a photograph of the water, knowing he would never be able to explain a photograph of the two of them. Kharouf snatched the phone off him, pointing it at Abbas, with the reservoir in the background behind a sandy shore, taking a photo of Abbas laughing in loving resignation. Kharouf handed the phone back, and Abbas looked at the photo: the first one he had seen of himself in years, and the first in his life with a smile so genuine. He gripped the boy in a tight hug.

"You deserve the gentlest love," he whispered into Kharouf's ear, and kissed him on the head as Kharouf turned his neck to look into Abbas's eyes.

C.

The War of Words

"These violent delights have violent ends And in their triumph die, like fire and powder."

—William Shakespeare, *Romeo and Juliet*

XXVI

The Heartbreak of Sodom and Gomorrah

The fact I can still barely bring myself to say his name is evidence enough of the fact I never loved Lewis. If you love someone, you want to sing and scream and shout about them every second. You want to envelop yourself in their world. You don't want to forget they ever existed, and you don't want to guard them and hide them from public view so no one else can see them or the scars they gave you, and no one can ever know how they broke you. But that didn't stop my heart from thundering every time a message from him popped up.

I had always been an avid texter, and as most texters know, you only have the capacity to text one person continuously. Trying to text one more would become a full-time job, rather than a full-time obsession. Whereas in the beginning I had compulsively texted Olivia, and then Marcus, and then no one, when the buzz of a new person flooded my veins, my fingers pounded away at my phone screen as Lewis and I made banal conversation about movies and music. He kept telling me he preferred video calls, but how ever I could, I would delay that happening. I preferred to text. To write.

The thing I remember about Lewis at the start was how he complimented me. He called me cute when I laughed. He told me he wished I was with him so he could see it in person. He reacted with a storm of heart emojis to every selfie I sent him, and I bathed in his attention, warming myself under his sun that kept on shining every moment of the day. I felt as though his hands were wrapped around me, and I fell asleep imagining I was wrapped in his embrace. I craved his affection, his praise, the feeling that I had been chosen by someone who was so above my station. That I should be grateful for every moment of his attention.

The first time I met Lewis in person, I had received sage advice from the few friends I had remaining after the Marcus incident. Mostly Saira, who had messaged me a few weeks after to check in and make sure I was okay and, as if we needed more proof I wasn't okay, I latched onto her and refused to let her leave. I wore my favourite white vest with a blue overshirt and skinny jeans. I put on the ring my grandfather had given me that had only just begun to fit on my finger, and I tied an old bracelet around my wrist. I slipped on the white trainers that had been scuffed to high heaven but were still my go-to for this outfit, and I closed my bedroom door on the way out.

The walk to the park didn't take long, and I was careful to have left early so I wouldn't break out in an embarrassing sweat in the heatwave that had struck our town that weekend. The air was still and as we reached the park, the sound of children laughing and screaming—*why are children always screaming?*—reached me, and the nerves pricked my skin. Lewis was there, as he said he would be, sitting on a bench by the entrance gate. He was shorter than I thought he would be in person, but just as beautiful as he was in pictures. His teeth were perfectly straight, whereas mine were awkwardly gapped in place, and his hair seemed perfectly styled in contrast to my increasingly messy bird's nest. He was wearing a plain blue t-shirt and black jeans with black trainers, but somehow the simplicity was mesmerising, and I scolded myself for having over-thought the outfit when clearly Lewis was more substance than style, though he wasn't lacking in the latter by any means.

I breathed a "Hi" that came out softer than I meant, and I

smiled awkwardly, reaching my hand out to shake his, whereas Lewis beamed at me, ignoring my outstretched hand, and wrapped me into a hug. My fingers were awkwardly jammed between our chests.

"It's so good to meet you," he said, holding me at arm's length as we separated, his hands on my shoulders. "You're even cuter in person."

I flushed a bright red, and he laughed. Somehow, even his laugh was perfect. I chuckled awkwardly, and he pulled me into him for another hug. He smelled of an aftershave I would never remember with a scent I would never forget, and I wrapped my arms around him, squeezing him a little to let him know I was happy for him to do it as much as he wanted.

The walk around the park started at midday, but it lasted eight hours, with conversation that somehow never ceased. We flowed from one conversation into another like a river winding its way through a valley. He told me about his family; a younger brother, his parents, and his grandparents, one of whom had emigrated here from South Africa, which is how he got half of his double-barrelled surname. He told me about his goal of studying at Oxford and working on the world stage; he told me about how his cousin was arrested, and how that spurred his interest in politics.

Somehow I found myself telling him things I never would tell anyone. I told him about Marcus and Olivia, and he listened sympathetically and laughed as I made self-deprecating jokes about the situation. I told him about Megan, and the accident, and how it still stays with me, and he interlaced his fingers with mine as I walked another lap of the park and he floated beside me.

"Floated?" Luce laughs.

"It felt like he was an angel. He wasn't real. He was so perfect, and so interesting, and so handsome, and so... perfect," I repeat with a half-hearted chuckle.

As the sun began to set and the park was flooded in our golden hour, our lap took us back to the gate, and Lewis paused, drawing me to a stop. I turned to look at him, and he was checking his phone. I had forgotten mine existed, and pulled it from my pocket too to see a couple of missed messages from Saira and my dad, and a news alert about some health food that I dismissed without a second glance.

Lewis looked at me apologetically and said that he had to go and meet his friends. They were all 18 and having something of a house party. He invited me, and though every inch of me longed to go, I made a polite excuse that I should be heading back home, and Lewis pulled me into his arms again. I buried my face in his skinny chest, feeling his sternum press against my nose, and when I pulled away, he wrapped me tighter, forcing a little grunt of surprise out of me. I closed my eyes and breathed in his aftershave, now mixed with his sweat. When he released me, I looked up into his eyes, and he smiled before pulling me in to kiss me softly on the lips.

As I walked home, I started to sing under my breath.

***

The walk home was silent for Abbas, as he considered the enormity of what he was feeling. His shoes dragged along the dusty trail back to his house on the hill and he discarded the concern that the white soles would scuff while thoughts of Kharouf floated through his mind. His heart was heavy and his soul hurt with the notion that anything could or would seek to separate him from the boy he had fallen in love with. Over the years of his young life, Abbas had barely considered boys, but now one boy consumed his every waking moment, and, like most first loves, Abbas had *no fucking clue* what to do with it. The sound of owls and crickets periodically broke the silence, with only the crunch of the gravel under Abbas's feet grinding against his ears until he stopped altogether and stood under the black sky, breathing in the cool night air with his eyes closed, trying to still his beating heart. It took another few deep inhales before Abbas felt eyes on the back of his head. He sighed, and turned around, tears ready to flood down his cheeks on meeting the stare of Kharouf, but instead he was faced with his brother, Suhail.

As Suhail had reached adulthood and stopped growing, he was no longer the scary big brother Abbas had grown up fighting. The stump where his hand should have been was still covered by a loose cotton wrap, but otherwise Suhail had grown back to his former self. His long black hair grazed his shoulders, with a stubble beard under his wide deep-set eyes and high brows, and cheekbones that could have cut a steak. Though he still had several years on Abbas, the younger could almost meet his eyeline, inch for inch, though as they stood in the night, the elder brother leant casually on his hip several feet further down the path to the town. Another screech of an owl pierced the uncomfortable silence.

"Hey, brother," Suhail said quietly, though his low voice seemed deafening.

"Hi," Abbas replied, breathing deeply into his chest.

"Where do you spend all these late nights?" Suhail asked, though his tone did not indicate a question.

"Alone. I just need to walk and get out of the house. I can't stay cooped up inside all day."

"Do you want to stay here?"

"What do you mean?"

Suhail gestured up the path to the house illuminated by lanterns. "Do you want to stay in this house with our family?"

"I don't know, man. What are you trying to say?"

A pregnant pause sat uncomfortably in the air between them.

"I know about you and that boy."

A sharp pain hit Abbas in his chest, and he tried to mask his wince, but Suhail's eyes narrowed slightly at the sharp intake of breath from his brother's nose. "What're you talking about?" Abbas asked, his voice shaking slightly towards the end of the sentence.

"You've been disappearing off at the same time every afternoon for weeks, Abbas. You don't tell anyone where you go; not that Mom or Jamila are going to ask," he chuckled breathily. "I was worried about you. You know all these fucking crazy people nowadays. I didn't want you getting mixed up with them."

"I thought you were one of the crazy people," Abbas shot back with a forced smile.

"Don't change the subject, baby brother. I was worried about you, so yesterday when you left—after stealing our bread, by the way—I followed you. I followed you up to the reservoir and I saw you and that boy. I saw you talking with him, and I watched you lie together, and you kissed."

The only word that spun around Abbas's mind was *'Fuck'*.

"I guess that's what you've been sneaking out and doing every day for weeks?" Suhail asked, but again, his tone did not indicate a question; it was more a resigned sigh.

Abbas's heart was pumping faster and faster. His hands were starting to prick with pins-and-needles, and sweat pierced through his forehead. His breathing was slowly getting shallower and shallower. Suhail stepped towards him, and Abbas flinched.

"I know what it's like to do something no one else wants you to do. I know what it's like to suffer for it." Suhail raised his stump with a grimace. "People here will not be kind to you if they find out, Abbas. People will kill you for that. God, they will kill you for so much less than that." He took another step forward, and this time Abbas was motionless, staring at him with wide eyes. "If you carry on with this, with him…"

"Kharouf," Abbas croaked. Names matter. They're what give you your humanity. Why do you think the Nazis made sure to take them away? He couldn't let Kharouf go without his name.

"With Kharouf," Suhail continued, "Then you can't stay here, okay?"

"I can't stay here?" Abbas felt a tear burst from his eye, and pinched his lids closed as he tensed his jaw and clenched his fists, hoping to stem the oncoming flood. He felt Suhail's hand on his upper arm.

"You're my brother, Abbas," Suhail whispered. "I need you to be safe. I need you to be sensible. If you want to keep doing this with Kharouf, then you won't be safe here. If you want to keep seeing him, you have to leave. Both of you. You have to go somewhere it is safe, okay?"

Abbas dropped his head to the floor and felt more tears breach the barrier and roll down his cheeks. Suhail wrapped him in a hug, and his body started to wrack with sobs. "I love him," Abbas cried, and Suhail held him tighter.

"If you love him, then for both your sakes, for my sake, too, you have to go. Please don't get into any trouble here, brother. I can't see you get hurt."

His brother held him as Abbas cried and cried harder and harder. The tears flowed freely, streaking his face as he buried himself in his brother's arms. Suhail held him silently, his grip on his brother not loosening even a little as Abbas sobbed for the first time in years.

The next morning, Abbas awoke in his bed with the sun creeping in through his shutters, and his eyes stung from the unwelcome light. His first thought was of Kharouf. He couldn't get the boy out of his head, but then the memory of Suhail dawned on him. Though Abbas had no loyalty to his country anymore, he knew Kharouf did from the way he spoke of his mother and her stories, his father and his garden. When they had gazed at the stars, Abbas had spoken of a map guiding them to a distant land, but Kharouf had giggled and pulled his eyes back down to earth. Kharouf was determined they would find a way; they would stay with each other, in their home, and stay in each other's arms. Abbas couldn't leave with Kharouf when the boy's heart could never be away from his home. Abbas didn't know how his mind and body could physically hurt from this, but he lay in his bed, pained at the very thought of his hopelessness. Of all the people, he had to fall in love with the dreamer. The peacemaker. The optimist. A *boy*.

***

The clouds were unpleasant in the sky, and I stared cautiously at them as I left the house without a waterproof jacket. My outfit wouldn't permit my god-awful grey cagoule, and I couldn't let something as stupid as rain ruin my aesthetic. Dad had watched with raised eyebrows in silent judgement as I tousled my hair in front of the mirror, running in my mind through all the things I had to talk about that would make me sound cool and sexy. I replayed my last conversations with Lewis in my head over and over: his offhand comment that he liked me with looser t-shirts and his dream of becoming a diplomat at the UN. I had spent all night reading Wikipedia articles of major foreign policy officials, from Boutros Boutros-Ghali to Henry Kissinger (whom Lewis idolised), memorising key facts about every single one that I could sprinkle into a conversation that I would artfully choreograph to highlight my newfound expertise. I left the house in a baggy white tee and grey skinny jeans that hugged my legs in a way that made me hate them a little less than usual, and I began the walk into town.

Lewis had invited me to chill at his house and watch some TV, an invitation I had eagerly accepted over message, and instantly relayed the news to Saira, who responded with some unwanted advice about not going too fast. I loved the girl—my only friend—but her comments enraged me. *How could she think I don't know what I'm doing? She knows how much I like him. I'll do whatever the fuck I want with him.*

It was a little too late before I realised I would actually do whatever the fuck he wanted me to do.

Lewis's house was a semi-detached brick monstrosity with a manicured lawn surrounded by pruned rose bushes and off-putting ornaments. I banged the brass knocker three times against the moss green door and waited for it to open, anxiously checking my phone to confirm I had the right house. A few moments later, the door opened.

"I wish I didn't remember it," I say to Luce, who watches with a glint of glee in his eyes. He wants me to tell this story. I know he does. I know he is absolutely fucking living for the drama, the gossip, the tea, and I know he loves how it feels like my insides are being eaten by maggots and my flesh is rotting off my bones. I know he likes how much I hate it.

"You have to tell it, kid."

I want to vomit.

Lewis stood in the doorway wearing some grey joggers—the kind that draw your eye right to the VPL (the male version)—and a black shirt of some band I had tried to enjoy but couldn't bring myself to. I decided I wouldn't mention it in case I wouldn't be able to fake it for him like I wanted to. He greeted me with a wide smile and a hug. He smelt like ash—the kind you get from wood, not cigarettes—and he buried my head in his skinny chest again. I breathed in deeply.

Lewis's house was big and empty. His parents were out for the day, and his older sister had long since moved to university in Edinburgh to study advertising. I didn't mention the fact it wasn't a real degree. I smiled and looked around awkwardly. It was like nobody lived there at all: everything was perfectly in its place with no clutter, no dust, no... *emotion.* You could have plastered it straight from a magazine page. The art on the walls was tasteful and personality-free, and the books on the shelves were suitably generic: a handful of classics, cheap thrillers, and self-help garbage. The temperature was a few degrees too cold. Through the hall I could see into the kitchen, and then into the garden. Nothing about it felt right.

I start to cry.

We walked into the kitchen and he opened the fridge to grab me a bottle of cider. This was the second time I had met Lewis in person, after about two months of talking every single day. I watched him as he popped the caps off of each with a stainless steel opener pulled from one of those drawers with the silent-close technology that my parents had always envied in peoples' homes. I sipped the sickly sweet liquid and hid my grimace as Lewis watched me intently. I made some comment about something, I don't remember what, and he chuckled. I relaxed a little and moved a step closer to him. He put his hand on my hip and took a gulp of cider from the bottle, where condensation was already clinging to the glass like mould.

He took my hand in his and turned, leading me up the carpeted stairs lined with photos of his family taken in one of those portrait studios. He was a handsome kid even back then, and I looked at his back as I followed him, the way his lean frame moved under his clothes, his athletic gait, the way his hair barely shifted as he walked. He was 18 and still had the body of a teenager. I wondered for a second what he would look like in ten years, or twenty, but couldn't picture his face. When we reached his bedroom, he opened the door without a sound—everything in this house seemed so silent—and led me in.

His room was big. He was rich, clearly, which explained his understanding that he simply would be studying at a top university with a prestigious career ahead of him. He had some odd knick-knacks on his shelf, from a small football trophy from a primary school match to a model of a video game character I had never heard of. A wide window looked out onto the back garden and the rows of houses behind it. There was a small pond at the back of the square of grass, and for a brief second it reminded me of my grandparents' house where my mum lived.

He dropped himself onto the bed effortlessly and somehow made it seem sexy and cool. He placed the cider bottle on a coaster, and shuffled across, making room for me on the pillow beside him. I smiled, looking at his hand patting the fabric, and sat down next to him. He wrapped his hand around my shoulder and pulled me into him. His collarbone dug into my neck and my arm was awkwardly crushed between us, but I didn't say anything. He kissed the top of my head.

I remember my heart was beating so fast. *I loved Lewis*, I told myself. I loved him and this is what I wanted. I hadn't even sent him nudes, nor had he sent me anything more scandalous than a shirtless picture where, in the lighting, he had looked more toned than skinny. I breathed in his ashy scent and closed my eyes, intent on remembering the warmth of his skin on mine, the pressure of his body wrapped around me, the way his thumb traced small circles on my back. All the things I wish I could now forget.

"You'll be good to me," he whispered.

I wasn't sure if he meant to say it aloud to me or just to himself, and for some reason the Tina Turner song burst into my head, ruining the carefully crafted presentation of the memory I was scorching into my mind, forcing myself to remember everything I thought I wanted. I wriggled deeper into his embrace and he kissed the top of my head again, then pulled my face up as he closed his eyes and pushed his mouth against mine. The taste of the sickly-sweet cider lingered on my tongue.

Kharouf seemed quiet that day, Abbas remembered. As their eyes met across the reservoir and they stalked the perimeter for intruders, Kharouf walked with his head pointed firmly at the ground. Abbas arrived about 5pm, but Kharouf didn't turn up for another three hours. This wasn't too unusual; sometimes their schedules and families did not permit them to meet at the same time, but they knew the other would be there waiting for them when they finally showed up. The summer was slowly turning into autumn and Abbas had worn a light linen shirt with the sleeves rolled down. Kharouf was wearing a pair of khakis and a more formal shirt than Abbas had seen him wear before, and when they reached the hollowed tree, it was the first thing Abbas asked Kharouf after they had embraced.

"It's the anniversary of my parents' death," he explained, his tone monotonous and emotionless, and Abbas nodded awkwardly. Despite his father having died, the grief had long since passed, and Abbas felt completely unqualified to be giving advice or comfort to an orphan when he, at least, still had a mother.

The pair sat down in silence, Kharouf picking a speck of dirt off his ironed purple shirt. The colour suited him and Abbas found himself staring at the boy beside him, reminding himself again how lucky he was. He decided not to mention the conversation he had had with his brother the day before—not today, at least.

They had spoken in the abstract before about leaving, but Kharouf was resolute in his desire to stay in his home country. When he told the story of the king and the merchant's daughter, he reminded Abbas that they could not run away from their problems. Even if they were killed, they had to stay and try to change things for the better. *Even if they were killed.*

The wind started to pick up a little, and the boys watched a pair of swifts dart about on the currents, twirling with speed and ease until they disappeared into specks in the sky. Abbas pulled Kharouf closer to him, under his shoulder. Kharouf leant his head on Abbas's shoulder and sighed. Abbas had brought some flatbreads along with him, as usual, and a plastic bottle of juice, but they remained in his bag, forgotten as the pair sat in silence with the enormity of the world around them.

The silence was broken.

We were on the third or fourth cider before Lewis suggested we move to something stronger. Music was playing, though I hadn't registered when he had turned it on, and I didn't recognise what it was either. I lay on the bed awkwardly, unsure of where the fuck I could put my hands that was a normal position, while Lewis ran down the stairs and came back a few moments later with a bottle of what looked to be the cheapest vodka ever produced. He poured generous servings into two neon pink plastic cups and the first sip confirmed that it was, in fact, crap. I looked over at Lewis as I winced from the burn in my throat and found him staring back at me with a smile on his face. His eyes looked pitch black. Or maybe that's just how I've chosen to remember it.

At least I remember that. Everything that came next is a haze.

A loud shout from behind Abbas and Kharouf scared them shitless. They leapt to their feet, slipping slightly on the sandy gravel surrounding the water, and their necks swinging rapidly to find the offender. Abbas can't remember what he said, or if he said anything, but he remembers what came next. There was a man with a potbelly and thick chest hair curling out from under a hideous striped mustard shirt, and he was shouting at them both, ringing off one string of Arabic after the next. Abbas's heart was pounding so hard that even though the early evening had been so quiet, he could no longer hear himself think. The thought of the swifts flying burst into his head, and no matter how hard he tried, he couldn't cram it out. Kharouf was running towards the man, closing in the several metres between them in seconds, and Abbas saw him grab the man's forearms as the stranger flailed wildly, so violently that for a second Abbas didn't know if Kharouf would remain on the ground or be thrown into the air. The younger boy was talking quickly and quietly as the man raged and in the blur, Abbas could only pick out certain phrases, or rather one phrase that the man was repeating over and over: "I knew it, you fag. You filthy fag."

Abbas was frozen to the spot with his eyes wide and his heart continuing to thump. He tried to take a step forward to go to Kharouf but his feet wouldn't move.

As the man yelled louder and louder obscenities, Kharouf's grip on his arms was loosening, and eventually the boy was thrown to the ground. Without pausing in his tirade, the man looked down at Kharouf and started kicking him wildly. Abbas could hear the beat of his boot against Kharouf's ribs as loud as he could hear the beat of his own heart. But still he could not move.

Kharouf had scrambled to his feet and back to Abbas, his shirt now smeared with yellowish mud. The boy was bleeding from his nose. Abbas didn't know if the man had hit him. He must have.

"It's my uncle. You have to go," Kharouf said, his eyes locked onto Abbas's.

Abbas stared back frantically, desperate to say something, do something, but finding himself paralysed. His eyes flicked over to the man—Kharouf's uncle—and saw he was marching closer, but his words had become muffled to Abbas.

"Abbas. You have to go." Kharouf was touching Abbas. His hands were on his shoulders and his eyes—those big deep brown eyes—were fixed on Abbas. In the light, they almost looked golden.

A hand smacked down on Kharouf's shoulder and wrenched Kharouf back, throwing him down onto the floor.

"GO!" Kharouf screamed, and Abbas finally found his legs moving before he realised what was happening. He was running, sprinting, back down the path he had taken, back up the road to his house. His muscles were shrieking at him as he burst through the front door. His mother and his brother snapped their necks in his direction—Abbas didn't know where his sister was—and his eyes fixed on his brother's. Suhail stood up suddenly and walked towards the panting younger brother.

"Kharouf..." Abbas whispered, and Suhail dragged him into another room.

I think I remember him kissing my neck. I remember my neck feeling wet and cold, like he'd licked it or something. I remember laughing. I remember him smacking my phone out of my hands as I tried to reply to a message from Saira, and I remember him tossing it behind the stack of pillows on his headboard. I remember him laughing at my drunk protestations, and I remember him batting away my playful swipes before pinning my wrists to the mattress with his hands. I remember looking into his eyes and how they looked so... *hungry*.

I wish I remembered more. I wish I knew what happened. I wish I could relive every single fucking God-awful minute it. I wish it wasn't all just in my head.

"I wish, I wish, I wish," Luce whispers. I don't know why he says that.

I remember waking up the next morning. That's the next thing I remember. My face had been buried in his sheets and when I opened my eyes they were so white. The curtains were still open. I don't know if they had been open all night. My feet were cold as well. My whole body was cold. I was only wearing my boxers, which I didn't understand. I didn't—I don't—remember taking anything off. *I wouldn't have*, I told myself. This was the second time I had met Lewis. *I've never had sex with anyone. I wouldn't do this.*

A hand wrapped around my shoulder and pulled me back. Lewis ensnared me in his arms again and I was trapped again against his ribcage. He kissed my neck, and I lay there motionless, just so confused.

Abbas had probably managed to articulate about three words before Suhail started throwing stuff into his bag. Abbas stared at it, dumbfounded. He didn't remember picking it up from where he had tossed it by the reservoir, but there it was, on his bedroom floor. Suhail balled up and crammed shirts, boxers, socks, trousers into it. Their mother stood in the door, asking repeatedly what was happening, but the boys ignored her.

He kept mumbling, "Kharouf?" but Suhail didn't even look up. He grabbed Abbas by the arm and hauled the boy through to the kitchen, pushing past Fatima, whose voice was creeping to a higher and higher pitch. Suhail climbed up on the counter and started rummaging in the boxes above the cabinet. Frustrated but silent, he began to pull the boxes off, dropping them on the floor with their contents pouring out: serviettes, Fatima and Shabaz's wedding cutlery, index cards with recipes scrawled on in Gidda's spidery handwriting. Fatima started screaming, pushing past Abbas who was still standing there quietly mumbling Kharouf's name increasingly desperately, and she pulled at Suhail's arm as he shook her off. Eventually, he found what he was looking for: a small shoebox with bundles of notes inside. Suhail grabbed at the money, stuffing it into the bag on top of Abbas's clothes.

Abbas finally managed to croak loud enough to pause the chaos before him: "Kharouf, Suhail."

Suhail closed his eyes and exhaled deeply. He zipped up the rucksack, and walked over to Abbas, putting his hand on his shoulder. "You have to go," Suhail said and tears started pouring down Abbas's cheeks even as he did not sob.

"Go?" Fatima shrieked. She threw herself on Abbas, yelling loudly that no one was leaving.

That was the only time he had ever seen a man raise their hand on his mother. When Suhail hit her, she fell with a cry to the marble floor.

That morning was eerie. It felt so wrong. I laid in Lewis's clammy arms, trying to work out what had happened, and coming up completely blank. After what felt like an eternity, Lewis released me from his grip and, with another kiss on my neck that prickled my skin, he padded out of the room and to the bathroom. I sat up, watching him go, and then grabbed my shirt that I saw lying in a pile by the bed. I pulled it over my head and began the hunt for my jeans, trying to do it as silently as possible so I could hear when Lewis was coming back.

"Why?" Luce asks.

I didn't want him to catch me off-guard. I wanted him to come back and find me fully dressed. I wanted him to come back and find me the way I wanted to be found. I didn't want him to come back at all, but if he had to, which I guess he did in his own house, it had to be at least a little on my own terms.

I heard the bathroom door click open and I hurriedly pulled the jeans up the rest of my legs, and managed to button them closed in time for Lewis to walk through the door. He smiled at me.

"Do you have to go?"

I smiled back and nodded. "I ought to get back, yeah." I paused. "Sorry."

"Can't stay a little longer?" He collapsed on the bed next to me, laying his head on my chest. He was still only in his underwear. I didn't look at him.

"Sorry, I didn't mean to spend the night."

"Yeah, we got a bit carried away," he laughed. I chuckled hollowly along with a vacant smile. "*We*"?

"I should just be getting back, y'know?"

"Alright, your call, baby." He lifted his head and kissed me again on the lips. He still smelt like woody ash. I sat there motionless until he had unlatched himself.

I walked home like I was in a fugue state. Like this was the first time I had ever walked home. It was still relatively early morning, and on a weekend, barely anyone was around. I wish I had brought my headphones with me, to drown out the silence where there should have been so much noise.

XXVII

Tread Carefully. Here Lies a Lover

The days after that passed slowly, yet all too quickly. My phone buzzed unanswered with messages and missed calls from Saira, from Lewis, from my mum, but I would swipe the notifications as soon as they appeared. I couldn't bear to face Saira, whom I hated with every fibre of my being for encouraging me with Lewis, and yet the thought of whom still stung with regret and embarrassment, as though I had let her down by failing to have a happy ending with the first boy I had ever sort-of dated. I couldn't reply to Lewis, whose messages got progressively more aggressive:

`Why aren't you replying to me?`

`Are you embarrassed?`

`Fuck you. You wanted it too. You just liked the attention, didn't you?`

`Whore.`

There was a message from Ella, Lewis's friend, saying that I needed to reply to him, saying that I was being cruel by ignoring him. I had never even met her before, but her messages made me cry more than the rest.

My mum's solitary message: "Hi darling, how is everything?" hung like an execution in the air before me. She didn't even know I was gay yet, so how could I even begin to tell her anything? Lois had long gone. My dad didn't talk about this sort of stuff. My sister blamed me already for not telling her about Marcus. I was alone.

I wanted to reply to them. I swear I did. I wanted to scream at them all, I wanted to hit them until they stopped moving, until the blood stained their face and my fists. I wanted to cry until the sobs hurt my lungs. I wanted to stand on a stage in the spotlight and I wanted to read out my list of sins. I wanted to wake up from this nightmare and to be a kid again, back when I was too young to understand that I was a bad person. I wanted to break every single person who had the nerve to stand before me. I wanted them to combust with a tensing of my muscles. I wanted, for once, to have power instead of having it taken from me.

"What happened?" Luce asks, and I tell him the honest truth, for once.

"I told so many people so many things about Lewis," I say, my heart aching like it had run a marathon. "I told them we had a falling out, that we hadn't spoken much for a while, that we were actually still friends. I never told them what he did."

"What did he do?"

"I don't know." The words scald me as I say them out loud. "I remember my heart beating fast, I remember my leg throbbing and my foot going numb, like my body was begging me to leave but cutting off the very means of doing so. I remember drinking cheap vodka and it burning my throat, and I remember him staring at me with eyes that glistened and flashed with darkness. I remember how he poured one drink after the other, laughing at me when I said I didn't want any more. I remember him placing his hand under my chin and lifting it up so I was looking him in the eyes. I remember him pushing his lips against mine and how it felt like every single part of me that mattered disappeared. I remember his tongue searching inside my mouth while my soul hollowed out. But I don't remember what he did. I don't know if he…" the sentence hangs in the air. "I don't know if he did."

I wish there was a more eloquent way to put it. I wish I could say it like how I have seen it in the movies or in the songs or how I have read it in countless books. I wish I could put it on paper in a way that makes me feel seen, rather than in a way that makes me hate myself more than I did before.

"Did you tell Abbas?" Luce asks, and for a second I feel like I could fall into his arms.

I shake my head without a word.

"May I ask you a question?" Luce says, and I nod silently. He is standing opposite me at his despatch box and I sit huddled on my bench. "Do you know what Abbas wrote in his witness statement?"

"His witness statement?" I ask, looking up at the man.

"For his asylum application. He submitted a witness statement that set out his story and why he had to leave Syria."

"Oh. Yeah. No, I don't."

Luce reaches inside his blazer pocket and pulls out a folded sheet of paper. "This isn't the whole thing," he says, as he sees me watching him. "The whole thing is about 80 pages long. It's all about his childhood, his grandmother, his father, the war, his brother, his sister, everything. This is the final page.

"In his final interview that he did with Mary for her to take his statement, she asked him two questions: What would happen if you went back to Syria, and what would you want your life to be like if you stayed in the UK?

"He refused to answer those questions. He said he needed to think about it, and he wanted to write it himself. He said he couldn't say it out loud because he needed to think about it carefully. But the truth is, he didn't need to think about it carefully. He didn't need to consider it. He knew exactly what his answers would be, because those are the two questions he had been asking himself since the day his brother drove him across the border to Turkey and to the airport with a bag full of loose change and clothes, still with a couple of squashed flat-breads and a bottle of apple juice crammed at the very bottom. After he threw up out the window of the car because Suhail refused to stop, even for a minute, while a song on the radio kept repeating the lyric "*Run, run, run, run, run*" and Abbas can't remember what song it was, but those words still haunt him.

"Those are the questions he asked himself as he looked out the plane window as they took off. They are the questions he asked himself as he landed in the UK, and as he took the train to see his aunt on an address that Suhail had scribbled on the back of an envelope he found in the glovebox of the car; as he was on the phone to Suhail days later, finding out that Kharouf had gone missing. Then finding out that his body had been found, riddled with bruises and gashes and cuts, with the only clear patches of skin being where the tears had washed away the blood. They are the questions Abbas never stopped thinking about as he never stopped blaming himself for doing, for *being* nothing.

"So he didn't need time to prepare. He just wanted to write it himself. He wanted to be the person to say it out loud, in his own words. He wanted to grapple with the enormity of what had happened, in a way that he had tried for so long to hide."

Luce looks at me, but I am staring at the floor.

"This is what he wrote, kiddo:

> *I dream that if I return to Syria, I will find Kharouf waiting for me. We will embrace and kiss and I will look into his deep, beautiful, brown eyes and tell him I love him, that everything is okay and I am here now. I will feel the touch of his hand, the warmth of his body, and the softness of his skin. I'll hear his laugh again, and see his smile light up the world like a sunrise across the desert. I will hold him tighter, closer than I ever let him get before. I will beg for his forgiveness and promise him that everything he*

deserves will be his. I will take him by the arm and we will, one by one, show everyone in that whole goddamn country that our love is just as pure, just as perfect as anyone else's. And we will build a life together there, among the olive trees, until we are ready to pass into heaven, hand in hand.

But the truth is that if I return to Syria, I will find Kharouf dead. Maybe he is buried in an unmarked grave or maybe his body will just have been discarded and left to the jackals. He will be gone because I was not brave enough to do something, anything to save him. There will be no forgiveness, no redemption, nothing to beg or cry for. They will kill me too in the most brutal way, and what is more is that I will not care. I do not intend on living in that country without him, and I will be happy because at least then I will be with him in death.

If I stay in England, I will spend the rest of my life wishing I was in his arms and dreaming about him every night. Every second, I will hide from the world under the fortress I built from the stones that rained down on him. I will live a quiet life in England, in the knowledge that my one great love story was stolen from me abruptly and unfairly so many years ago. Maybe one day I will have a family of my own and maybe I will give my son the name of Kharouf. Maybe one day I will tell him of the boy who shared his name: the boy with a heart so pure and a love so great they had to kill him rather than confront that they will never be able to understand it themselves. The boy who deserved the gentlest love and was met with the world's ugliest fury. The lamb with whom the lion fell in love.

My Kharouf.

I stand up and walk from the room.

***

Rebecca is standing by the door as I leave and I almost knock her over with the force of my stride. She lets out a small cry.

"Shit, sorry, are you okay?"

She brushes the hair from her eyes and looks up at me without a trace of a frown on her face. "I heard what you were talking about in there."

I nod grimly, looking around to avoid her gaze.

"Is Abbas the reason you don't want to go back?"

My head swivels to look at her—the deep fucking ache in my heart replaced momentarily by the bittersweet release of confusion. "What?"

"Is Abbas why you don't want to go back?"

"What are you on about?"

"Is it because he's still in love with that boy?"

That boy. The words sting like vinegar dropped onto an open wound.

Sometimes I feel my world is taken up by that boy. If it's not Marcus, it's Lewis. If it's not Lewis, it's Abbas. If it's not Abbas, it's Kharouf. *That boy.* Would it ever be so fucking hard for me to be that boy for once? For me to be the sun that they all revolve around, rather than being tossed from one orbit to another like an asteroid that's just waiting to enter an atmosphere, *any* atmosphere, to burn up. My heart flares. I don't even know this kid, and yet my life—fuck that, my death—is becoming defined by him. By his life. By his death. By his fucking love story.

"I hate him," I say, my eyes dropping to the floor in slow realisation.

"Who?" Luce asks. We're back in the Commons and I don't know how or when I got here. It feels like I've been stuck in my brain for an eternity since I saw Rebecca.

"I hate all of them. I hate them all."

"Kiddo," he says softly and I look up at him. He's staring at me softly with his deep brown eyes. His expression is so gentle I want to cry. "We have one more story. Then we have to decide."

I don't even need to ask. I know exactly what he means. I nod.

XXVIII

Better Safe Than Lorry

It's a ridiculous saying. My dad came up with it when I was a kid and I remember him using it as far back as my memory goes. Before we'd cross a road, my dad would squeeze my hand and say, "Wait, kid. Better safe than lorry." We'd then check to the left and to the right before we concluded with a synchronous nod and grin that we could once more step into the breach. It's devastatingly ironic that, given the circumstances, the thing that would bring me here, to the Commons, the Interlife, and to Luce, would be the one thing my dad would always warn me about.

Wait, kid. Better safe than lorry.

***

Somehow, I had started my final year of school with a positive attitude. It was the first time ever. I had no nerves walking into form on my first day, greeting Tom, Alonso, Lukas and Liam with a smile and slaps on the back. They discussed their summers with outrageous stories and much ado about nothing, and I joined in the laughter when Lukas recounted his horror story of losing his virginity to Cath and having his younger brother walk in—and I quote—"mid-stroke" (once he finally got it up, that is). Mr Nathwani grimaced at overhearing the news, which brought another chorus of hooting laughter from us all. The other three were still single, though Tom was heavily compensating for it in the amount of people he had made out with at a club the night he turned 18; the first among us to hit the milestone.

When Abbas walked in, the four boys cheered and Abbas did a mock victory dance for his adoring fans, myself included. I stood from my perch on a desk and met him in his walk across the room. I wrapped my hands around his waist and kissed him 'Hello', even though we had seen each other two days before. Mock 'aw's filled the room, led by Tom to Alonso's chastisement. Abbas shook his head with a grin.

The school days passed pretty quickly, with endless coursework, exam prep, and university applications. I was applying to study politics, of course, while Tom went with psychology (fitting for a psycho), Alonso was looking at fine art schools on the continent, Lukas was torn between biochemistry and biomedical sciences (the difference between which I'm still not sure), and Liam had taken an apprenticeship in an architecture firm. Abbas was the only mystery: he remained mum when pressed by our friends and teachers, and it was only after weeks of personal statement drafting that he confessed to me he was torn between engineering or English literature.

He told me he wanted to build something that would last. I said I understood, and there were very valid arguments for both courses, but as a humanities student through and through, I was of course secretly wishing he would choose English. I knew he admired engineering, with its precision and efficiency, and I'd seen him bury his head in complex calculations for hours before coming up for air. But I'd never seen him relax as he did when he was reading. When he opened the latest battered charity shop copy of a novel and lost himself in thought, with his body twisting in contortions that could only feel comfortable when you were transported to a whole other world. In truth, I knew what literature had done for me and what it had done for Abbas, and how it bonded us together. Books had saved my life, just like Abbas had. Well, until the end.

The end began as it always does: with a day like every other. There would be nothing you could use to distinguish it from anything else at first, until your world comes crashing down around you. It's not like a tsunami, when you see the animals fleeing for higher ground, or like a hurricane when the winds gradually pick up speed around you. It's like an explosion: complete normality, followed in an instant by utter destruction.

If I had known what was coming, I think I would have paused a little, and thought about things a bit more. I would have remembered which cereal I had for breakfast, which underwear I put on, which playlist pumped through my headphones on my bus ride to school. I would have messaged my mum, just to say 'Hi'—I wouldn't have wanted to worry her, but I wanted her to know how she was always on my mind. I would have given my dad a hug before I left, with no words needed to be spoken. I would have probably given my sister a bit of a rest, instead of sarcastically sniping at her while she rolled her eyes and gave me the finger. I would have scrolled back on my social media and seen the countless photos of me and my friends: from Saira, who I, for no reason other than my own shame, hadn't spoken to in over a year, to Lukas, Liam, Alonso, and Tom. I would have rubbed my dogs' heads and given their belly a scratch as they rolled around on the kitchen floor as I made breakfast. I would have straightened my school tie, and maybe shaved a little closer.

But instead, my last day only became important when it was too late.

The weather had turned freezing, with a frost gripping the town for the last week that it could not shake, with perpetual ice warnings on the roads and salt on the pavements. The winter sun burned down on the biting cold and turned my cheeks red as I pumped out steam before being assaulted by the moist heat of the classroom. I took my place among my friends and tried to concentrate on the last few scenes of *Romeo and Juliet* that I needed to annotate before English class that afternoon. I had never been a fan of Shakespeare, and studying his works was my least favourite aspect of English, but I couldn't let Mr Wilson down; I'd hate to be the reason his enthusiasm finally waned. *Fuck it*, I thought, *I'll just copy from Abbas.*

But Abbas didn't show up that morning.

Politics dragged on as Abbas didn't reply to my texts asking where he was. Mr Whyssler called my name twice, and I was left stumped, having completely ignored the question both times. His squirrelly face gave me a disapproving stare, but I quickly went back to looking out the window, wondering where Abbas could be. It's hard to balance not appearing to be needy when you're naturally a very needy person, and though we hadn't argued since the debate incident, I lived with the perpetual worry that one day he would stop speaking to me again.

Mr Wilson's English class started late, as he hurried in 10 minutes after the lesson began, with a red-faced apology and a stack of marked essays that it looked like he had only just finished. It was our *Jane Eyre* work. Apparently we hadn't been "engaging" enough with the text, and in a fit of desperation—with only six months to go until the exam!—he had assigned us the task of producing a creative work inspired by our favourite *Jane Eyre* quote. Mine was a short story about painfully enduring a smart in which the protagonist found himself in a situation where he wanted to do nothing more than scream, but had to sit in silence and watch his world fall apart. *Sound familiar?*

He handed them out, giving generous compliments on the papers as he did so, and I was sure to notice with some poorly disguised relish that the praise he gave to Tony was far beneath that which he bestowed onto me. He particularly liked the parallels I had drawn between the heteronormativity of the modern day with the patriarchal themes that penetrated Brontë's work. I thanked him with a smile and turned to the back to see the grade I had been given: an A. I nodded in approval.

"It's a dear shame that our Abbas couldn't be here. I think his was one of the best pieces of writing I have seen in a long time." He slapped his sheets down on the desk beside me with the instruction to pass them onto him when I see him next. I don't know if he knew we were boyfriends or if he just knew we sat next to each other in his class. What teachers know about their students, what they discuss and gossip about behind the staff room door, is the perennial schoolhouse mystery.

I glance over at his essay with curiosity, and find myself unable to look away. That was the first sign the day was going to go wrong.

Abbas had written a poem entitled *Reader, I married him.* Perhaps the most famous quote from *Jane Eyre*, but nonetheless one that I didn't realise Abbas would have written about. I can still feel, in the memory, the pit in my stomach choking my heart. The words seared through me with visions of Lewis and Marcus. Of Abbas and Kharouf. He deserved the A* he was awarded. I *knew* he had to pick literature.

<u>Reader, I married him.</u>
Abbas Rahim

What hold he has on me
His hands are open but grasp my heart
until my pulse stutters and faults
Reader, I love him
But we both understand he forgets I am here
It is with a glimpse of surprise he remembers
When something forces the memory upon him

Reader, I remember him
With every train that passes through my mind
With every step and every breath
The pit inside me deepens and churns
The black he cannot see, that I keep hidden
The tumultuous waters and currents within
What a hold I keep on him Desperate to not let him go

His life moves on and changes and fades
With every fresh morning, I grasp at the blades
Tugging halfheartedly for him to withdraw
But the very thing that pains me so
is what stops me bleeding out, reader
Reader, I can't

Reader, I can't
With every song he sings,
whether of triumph or heartbreak
I feel the music in my skin, and I cannot mute it
I long for the silence, the absence of my guilt and regret
But the melody crawls into the crevices of my skin
and embeds itself in my muscles
With every note, he shreds me

With every note, I shred the memory of him
But the mosaic it leaves is too beautiful, too painful to look away
He morphs into dragons and beasts and nightmares that haunt me,
but eventually the scattered pages will flutter like petals in a breeze
They soothe, and seduce and slay me.
I burn the pages. I kiss the ashes.

Reader, I bury him. Reader, he buries me.

***

"You remember now how it happened, don't you?" Luce asks, and I nod quietly. My leg aches and throbs with waves of pins and needles, and I try to ignore it, but every time my emotions flare, it comes back to haunt me in a frustratingly unwelcome reminder of who I am.

I stand up, steadying my jellied legs by gripping the despatch box before me. My stomach feels like it's about to explode, but somehow I know that it will last me long enough to finish my story.

"I read his poem, and I knew it was about him. I knew it was about Kharouf and I wanted to throw up. I wish Abbas knew how much I loved him and wanted him and needed him, and I wish he felt the same about me. I can't change what happened to Kharouf. I wish I could, but I can't, and neither can Abbas. I know it's selfish and it's so stupid to be jealous of a dead boy, but Abbas was never going to love me like he loved Kharouf. In all the months we were together, since the very first time we kissed on my bed, and the times we fucked, or held hands, or spent hours and hours with each other. For all the time I knew him, Abbas never told me he loved me. I told him every time we spoke, but he would only ever say, "You too." That's not the same.

"I excused myself from Mr Wilson's class and went to the bathroom. I don't think I was even going to be sick, but I just wanted some privacy where I could sit, and put my head in my hands, and just try to breathe. And I wanted to text Abbas. I wanted to know where the fuck he was and why he hadn't told me he wasn't going to be in, and why he had written that poem. I wanted to scream at him and cry and hit him until he loved me as much as I loved him. I wanted him to hurt so he could see how badly he was hurting me.

"I called him instead. I didn't want anything to be lost in translation through texts. He picked up after the first ring, well, I guess, the first buzz. He always had his phone on silent. His voice sounded gruff and gravelly, like he'd just woken up. He told me to meet him in the park at lunchtime. We weren't technically allowed to leave the school grounds during the day, which was a fucking stupid rule that none of the years before us had to follow..." I don't know how I get sidetracked at a time like this, but I still manage to. "But I told him I would, and he hung up pretty quickly. Didn't even say goodbye. I went back to English and sat in silence for the rest of the lesson, even though Tony was still making his snide little remarks about a novel I doubt he would've even read. I just stared at the pages until my eyes blurred and stung dry, and waited for the hour to be over as soon as possible.

"I didn't wait to let the guys know where I was going. I just put my head down and hoped none of them would pass me in the corridors as I walked as fast as I could without running. Mr Wanker tried to stop me. He yelled as I was just about to turn out of the school gate, but I ignored him and just kept walking. I knew he wouldn't follow. He was a dick, but a limp one.

"When I got to the park—the same one that put a pit in my stomach because I could still feel Lewis there and, even though I knew he would rarely, if ever, go, a part of me always dreaded the possibility that he might be waiting at the gates like before—Abbas was sitting under a tree. He looked pale and tired, like he'd been sick, and he was clutching a crumpled piece of paper in his hand, which was weird because I don't think I'd ever seen him treat the written word so carelessly. He even straightened out his crisp packets before putting them in the bin. He glanced up at me when I sat beside him, but he didn't move or say anything. He just stared into space. I twisted my face into a smile that probably looked as forced as it felt and asked him as casually as I could what was up. His fist tightened around the piece of paper.

"'They didn't believe me,' he said, and I didn't know what the fuck he meant. I mean, why would I? Everything had been fine the day before. All I knew was that he had skipped school that morning.

"I asked him what he was talking about, and he just handed me the paper. It was a letter from the Home Office, and on a first scan, I saw that his application had been denied. He hadn't been granted asylum. I mean, I scanned it so quickly I didn't really take any of it in, but they said that his witnesses—that was me—weren't credible. They didn't believe us. They didn't believe him. I looked over at him; his steely face and strong jaw were clenched into a mask. He said again that they didn't believe him, and I don't even know what I was thinking. None of it felt real. It was like a sick dream, but because it feels like a dream, you still have that tiny bit of delusional hope that things will be fine and you can just wake up.

"I'm not dumb, y'know? And I like politics. I knew exactly what the Home Secretary had been saying, what everyone had been saying, about asylum seekers and refugees and immigrants. I knew, you know I knew, about the small boats and what everyone was saying we needed to do. And even though I knew what Abbas had told me, everything about his life and his home, I guess I didn't think that anything could happen to him. He was mine. He was good, he wasn't like the others. He couldn't leave me."

Luce shifts in his seat a little and I realise I'd forgotten he was there. I'd been staring at the despatch box, caught in my memory. He is looking at me with no expression other than a slight narrowing of his eyes. I can tell that he's been waiting for the end of this story.

"I turned to Abbas and I told him that we could appeal. His lawyer, that Mary person, had told us when I was there that he could appeal if he was denied. We would appeal, I told him.

And we could write to our MP, they could send letters to the Home Secretary or someone. They could raise it in Parliament. I mean, I was literally overflowing with these ideas; my own little political shitstorm I could solve like someone in a Shonda Rhimes show. I said that we could speak to the press, to a journalist and he could tell them his story. If people knew about him and about what he'd told me—I neglected to name Kharouf, but his name hung between us like a phantom—they would stop anything from happening. Fuck it, we could drag it all out so long that he could just marry me and he could stay. I even laughed. It was all fine, I was telling myself. I was telling him.

"I'd been so wrapped up in this whole little tirade that I didn't notice him staring at me with hollow fucking eyes that looked black and dead. It was like I'd never met him before. He snatched the letter away from me and tightened his fist around it til his knuckles were white."

"Didn't you fucking read it?" He snarled, and I turned bright red. My mouth hung open like a fish. "It said they didn't believe me. They didn't believe that I'm fucking gay. They think I'm lying to them about it all. They say," he gestured forcefully, "that I'm not fucking *'credible'*. They say that if Syria is as fucked up as I say it is, then I never would have looked at Kharouf. They say I wouldn't have spoken to him. I wouldn't have kissed him. I wouldn't have fucking fallen in love with him. They say that if Syria was dangerous, I would never have entertained the fucking notion I was gay while I was there. That I would have kept it hidden and never fucking done anything about it until it was safe or until I was dead. That I wouldn't have fallen in love. They say that I'm making the whole fucking thing up."

I stared at him. Each mention of Kharouf was another puncture in my heart. The reason why this letter was ruinous wasn't the same for us. For me, it was because I would be losing him.

For him, it was because he was losing Kharouf. *Again.*

He thrust the pages in my face and I flinched, but didn't break our eye contact. I wanted him to see me. I *needed* him to finally see me.

"I'm sorry," I said. I don't know why I apologised. I hadn't done anything wrong, but I hated to see Abbas so upset. "We can fix things, though. This isn't the end of it. Like I said, we can appeal and we can make a fuss about it and get people to notice..."

"Shut the FUCK up," Abbas yelled. Screamed. Shouted. I flinched again. "This isn't one of your fucking games. This isn't a fucking picture book where everything works out fine in the end. I don't fucking want to be in the news. I don't want to be a fucking story. I don't want to be a fucking FUSS." My heart was beginning to beat faster and faster. I was starting to feel faint. "You're so wrapped up in your fucking fantasy world," he said, spitting my name. The first time he called me by my name, it sounded so sweet, so smooth, so safe. Now it was a bullet. "This is my fucking life. Can't you see that? This is real life."

"I know, Abbas, but I just thought..."

"Yeah, you 'just thought'," he scoffed. Tears were beginning to form in the corners of his eyes. I hoped that if they spilled out, he might calm down. "That's all you ever do, isn't it? You just think. You never actually fucking do anything." The vein in his neck was throbbing angrily.

"I want to help you, babe, but..."

"Don't fucking call me that. You're so fucking stupid. You think this is just a fucking game. You think this is one of your books or one of your stories." He didn't mention the fact that he loved books, too. The thought of his poem flashed into my mind. My heart was pounding. He waved the letter around as he gesticulated in fury. "This is my fucking life. This is *my* fucking life. I am going to be sent back and they are going to fucking kill me. But do you know what? At least then I'll be with Kharouf." He turned, throwing his arms up in frustrated resignation.

"Don't you want to stay here? With me?" My voice came out as a whisper. Abbas turned around.

"I don't give a shit about you."

"Then what?" Luce asks. I take a deep breath in.

"I love you."

"You love him?"

"I. Don't. Care." Abbas fumed. He was centimetres from my face as he spat out the words. "You're pathetic."

Luce leans forward. "Then what?"

"I run."

"You run?"

"Yeah, fucking run away as usual," Abbas shouted after me.

My leg was splintering and pins and needles shocked up the limb like a mutiny of my own body. I stopped running by the time I reached the traffic lights and I was practically doubled over, gasping for air as the pain from my leg ripped through me. Tears stung my eyes and though I started counting, "One... Two... Three..." nothing would stop them from bursting forward. I sobbed silently, silently praying and pleading that Abbas would come running after me, that he would tell me he was sorry. That he would say we could fight together. That he didn't want to leave me. He didn't.

For the first time in months, I wanted to bleed. I wanted to cut myself and keep cutting until there was no skin left. I wanted to cut through my muscles to the bone. I wanted to shred every nerve until there was nothing left that could hurt. I wanted to bleed and bleed and bleed until everything inside of me had spilled out. I gasped for air as my vision went foggy and I squeezed my eyes shut.

One... Two... Three... It wasn't working.

I stepped forward and I barely registered the horn and the screech of the tires. I barely registered the force crumpling my body like a ragdoll.

Ironically, it should have been, "Better safe than van."

XXIX

The Death of a Secondary Character

I stand in the Commons. There is no other sound but my shaking breath. I stare down at the despatch box and slowly run my fingers over the bronze edges, tracing the patterns and engravings with the tip of my index finger. I can feel Luce looking at me, but I'm scared that if I meet his eyes, I will start to cry. I simply breathe instead.

"And now we're back to where we started," Luce says softly, and I nod in response.

I don't know how I forgot how I got here, but now that I remember every single moment, the feeling of every single cell in my body being hit by a completely nondescript white van, the split-second of complete agony before opening my eyes to the hazy white lights that hang over me now. I don't remember how long it has been since then. I don't know if, while I'm lying in the hospital room, there is anyone beside me holding my hand. My father, who I had pushed away? My mother, who I had lost so many years ago? My sister? I try desperately not to think about Abbas sitting there, but that's all I can really imagine. I hope with every fibre of my being that he is the one next to me, that he has forgiven me. That he loves me.

"When you first stood in front of me, kiddo," Luce says, his voice low and melodic, "You told me that you wanted to live. You told me all the reasons: your family, your friends, how much you loved politics, all the things that you wanted for your future, and everything that you loved back home. You told me about Abbas, and how much you loved him and he loved you." I nod again, slowly and shakily.

He says my name. "Your last moments were you begging to be hurt. Begging to die. Not even die quickly and painlessly. You wanted to be ripped apart piece by piece so that you could feel all the pain you knew existed for you. It wasn't enough that you were torturing yourself in your mind; you wanted to be in absolute agony so that you could externalise everything and completely combust.

"Kiddo, the pain you feel is okay. I know how much it hurt you. I know how much it all hurt you. From Olivia, to Marcus, to Lewis, to Abbas. From Megan to your parents to your best friends. I know each and every moment that made you break down, and I feel how it ground you more and more into the dirt and, more than anything else, I know how you hurt yourself. I know how you replayed every moment over and over until the words were memorised like a line in a play. I know how you relived every single time you were hurt, and how you cut yourself and made yourself bleed so that it might leave you, even for a second. I lived all of it with you."

I wipe my nose on the cuff of my sleeve and it leaves a slime trail behind it. Luce stands up and leans on his despatch box.

"I told you when we started that this had to end in a choice. That you had to convince me and yourself of whether you wanted to go home or not. I know what you said back then, and I know everything you have said since. You should go now and take some time and think and reflect on everything you have said here, and then, when you come back, we can talk it through. Now we have the full story in front of us—from beginning to end—we can start to make a decision. Okay?"

I nod.

Luce walks out of the room and leaves me standing there, still staring at the despatch box like a genie might pop out and give me three wishes. Not that I know what I would even wish for. Maybe some help.

***

The atrium is quiet, but not in an eerie way. It feels secluded—peaceful, even—and desperately needed after the story of my death. Well, almost death. I wander up to the third floor, having long started ignoring the dim glow of the shops that I can never go in, and find my bench sitting in the ceiling's shadow. I take a seat and lean forward, my elbows resting on my thighs with my hands loosely clasped in front of me. There's the kind of silence that feels safe. I read once that when films are trying to cover up background noise in a scene which they have to record silence in the same place because people can tell the difference between silence in one place compared to silence in another place. I don't know if that's true, but this is the kind of silence that fits this place. There's no background chatter, footsteps, echoing, nothing. There's just silence, like a light blanket shrouding me as I sit on my bench and look through the glass barrier down to the ground floor.

I feel a presence next to me, and look across to see Rebecca shuffling backwards onto the bench. She's wearing a white dress. I still don't know where everyone gets their outfit changes from when I am still in my socks, joggers, and tee, but it doesn't feel like a problem anymore. I'm even kind of glad to see her.

"Have you finished your story?" she asks, and I nod wordlessly. She takes my hand in hers and my long fingers—Tim Burton fingers—curl around her tiny ones. She's warm to the touch. "Are you going to decide soon?" I nod again. "Do you know what you'll do?" I squeeze her hand softly and she squeezes back before releasing a few moments later. I shake my head slowly.

It feels so fake to make this decision. It feels so artificial and so wrong, like a chapter in a book that's been cut and pasted into another, and the tone change is jarring. It feels like it doesn't fit, but looking back, I guess, in a weird way, it's a logical continuation. Through the invisible string linking every moment, there's a thread that tapers off to this place. I don't know what I'm going to do, or say, or want.

I have spent hours, days, wishing for this moment; for an ultimatum to be handed to me so I could finally decide whether my life was worth living and now I am here, I'm drowning like a bee in honey: slowly and sweetly in a death of my own making. We sit silently for what could be seconds or hours, holding each other's hand until our fingers cramp and ache, but still we hold on. It's not until I feel a hand on my shoulder that the trance lifts and I see Luce standing above me, looking down on me with his eyes creased into a sympathetic smile.

"Hey," he says, in almost a whisper. I smile back fleetingly. "It's time, kiddo." Rebecca and I stand, and while I stuff my hands in my pockets, Luce takes Rebecca's hand tenderly and together we walk in silence down the stairs to the doors that are there some moments and gone the next. He pushes them open, and though they look old and wooden, with big brass handles, they do not creak. What is inside surprises me.

It's still the Commons, still the place I've been this whole time, but this time, instead of being empty, the benches are full of people sitting in neat rows, dressed in faded pastel dresses and suits like a heavenly mirage. They have all turned to look at me, soft smiles on their faces. I stare back at them, looking around the room in something that would have been akin to wonder if it was not so devastatingly melancholy. I take my place on the bench behind the Government's despatch box, Rebecca sitting in the space to my right and Luce standing opposite me. He has no papers and I wonder what is going to come out of his mouth, but he winks at me with a smile.

"I have a surprise for you, kiddo." I look at him quizzically.

"Remember how we started this whole thing?" I nod slowly, my eyebrows furrowed as to what could possibly happen. "Remember that little.., faux pas about the decorum of the House?" I nod again, my face reddening slightly at the memory. "Well, because this is so important to you, to us, I brought someone along… just for you."

The door to my left swings open and in walks a woman. She wears black and white robes, her silk shirt tied into a perfectly coifed pussy bow below her neck and her blonde hair flowing in loose messy waves from her head. She would be probably late thirties, with eyes as blue as the ocean on a clear day and fair skin unblemished by spots or scars. Her lips are pink: too vibrant to be natural, but not bright enough to be evidently lipstick. She sits in the Speaker's chair expressionlessly, looking straight at Luce, who is smirking back at her.

"Except this time, it's *Madam* Speaker," he grins. I laugh in spite of myself. No one else reacts in the slightest. Luce closes his blazer buttons in front of him. It's only now that I notice he is wearing a suit; a deep black jacket with a white shirt and a black tie that seems to glitter like the scales of an iridescent snake. I look to my right, then my left, and realise that I am the only person not dressed formally, completely against my ethos of always dressing one step nicer so as never to be out of place. If you're not above, you're below. First among equals.

He clears his throat softly, but the sound still echoes around the Chamber. "Madam Speaker," Luce begins with a glint in his eye as he looks at me. "I beg to move that the motion laid before this House on this date be approved: that the honourable Member opposite be refused permission to return to his life; that he has squandered each opportunity to take full advantage of his life. More than this, the honourable Member opposite does not even *wish* to return. He knows this to be true: he does not wish to pass any further through life; to return to the home which he has left and to which he cannot return; the consequence of his every choice and every moment has been hanging in the stars; and he knows himself what I say to be true. Madam Speaker, I beg to move that the honourable Member, the *boy* sitting across from me, be granted the permission to die."

***

The role of the Speaker is almost as old as the Commons itself. It became apparent, as it does in most things, that chaos without order is not a long-term strategy. Though there are a few instances of contested election, and undoubtedly more as the years marched on, the decision about who would preside over the House was generally a pretty settled one, and rarely has it been a matter of much controversy and acrimony. The individual who sits in the chair, of whom there have been over a hundred, commands the respect of the House and its Members, and, indirectly through their representatives, commands the respect of the people.

Though there are, of course, occasions in which the Speaker—all but one of whom have been men, not including the lady sitting before me in this moment—has been accused of playing games and political trickery, it is the Speaker who is the representative of the representatives, first among the commoners, and the voice of the people to the nobility and to the Crown. Originally, in fact, the Speaker was usually the choice of the monarch, but over time, as the royals faded and democracy grew, the Speaker's loyalties migrated from the head of state to its subjects. It is now that we find ourselves with a Speaker in its purest form.

Ironically, the Speaker does very little speaking, though I'm sure John Bercow gave people a run for their money. Instead, they simultaneously act as the head of the House and its servant. Indeed, it was William Lenthall, the Member for New

Woodstock, who, in declaring his allegiance to the Commons and not the Crown, said, "I have neither eyes to see nor tongue to speak in this place but as the House is pleased to direct me, whose servant I am here." Of course, it's easy to be badass when you speak in so convoluted a tongue that Charles I probably didn't even know what he was saying, but in saying whatever he did, Lenthall solidified the shift in the speakership from king to country. Executing Charles probably also helped in this.

In sitting on the front benches behind the despatch box, it's clear why kings and queens would have wanted an ally in the chair. Their height is imposing, and their centrality in the chamber unnerving, with a great canopy hanging over the emerald-green leather. The fact also that you do not address the speaker by name, but rather by their position. I do not know the name of the woman in front of us, and yet I am bound to direct my arguments to her, and not to Luce, the man who put me in this place, and the man who is now trying to get me out of it.

***

"Okay." He grins wickedly. "Let's dispense with the formalities and get down to the real thing. The truth is, kiddo, that you don't want to live. I know when you got up here for the first time, you said you did, and I get that: it's a reflex, like someone asking you if you're okay and you just say 'yeah' when you're not, or if I tried to hit you, you'd duck, even if you wanted to be punched. You're English, I get it: you're a stickler for tradition and a stiff upper lip, and you're incapable of expressing emotions beyond those that consist of perturbed or amused. But this isn't a time for those things. This is the single most important decision you'll ever make, and you can't do it based on an impulse. You have to dig a little deeper and look at the evidence, the facts, the figures, the truth. You can't just jump and fall back into life, kid. You have to be sure, and until you are, we won't be done here. Sure either way, that is.

"So let's look at it. Let's look at how you actually feel. Let's start at the beginning with your family, and how they moved from their Little Eden," this he said with something bordering contempt, "to a farm they didn't want, to care for parents who died before you could know them. Your father was absent and drove your mother to depression, and when he fucked some whore he met in a hotel bar on one of his dozens of business trips, he put the final nail in the coffin they'd been building since the start. That's the thing about Eden: there's always the snake in the grass.

"Not only that, but your mother, knowing what he had done, blamed herself and a part of her died, and you watched that part die. You heard her beg him not to leave and promise to improve on a situation she had no hand in making. She left her home, her family, and got to see her kids every few months if that, and you didn't even want to see her. You resented her for leaving, more than you resented your father for it, and every second you spent with her was just a reminder of how you longed for that Little Eden when everything would have been okay. I don't know if it was a coping mechanism to blame the person you didn't see as much, but your relationship with your mother never recovered. She never knew you, and how could she if she never saw you? Hell, even though your father stayed at home the whole time, he didn't even know you. You wouldn't let them know you.

"You had a chance with Olivia to tell them who you were and you ducked and you obfuscated and you lied until your dark, secretive fantasy would wrap itself into a noose for you to hang yourself on when you would throw yourself over the nearest boy who showed you the slightest bit of decency. You admitted yourself you didn't love Marcus, you were just lonely. But still you kissed him, without his consent, when you had a girlfriend. You cheated, you assaulted, you lied, and you got hurt. You did that."

"I didn't assau—" Luce holds up a hand and my voice dies in my throat.

"Then the one person you tell—I mean, the first person you ever come out to and tell them who you are—leaves. Do you know why Lois left, kid? It's because your sister told her to. When you left Lois on the sofa to go to bed, she woke your father and told him everything and the next morning, when they hadn't slept a wink, your sister walked in on them discussing it all in the kitchen, and when they caught her eavesdropping, they had to tell her everything. They sat Penny down and told her how you had been hurting yourself, how you had cut yourself within an inch of your life every night for months, and how you had kissed a boy and it all came crumbling down.

"How the fuck is Penny meant to react to that? You're her big brother. You're meant to be a constant. It's meant to be you and her against the world. That's what siblings do, and yet here she was finding out that her big brother was mutilating himself, that he was gay, that he had been lying to every single person in his life, except the one person in that room who was not part of her broken little family: Lois. Your sister told Lois to leave. She said that she had no place here. You know what Penny said to you when you spoke to her after that day; she said that you should've told her first, or that you should have told Dad or Mum, or anyone that wasn't some stranger living in their house. Do you have any idea how much you betrayed Penny? She thought you were a family, at least the two of you were what was left of one, and then she finds out she doesn't even know you, and she finds that out from someone she barely fucking knows, anyway.

"In that one night you hurt so many people, kiddo." Every single 'kiddo' grates at me like my skin is being shaved off layer by layer. "You hurt your dad, who found out one of the two people he had sworn to protect was dying on his watch. You hurt your sister. You hurt Lois. How do you think she felt with having all your shit dumped on her and then being kicked out of her home? You hurt Marcus, who had to carry the burden of being assaulted alongside the knowledge that you had cheated on his friend, and that you had been lying to them all the whole time about who you were, and if he dared tell anyone what had happened, he would risk outing you. You hurt Olivia. The only people who weren't hurt were the people who didn't even know these whole facade had fallen.

"And when you did that—when you broke their trust and when you pulled off the mask to show that they had a stranger in their family—you forced them to take away your privacy, your bedroom door, your intimacy. You were no longer their son or their brother: you were a problem, a risk, a situation. Ironically, in revealing your true self, you destroyed your whole identity in their eyes. You paid the price for the truth with your humanity, and in your desperate, lonely attempt to patch yourself back together, you clung onto the only person you thought saw you: Lewis."

Fuck me, I feel sick.

"You thought he was the only person to see you as a human being anymore. He complimented you, he showed you attention, he made you feel like maybe there was a fairytale that could be made out of the ashes of your life, but then you found out too late—breezing past all the red flags—that the only reason he showed an interest in you is because he was bored and needed a new plaything. You don't even know what happened."

"What happened?" I ask, stuttering.

"You never said what happened. You said you woke up. What did Lewis even do to you?"

My stomach is pulsing into my throat. "I..." I swallow it back down, but it lurches back up again. "I don't know."

"You don't even know what happened, kid! You just woke

up feeling dirty, like a cheap fucking whore, but you don't even know what he did."

"You don't think I want to know what he did? You don't think that would make me feel better? If I knew exactly why I woke up feeling like I had lost the last single fucking scrap of who I am instead of just filling in the blanks myself? You don't think that tiny bit of knowledge would be so much better, so he wouldn't keep having the upper hand over me when he remembers what he did and I have no fucking idea?" I'm screaming now.

"You'll get your chance to reply," Luce says, and holds his hand up, silencing me again. He ignores the Speaker. This is his House. He continues:

"And it's Lewis who forces you back into therapy, back to Jo, because your dad is so worried you'd solve his little problem for him. You end up in hospital because he comes home to find you sitting on the stairs with tears streaming down your face and blood pouring onto the carpet from your wrists while your sister was asleep upstairs.

"But then we come onto the worst part: we come onto the story of Abbas."

"You have stood here, where you are right now, and you have told me that the story of you is the story of Abbas. When you told me that for the first time, you didn't even remember that the story of Abbas would become the story of how you got here. When you first met his eyes on that first day of school, you took the first step down the path that led you here: to your own destruction. No... Not even destruction. *Dissolution*. Every step you took, every page turned in that story, was one closer to the end. You know that now. You knew it then.

"But you also know now the missing piece in everything you had back then. You know that Abbas didn't love you. He loved Kharouf. You know what he wrote in his witness statement: 'The boy who deserved the gentlest love and was met with the world's ugliest hatred. The lamb with whom the lion fell in love.' *His* Kharouf. And now it makes sense why he never said he loved you. It makes sense why every time you looked into his eyes, there was something blocking the window to his soul."

I'm crying now. Not sobbing, just sitting motionlessly staring at Luce as he dismantles every moment of my life.

"I know this hurts you, kiddo. You think it doesn't hurt me too? What do you think I am if not just a part of you? If not just an extension of everything you are? You think I want to know all of this? You think I want to be standing in front of you, standing in the House of fucking Commons, confirming every single one of your doubts and fears? You think it doesn't break me like it breaks you? You think it doesn't kill me like it kills you? I am you, kid. I am you." Tears are falling from Luce's eyes now too.

"You said the story of you is the story of Abbas, but that's not true. His story is the one you have told me, the story of the lion and the lamb. The story of him and Kharouf.

"The truth is that his one great love story has ended, and you don't get a second one. After Romeo, there was no Juliet and Paris. You don't get another great love story. His story ended with Kharouf. You are an afterthought, an epilogue; your death is merely the lesser crime of killing a secondary character."

The chamber is silent except for Luce's shaky breath. I have never seen a fibre of weakness in him until now. He is falling apart as he tears me down.

"Your words, kiddo. You told me this: 'I wanted to bleed. I wanted to cut myself and keep cutting until there was no skin left. I wanted to cut through my muscles to the bone. I wanted to shred every nerve until there was nothing left that could hurt. I wanted to bleed and bleed and bleed until everything inside of me had spilled out.' You don't have to feel that way. That's not the way you have to live. You have a choice here. You don't have to go back. You don't have to leave here.

"Maybe if we had gotten here sooner, maybe if that van had come two years earlier, you might want something different. But this wasn't something that happened overnight. You didn't wake up having lost every single part of who you are overnight. Your dreams didn't take that from you. What happened was years and years of slow erosion, of lying to yourself because you never thought that you could be happy. Of screaming silently every night because you didn't want anyone to hear just how much you were hurting. Of Olivia tearing you apart, of Marcus leaving you behind, of Lewis's games, of Abbas's indifference. All of this, until you were nothing but the blank sheet of paper you started with. You don't deserve this. You didn't deserve any of this. You were punished because you were born loving someone society told you not to, and that weight shackled you to the ground when you should have been climbing up. I've seen it so many times: this slow, painful degradation and dehumanisation—of being a prop, a political statement, a problem—until not even you know who you are. Everyone is just as messed up as you, but that doesn't make you feel any less lonely. That doesn't make the weight of the world on your shoulders a little less easy to carry.

"You think that I hate you, but how can I hate you when we're just as broken as each other? How can I hate you for that? You think that I'm forcing you to make this choice, but you forced us to think it up in the first place.

"The first time we met, you looked me in the eye and told me you wanted to live. You do. I know you want to live. I know you want to go back and wake up and take over the reins and be everything you want to be. I know you want your life to be everything it could be. I know how much you want it. But I can't stand here and lie to you and say that that will happen. There comes a point when you have to look back and say goodbye. That's not a bad thing. It's not giving up. It's letting go. It's okay."

XXX

When Jesus Gives the Wheel Back

The election of a speaker takes place at the start of every new Parliament following a general election or a vacancy left by the incumbent's death or resignation. Under the new rules, implemented in 2007, a candidate requires the nominations of 12 of their colleagues representing at least three different parties. If there is more than one candidate, a secret ballot will eliminate the candidate with the fewest votes until a victor emerges with a majority of the votes cast.

A weird thing about the election of a speaker comes from its history as the voice of the Commons to the monarch. It would be the speaker who would suffer the king or queen's direct fury if the people diverted from their ruler, and so the speaker, even in modern times where the king does not opine on political issues, is expected to be reluctantly dragged by their colleagues to the chair, even though they would have put themselves forward for election to the position. For a person who does very little but chair, the direction of the monarch's displeasure at the only person who has historically sworn to serve the Commons, not the Crown, is a pretty sad indictment of the ability of a king to distinguish between the representatives and their representative. It's also quite depressing that the person who serves those who serve must suffer as part of his service.

Luckily, nowadays the speaker is much more likely to be

criticised by everyone but the king, and the speaker—but for their name—speaks so little.

***

Usually, before a debate, I would prepare endlessly. I'd have my crib sheet of facts and figures, and I would methodically work my way through the structure of beginning, middle, and end, dusting the rhetoric with data as I went. When I had finished, I would pull up an online thesaurus and go through removing the repetition, trimming the fat, and changing the words to hone my argument to say as little as necessary. The more you said, the more you could be criticised for it.

Standing in the Commons, I had no luxury of time, even though I still hadn't figured out how time worked here. Luce sat down, and the Speaker gestured gently for me to stand. She said nothing, but I obeyed. Another historical quirk, since removed, is that when a vacancy arose in the chair, the clerk of the House would act as interim speaker, but as they were not a Member, they weren't permitted to speak. They would simply point at whoever's turn it was in the debate. I guess she is not a Member. Either that, or she just really doesn't fancy a chat. I get that.

"Madam Speaker," I begin. My face doesn't flush this time, and Luce smiles at me, the tears drying on his cheeks. That's as far as I get before I walk from the room, swinging the door closed behind me.

I hear my name being called, but I ignore it. Rebecca keeps repeating it nonetheless and eventually she catches up with me, tugging on my tee to slow me down. I don't even know where I'm going, but anywhere has to be better than in there. I kept walking and walking until I stopped suddenly, staring at the floor in front of me. Rebecca was still only a few steps behind me. As I stop, she stands in front of me with a serious expression on her face.

"You have to do this," she said, my name dropping from her lips to my ears like a lead zeppelin.

I stare at her, my jaw clenched and my hands opening and closing as I struggle to find the words. "You keep saying that, Rebecca. You've been saying that since I got here, but I still don't know what *'it'* is. I don't know what I'm even doing here. I've got to make a choice to go back to my life, or some alternative that no one will explain to me. And this is a choice I have to make with Luce, who I know nothing about and I don't know what the fuck he's going to do. Is he even reasonable? Will he actually listen to whatever I have to say? I don't even have anything to say. And you keep saying that I have to make the right choice, but you won't tell me what that is and you won't tell me why. You keep pressuring me to make a decision but you won't tell me what you want from me. How am I supposed to know any of this? How am I meant to act or speak or anything when I'm completely in the dark? I don't know what is happening. I don't know, I'm just..." I look around in desperation. Rebecca takes my hand in hers again.

"You're just scared."

I nod. Scared. The word feels like a weighted blanket dropped on me and I'm not sure if it's comforting or claustrophobic.

"I told you there are rules here," Rebecca says. "I don't know what they are, but I told you that you can break some of them, and some of them you can't. But Luce told me you can make the rules yourself. You already did that, in a way, but picking that place we're in, by picking Luce, by picking what story you tell. You made all these rules up.

"I make them up too. I let myself go to the beach, and bring you there as well. This is your life and, no matter what Luce says, this is your decision. You get to decide how you make it."

The words, the sense coming out of her is creepy from an eight-year-old, but I appreciate it nonetheless. I nod quickly in reply, and take a deep, shaky breath in.

"Do you want to go back?" she asks.

I shake my head. *I don't know.*

"Come with me," she says.

The clearing is exactly how I remember it: quiet, peaceful, and alive in the tamest way. I sit on the ground and Rebecca sits beside me. I breathe in the fresh air as the leaves and blades of grass rustle softly in the breeze. There's a sparrow again, which flits from one branch on the edge to another, chirping softly, and I watch him as he dances in the fringes of the forest. I want to stay here until my veins become roots and plant me where I am.

"I'm sorry I haven't been clear," Rebecca says and I smirk.

"It's okay," I tell her. Not much to do about any of it now.

"Is this like your beach?" She is watching the sparrow too.

"Yeah," I reply. "I used to come here whenever I needed to think. It used to be all the time when I was a kid, but then not so much as I got older."

"I want you to live," she says. It's the first time she's told me this. She still isn't looking at me.

"Thanks, I guess," I chuckle.

"Remember my dad?" My heart goes cold again and I nod. "I was always so scared when he came into my room. I could smell his beer on him when he was walking up the stairs. But the only thing that scared me more than that is if he ever stopped coming to my room. I didn't want him to go to my sister instead. I didn't want him to do it to her as well.

"I didn't remember until just before Luce said I was ready to make my choice, but I remember how I got here. I was at the beach with my mum and my sister and Mummy said that we had to run. She told me she was scared that he would do it to my sister, too. Her name is Abigail. That was the first time I knew that my mum had known what was happening to me. Daddy always said that he would hurt her if I told her, but I didn't need to. She knew anyway, and she didn't try to stop him hurting me until she was scared he would hurt Abigail.

"I was crying, really crying hard, and then I started to run. She tried to grab my hand, but she got my sleeve instead and she pulled my cardy off me and I ran away. I didn't even get far before I was in the road and before they could stop, a car hit me."

I sit silently and listen to her story, each word breaking my heart more than the last.

"I want you to live because the man driving the van that hit you was my dad. He didn't mean to. It was an accident. But that's how I met you. You're the first person I've met who can help me. I need you to go back and make sure my sister is okay."

Luce grabs my arm and pulls me up. Rebecca is suddenly missing. He doesn't look angry, just tired.

"She told you then?" I nod quickly. He turns from me and clenches his jaw. "The amount of times I've had to stop her doing that."

"Why were you trying to stop her?"

"This is your choice. This isn't about her."

"But if I can help her, then I need…"

"She doesn't need help!" Luce exclaims and I stare at him in shock. He lets go of my arm and walks a few paces, his head in his hands. "Rebecca is a sweet kid, and I know she wants her sister to be safe, but I keep telling her that her sister is okay and she won't believe me. She has this inability to take that in."

"How do you know her sister is safe?"

"You lived close to each other, right?"

"Yeah, I think she lived a couple villages over. Near where my mum lives."

"Did you ever hear about her?"

"What do you mean?"

"A kid gets hit by a car. Is in a coma. That's news, right? Did you ever hear about it?"

"I mean, no?"

"Do you know any of the same people?"

"Yeah, she knows the ice cream shop and the statue in town..."

"Those aren't people."

I wrack my brain. "I guess not, but..."

"Rebecca was hit by a car when she was eight-years-old. Back in her life, in your life, she's now almost 35. Her dad never touched her sister, definitely not after what happened to Rebecca. Abigail is a grown woman now, and lives in Connecticut with her family. Her mother died a few years back from breast cancer. Her sister doesn't need protecting. Rebecca knows this. I've told her this. She is just scared to let go.

"You need to focus on you. You need to focus on why you want to go back. You need to focus on whether you want to let go."

***

Back in the Commons, it is quiet, and I feel awkward as fuck walking back in with everyone staring at me. Usually when I run away from a problem—and it's something I've made a habit of, apparently—there isn't such a big audience. Again, I curse myself for feeling awkward in what may just be my subconscious. But, *oh well.*

I take my place behind the despatch box and look up to see Luce watching me with amused disinterest. He is sitting with his legs wide apart on the front row, but the people to his left and right don't seem to mind. At least, they don't wear their displeasure on their faces. A blank expression is also an attribute I lack.

"This isn't going to be easy," Luce says. Ordinarily, he would be expected to stand if he is going to speak, but the Speaker doesn't say anything, and who am I to mansplain Parliamentary procedure in the Interlife? *Not my place.*

"I know."

"Are you ready for it?"

"Yes."

***

"I get what you mean, when you say that I don't want to live. And maybe that's true, I really don't know anymore. This whole thing has just wrapped my mind up even more than it already was. It's like I'm running in circles and tangling up everything behind me, but I know when I set everything out, like I'm gonna do here, it's pretty clear:

"I have tried to end my life at least once... I'm not even sure how many times I have attempted suicide. I don't know where the line is drawn between what I've done and what people *should* do when they attempt it. But I know that I didn't want to live, and I didn't want to live for a very long time. I used to sit in my bedroom and wish and hope and pray—pray, to a God I don't even know exists—that somehow the pain would be taken away.

"But who I was—the person I was with Olivia, and Marcus, and my parents, and Lois and Lewis—that changed when I met Abbas. It changed me. He changed what I wanted. He took that pain away. Nothing heals you like safety, and Abbas was my safety. With him, I could be me. I could be who I so desperately wanted to be..."

"Let me ask a question." I knew it wouldn't be long before Luce interrupted me.

"Sure." I throw my hands up in surrender.

"Do you think it's weird that when I asked you your story, you spoke about Abbas? You kept saying the story of Abbas is the story of you, but that's not true. Your stories may be, I mean, they are interlinked. He's a big part of your life, I get that. But you are different people…" The way he lets the sentence hang irritates me.

"I don't get what you mean by that. You said yourself that Abbas is the reason I'm here. How can that not be my story? How can everything that led him to do the things he did, and say what he said to me, which all ended up with me in front of a van, not be my story? If he hadn't met Kharouf, if they hadn't killed him, if he hadn't gotten out, if he hadn't ended up in my town, in my school, in my class, then I wouldn't be here. I can't tell the story of me without telling his story, too."

"That's not true. Why do you keep doing that?"

"Doing what?" I splutter.

"Every time I ask you about you, you turn it back to him. Every time I ask why you got here, it's him. Every time I ask you who you are, it's him. Always. Fucking. *Him*. Who even are you?"

"Who am I?"

"You're the reason you're here. Why can't you see that?" Luce's eyes are black now. Scarily.

"But without him, I wouldn't be here. I keep saying that."

"No. That's not true. You are the reason you're here. If it wasn't for everything *you* did, you wouldn't be here. You can't keep blaming it on Abbas. You can't blame it on him, or Olivia, or Marcus, or Lewis. Maybe the reason you're here is because you have no identity. You have no story. You are just a passive fucking figure moving through something that could only generously be called a life. You don't exist outside of the people you're hurt by. If it wasn't for Olivia and Marcus, if it wasn't for Lewis, if it wasn't for Abbas, you wouldn't exist at all.

"I have spent the last however fucking long we've spent doing this trying to get you to tell *your* story, trying to find out who *you* are, trying to uncover the reasons *you* want to live, but there are none. You are nothing. You haven't actually given me a single reason you should live. You went on and on and for a second you had me going. For a moment, I was actually looking forward to hearing Abbas's story. Him and Kharouf: now *that's* a love story! But that is all just deflection from the fact that you have no story. You're just reading someone else's and getting so caught up in other people that you convince yourself that you have some kind of vicarious narrative.

"I reckon if you sat down and wrote the book of your life, it would turn into the story of Abbas and Kharouf. '*The gentlest love*', who even says that shit? That's gold. But even in the event that you once had an identity—you were once a person—now, you define yourself by the people who hurt you. You define yourself by what broke you. You define yourself by tragedy. That's not a reason to live."

I stand there, withstanding the barrage coming at me from Luce and staring down at the despatch box.

"That isn't fair."

"What isn't fair?" he asks, his voice dropping from the yelling I had been subjected to since he interrupted me.

"I don't think I define myself by what breaks me. I think I define myself by what didn't break me. I think it's okay that I define myself with reference to other people, who doesn't? If it wasn't Abbas, if it wasn't... the others as well, it would be my parents, my friends, my family. We're all the sum of everyone else's parts. That's what being human is. Otherwise, it would just be nature and no nurture. What else is there to do when your happiest memories revolve around the people who hurt you most? You can't just get rid of them, take them out, hate the sin and not the sinner. They become you and you grow." I speak slowly, the words finding me as I come along. I hate not being able to prepare in advance, but for some reason, this feels like a multicoloured handkerchief that won't stop coming out of the magician's sleeve. "I don't think my life has been one reaction after another." I look around. "I made this place. I mean, I didn't make the House of Commons, but you said I decided where we would do this, make this decision. You said I decided how we would make the decision, and you said I even decided who you would be."

My next statement would make Ms Badden cringe: "I disagree with the premise of your argument." I can picture her curling her face up in disgust right now. She hated people disagreeing with the premise of an argument. "I don't think that I define myself by what broke me. I define myself by the people I loved. I loved Olivia, and Marcus, and Lewis, and Abbas—I loved them all in my own fucked up, human way. I don't define myself by tragedy. Tragedies are inevitable: they're built into the narrative structure. They're impossible to escape from. I define myself by possibility, from the scars of getting hurt so many times, but still with the hope that one day it will stop. I define myself by choice. I choose to love Abbas, just like I chose everything else.

"Yes, each one of them hurt me, but even though people are incapable of not hurting each other, people are incapable of not loving each other, too. I don't think it's a bad thing to just want to love and be loved.

"I spent my childhood scared shitless that would never happen. They say that people can't love you completely unless they know you completely, and I thought no one ever would. But with Abbas... I have never been so unafraid of loving someone so completely. If he never felt the same about me, if he could only ever love Kharouf, I would be okay with that. If I could go back right now and give myself, put myself in Kharouf's place, take the heartbreak and unimaginable pain from Abbas and give the lion back his lamb, I would. But I can't. So instead, I would be so happy if by me loving Abbas, by keeping him here with me, he could carry on loving Kharouf. It's not a competition between us all. It's not some sordid love triangle made up of hormones and homosexuality. Kharouf is part of me, too. He gave me my Abbas. I felt every mark on his body, every blow they dealt him, every tear he cried and every drop of blood he bled. Fuck, find a queer kid alive who didn't. I don't lack an identity, Luce. I am *everything* I have been made to be."

I turn to face the Speaker, who has been sitting silently this whole time, watching us with a quiet expression. I sigh shakily, holding back the tears that I'm not sure I have the energy left to cry.

"Madam Speaker," I say, "The story of me is the story of Abbas. The story of me is the story of a reader who fell for a lover. It is the story of a young boy with a crush, a boy with a secret, a boy who gets hurt, and a boy who, in spite of all of that, finds a fairytale. It is the story of a boy who fell in love with a boy. It is the story of how the gentlest love can overcome the greatest fury. It is the story of being his, even if he is not mine.

"If I go back to my life, I cannot guarantee I won't cry. I cannot guarantee my heart won't get broken. I cannot guarantee that I won't hurt. But I can guarantee, I promise you that I will love regardless of who loves me. Whatever happens, I will feel the highest of the highs and the lowest of the lows. Isn't that what life is meant to be about? I refuse to believe I cannot define a life by the love inside it. I refuse to believe I shouldn't want to live because of that love, because of Abbas. Everything I am is from him. Everything I do is for him. Dear Speaker, that's all I want. He is all I want. That life is all I want."

The Speaker nods silently.

D.

Requiem

"He wanted people to like his mind again—after a while it might be such a nice place in which to live."

—F Scott Fitzgerald, *This Side of Paradise*

XXXI

Dear Reader

I don't get a chance to say goodbye to Rebecca, though I start crying when Luce tells me this. I try to struggle away from his hands, but then everything blacks out. The last thing I see is his face looking at mine; handsome and stoic, with traces of smile lines around his brown eyes, and the scent of pomegranate shampoo.

***

"We're his brothers. You have to let us in. We need to see him."

I open my eyes wearily and the light above me is painfully bright, though dulled by how heavy my eyelids are. Everything hurts. My head, in particular, is thudding with pain and I want the shouting to stop. I don't know where it's coming from, but it keeps getting louder as the people insist, "He's our brother." The voices are male, so I know they're not talking about me. I don't have brothers.

I can hear a slow and methodical beeping which is pitched low enough not to drive me insane, and for this I am grateful. I want to speak, but I can feel something lodged in my throat. I try to move my tongue around to fish it out, but my tongue seems jammed at the bottom of my mouth. Probably by the same thing that's stopping me from talking. I don't even register this with much annoyance or fear, just a little confusion followed by acceptance. I guess you move through the stages of grief a little quicker when you're the subject of it. I can move my hands though, and I lift my right in front of my face. My left seems to be under a little more pressure, but I can't bend my neck to see where it is. I'm not sure why, but it feels reassuring to know that I do still have something of use around here. I hear a scream.

The face that appears in front of me is not the one I expected, and I'm a little disappointed at first, but as my vision swims into focus, I can see my mother staring down at me. She's crying and for some reason that makes me want to cry, too. I can feel the tears start to burst from the sides of my eyes and roll down my temples. I hear a voice yelling for a doctor, and I recognise it after a few moments as my father's, but that wouldn't make sense; my parents don't sit in the same room as each other. I'm right though. My dad's face appears beside my mum's as they look at me. He's crying too. It's weird. I give them a little wave. I'm not sure why, but it only makes them cry a bit harder.

They are pulled aside by someone else, someone I don't recognise. She's tall with jet-black hair pulled behind her brown, freckled face in a harsh ponytail. She starts shining a light in my eyes, which doesn't best please me. I wave at her, using my only method of communication, to try to get her to stop. She holds my arms down with her hands though, and I give up the fight pretty quickly. Best to just leave it, I think.

The door bursts open and there's a cacophony of hooting and hollering. I wince, but it gets worse as the woman above me—she's wearing a stethoscope and a pocket protector, so she must be a doctor—starts ordering the cause of the noise to leave. I recognise their voices as they try to argue.

"You're not his brother," I can hear her saying to their earnest protestations. "None of you are the same colour."

"Hey, I'm white too," I can hear Tom say and it makes me want to laugh.

"I never said we were biological brothers," Alonso agrees.

I can hear Liam telling her that they're as much family as anyone, and Lukas just loudly repeating "Yeah! Yeah!" I listen for a fifth voice, but I can't hear one.

"You can't be in here," the doctor is shouting over them, while my mother and father grip my right hand in their fists. I start to wave again, realising pretty quickly that a silent wave isn't the best means of intervening in a spirited debate. I try grunting, but it hurts my chest.

"Let them stay, let them stay," my mother starts saying, and the doctor tells her that she needs to examine me.

"You're always examining him! Give him a break! We need to see him! We've barely seen him since he got in here." I hear Liam say. I've never heard him speak so loudly. I've never even heard him disagree with someone.

"There's a reason," the doctor articulates. "I need you all to leave." I can see none of the blurry figures move. "He's awake."

He's awake. The words are creepy to me, as if I'm some kind of long slumbering leviathan about to destroy the world. It's like I've been buried alive but without the peace and quiet.

"He's awake?" Tom whispers. I can feel their eyes all on me and I lift up my arm again and give them—yep, you guessed it—a wave.

I'm so tired. I close my eyes, but then the doctor is prying them open and flashing her torch in them again. She seems a little sadistic but, then again, what doctor isn't?

"Can you hear me?" she asks. She says my name. *Caleb.* "Can you hear me, Caleb?" I nod a little. "I'm Maddie. I'm your doctor here. Do you know what happened?"

Do I know what happened? I close my eyes and squeeze them tightly shut. *I know what happened.* I remember the van. I remember the pain. I remember...

ABBAS. I want to shout his name. I want to start screaming. I lift my heavy arms up and start waving. I can feel cables and tubes and God only knows what else tug at me.

"You need to rest, Caleb," the doctor says. I feel something cool in my hand, and I close my eyes again.

When I open them again, my vision is a little less blurry. I start to cough and then I notice that whatever was inside my mouth has gone and my throat is clear. My head is still painful, and I can't really feel my lower body, but I see my toes twitching under the white blanket, so I know it's there at least.

There's a hand on mine, and I look to my right to see my mother looking at me again. She looks tired and her eyes are red and rimmed with tears. "Hey, you," she says. My dad is next to her, looking much the same as she does. "Hey, kiddo." The pet name feels so familiar to me again, but I can't really place why.

Doctor Maddie walks in again with a clipboard that she sets on my legs. She takes a seat on my left and I swivel my head to face her. She smells like some kind of fruit shampoo. She says my name—*Caleb*—and the more I hear it, the less foreign it sounds to me. She starts to tell me what is happening to me but I can't concentrate on the words which sound like gobbledegook, anyway. My throat is so dry and I look over to my mum and nod slowly and jerkily at a jug of water I can see on the side table. She picks up a weird little pink sponge on a stick and dips it in the water. I try to protest that I don't want that gross shit in my mouth, but she pushes it past my cracked lips and it turns out I'm grateful for the moisture it brings. I suck at the sponge hungrily, though it burns my throat.

I turn back to Maddie—Dr Patel, as I can now read on her name badge. She's quite pretty, I notice, but she looks just as tired as my parents do. I try to speak, but it feels like a thousand needles pushing up my throat. I give it another go and fail miserably again. Third time's the charm though, and I manage to croak out an "Abbas."

The doctor looks confusedly over to my parents, and my mum stares blankly at me. I don't think she remembers. My dad leans forward and clears his throat slightly.

"Abbas left about an hour ago."

He was here?! My eyes widen, and I think my dad understands.

"He's been here every day since the accident, sitting by your bed and holding you hand. He keeps trying to stay overnight too, but they kick him out." He jerks his head in the direction of the doctor with a gentle smile on his face. "We have to pry him away from your bedside every evening."

Tears prick my eyes again, and I think momentarily that I seem to be having some type of emotional crisis the amount of times I've cried in the 10 minutes I've been awake today.

"Oh, yes," my mother says quietly. "He's a lovely boy. He'll come back in the morning. When he saw that you'd woken up, he had to leave early, and he took all your friends with you. They come almost every day too, yelling at the nurses and doctors to let them in. They tell everyone you're their brother." She smiles. "They only let family see you, but they made an exception for Abbas. He wrote them quite the letter, I hear. Even threatened to have his lawyers sue the hospital. Put up quite the fuss."

I turn to Dr Maddie and she's nodding with a serious look on her face. She looks down at me and says, "None of them have made it very easy for us. They clearly care about you a lot." She smiles, but it comes across grim and exhausted, the kind of smile that comes from having to deal with Tom. I don't envy her, but the thought of my friends and Abbas—*Abbas!*—floods my brain like honey and I drown for a second in its bliss.

"They'll all be back in the morning," my dad adds, "with your sister."

Once the doctor has finished explaining the medical side

of things, the majority of which I zone completely out for, she leaves me with my parents. My dad helps me sit up in my bed, and though my body is aching, bandaged, and probably broken beyond repair, the pain medication is definitely working. I feel deliriously happy. I can see the cabinet next to my bed is littered with cards, flowers, teddies, and more, but my dad assures me I don't have to read them until I'm a bit better.

He then hands me a piece of folded paper, and lodges it between my thumb and forefinger. My hand is still quite heavily bandaged as well. "Before you do, you should probably read this one first."

I unfold it and stare at the tiny, neat handwriting, smudged a little in places, and read:

Dear Caleb,

First of all, I love you.

I am so sorry for the things that I said. I was hurt, not by you, but by everything else. I was so scared that after losing Kharouf, I would lose you too. I hurt you because I was hurting. I did not mean what I said, and I hope you know that.

I have never known someone with the capacity to love like you do, despite the fact that you may not even know it. Even if I have to scream it in your face or shower you with kisses. You love fearlessly, without pause and without bounds. You make mistakes, as do I, but you have shown me that to err is human, but to grow is divine. You are divine.

You have taught me more about myself than I thought possible. You have shown me what a life without fear can look like, and what a world without shame could be. You take every scar and every bruise on you and on others and you weave it closer and closer onto your heart until the pain becomes enveloped and overcome by the good in you.

Kharouf once told me the story of a king who gives up his throne because he falls in love. I always thought my story would end there: I thought I would have to give up what I loved and what was mine so that I could be with my soulmate. But the story didn't end there: the king returned to his palace with his love to make the world a better place, so that everyone could love someone the way he did.

Kharouf's story does not end with him. My story does not end with him. I thought after he was murdered that I would never be able to love again, until I met a boy who turned words into poetry and stories into art. A boy who could talk for days, but whose silence could speak for longer. A boy with a heart that could grow and heal and sing louder than any I have ever known.

You were right, as usual, though you must learn to find a more pleasant way to break the news to everyone else. I do have to fight the Home Office decision, and I will, but only on the condition that you are by my side, arms to shoulders, as I do it. I will stay here, but only on the condition that I stay with you. I will love you, but only on the condition that you love yourself too.

You are my next great love story. You are my everything.

I am yours,

Abbas

XXXII - Dear Speaker

The coma hadn't lasted too long, just a few months, but it felt like an eternity. Tom was keen to know if I had had any crazy dreams or if I could hear what was happening around me, but I couldn't remember anything other than a sense of loss, like I had forgotten a friend.

My teachers came and saw me—Ms Badden, Mr Whyssler, Ms Robertson and Mr Wilson. They brought chocolates and more cards, but my dad gently ushered them out before long, for which I was grateful.

I had decided, against the advice of my doctor and my parents, not to take the rest of the school year off, and so, from my hospital bed, I read through textbooks, drew multicoloured mindmaps, and drafted essay plans. Abbas came to see me every day, joined by Tom, Alonso, Lukas and Liam when they were able, and he would sit by my bed as we worked on our coursework or made up flashcards that we would probably never use.

He told me that he was working with Mary, his lawyer, on his appeal, and she was hopeful it would be successful, but if not, he was determined to go to a judicial review. I offered to give another witness statement, but Abbas laughed and told me not to worry or overexert myself. Each night before he left, he kissed me and told me that he loved me and he would see me tomorrow, and he did.

It is one of those nights that, after Abbas has left, I open my laptop to the UCAS page and stare at my options. Politics. Politics and Government. Political Science. They all mean essentially the same thing, but none of them sit right with me. I open a new tab and start Googling, and before long I've found something that piques my interest: a class on grief and romance in literature at Yale University, taught by a Professor Abigail Heath. It can be taken as part of a degree, or a standalone bit of fun. The admissions requirement is an essay on what we would want to write about.

I close the page, open up a Word doc, and start typing:

This is a story of love.
The story of a boy who deserved the gentlest love and was met with the world's ugliest fury.
The story of a boy who loved him, with the heart of a lion and the arse of a Greek god.
And the story of the boy who told their story.

It needs a little work, but I like where it's going. I flick open Spotify, select a playlist that starts to pump through my headphones, and I carry on.

Acknowledgements

I never seriously thought that I would ever publish a book, let alone one that means so much to me.

The first thanks have to go to the people who made this possible: the Spectrum Publishing team, including Andrew, who has been so helpful and supportive, and Carl, who first took a chance on Speaker and on me.

I'd also like to thank Radek for his generosity and talent in designing the beautiful cover art and supporting this project with such understanding, skill and care.

The story of Abbas wouldn't have happened without Olivia Clark, and her incredible and meaningful work with refugees and asylum seekers, as well as her non-stop encouragement of me.

Thanks also have to go to the Rainbow Migration team for their support of LGBTQ+ asylum seekers and refugees, without whom so many wouldn't be alive today. A special shout-out to the lawyers who donate their time, energy and expertise to fight for the real-life Abbas's, keep them safe, and give them a chance at open and authentic happiness. The law has saved me so many times, and without it and Rainbow Migration, so many wouldn't have a chance.

I couldn't possibly list them out here, but I will rave about them if ever asked: the authors, filmmakers and musicians that inspired me when I was struggling with writer's block, and to my playlists, the treadmill and my trainers who helped solidify the storylines and crystalise the characters. The book never would have been finished without them.

Thanks to my family, who have saved me from myself more times than I can remember, and to whom I can never repay my debt. Above all, thanks to my mam, for discussing theories with me, listening to me moan about boys and work and more, and for being everything I hope to be when I grow up; and to my dad, whose encouragement, love and support has never wavered for a second, even after 3am phone calls and countless interrupted naps. Thanks to my big sister, and also to my nan, for being my everything before she passed.

This story is also inspired in large part by my friends—my chosen family—many of whom have namesakes in this book. I love you all so much. Special thanks go to: Megan C, who did it first and better; Douglas, who was the first to know; James, my long-suffering flatmate; Srihari, my brother; and Megsy, my best friend.

There are too many people to thank individually but I am confident that those in the know will accept my love, gratitude and appreciation. I'd also like to thank the haters, the assholes, and the people I'd rather forget: you were part of the story too, and I hope you regret it!

And finally, to myself: it's been a wild 24 years, but we're just getting started. Lots of love.

Cai Cherry is a lawyer in England and Wales and New York, specialising in litigation and regulatory advice. They worked with a team at King's College London researching for Lord Neuberger and Amal Clooney's book Freedom of Speech in International Law. They are also an LGBTQ+ leader and an award-winning disability advocate.

From growing up in Lincolnshire, to starting university and his career in London, Cai was inspired to write Speaker based on their own experiences of queer identity, disability, mental health, and his work supporting LGBTQ+ asylum seekers and refugees with Rainbow Migration.
Speaker is Cai's debut novel.

RAINBOW
MIGRATION

Founded in 1993, Rainbow Migration supports LGBTQI+ people through the UK asylum and immigration system and influences policy and practice. Today they are the longest running organisation in Europe seeking asylum. They provide practical and emotional support to reduce isolation, improve resilience and help to access housing and healthcare. They deliver the UK's only specialist legal advice on LGBTQI+ asylum, to help LGBTQI+ people seeking safety secure their futures here. They undertake campaigning and policy work to advocate for a more humane and compassionate asylum and immigration system.

100% of author royalties from each copy of Speaker sold goes directly to supporting Rainbow Migration's work.

Scan here to donate to Rainbow Migration and learn more

Printed in Dunstable, United Kingdom

80156894R00184